On This Harvest Moon

A Moonrise Inn Novel

Book 1

JENNIFER SAFREY

Sibylline
DIGITAL FIRST

Sibylline Press

Copyright © 2025 by Jennifer Safrey
All Rights Reserved.

Published in the United States by Sibylline Press,
an imprint of All Things Book LLC, California.

Sibylline Press is dedicated to publishing the
brilliant work of women authors ages 50 and older.
www.sibyllinepress.com

Sibylline Digital First Edition
eBook ISBN: 9798897409877
Print ISBN: 9798897409914
Library of Congress Control Number: 2025938489

Cover Design: Alicia Feltman
Book Production: Aaron Laughlin

This is a work of fiction. Names, characters, places, brands, media, and incidents are either the product of the author's imagination or are used fictitiously. Any resemblance to similarly named places or to persons living or deceased is unintentional.

HUMAN AUTHORED: Any use of this publication to train generative artificial intelligence (AI) technologies to generate text is expressly prohibited.

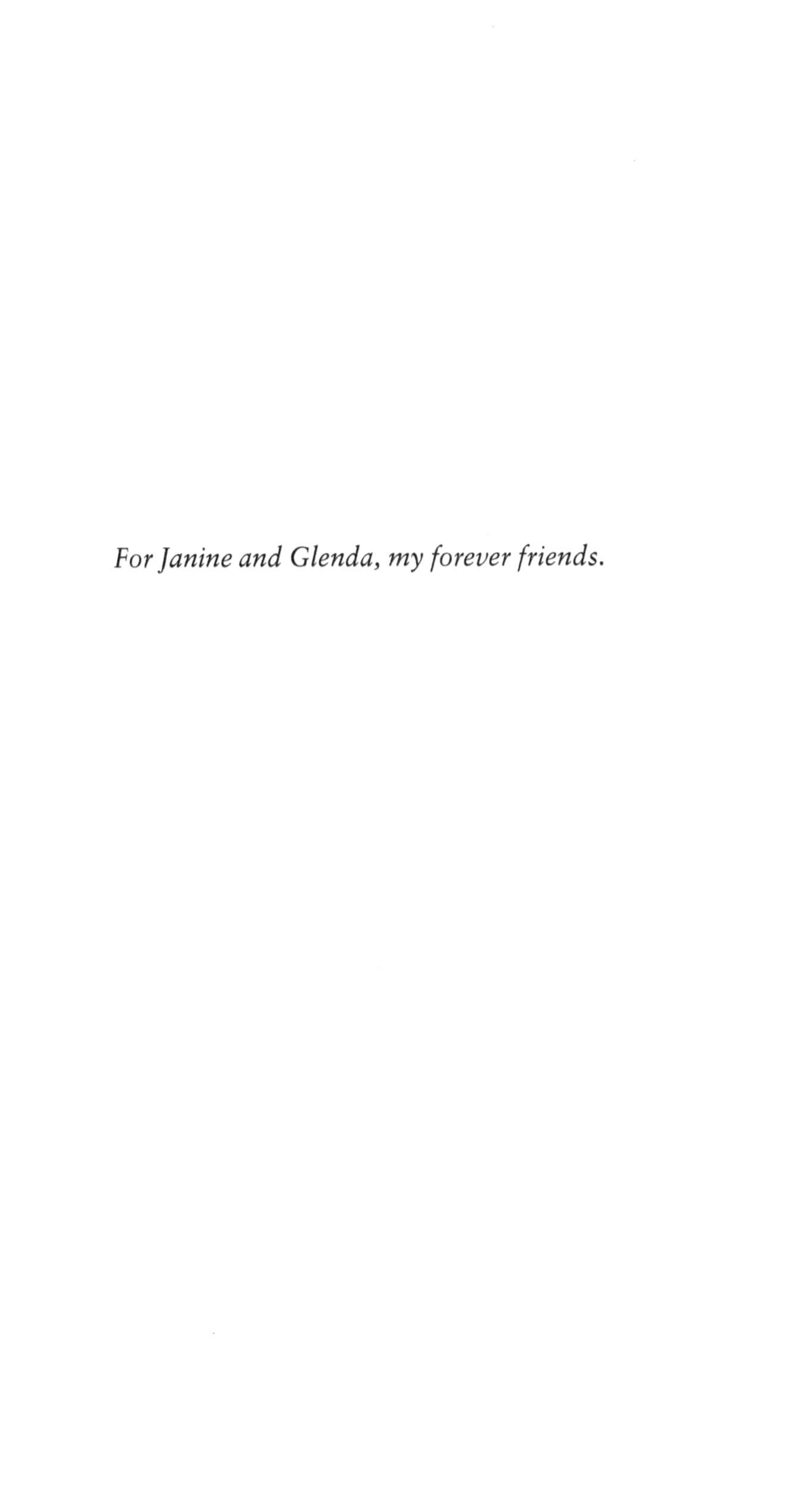

For Janine and Glenda, my forever friends.

CHAPTER 1

Roman had only worn a tuxedo three times before in his life, and each one of those occasions had ended in disaster.

The first tux was ten years ago, at Seasalter High School. The tuxedo rental shop two towns over offered a significant discount to any boys who wore one of their tuxes for a full day of class and handed out the shop's card to all the senior boys. Roman asked for a garishly floral, hot-pink cummerbund and sat through math class and physics class—which he ordinarily hated—with girls passing him notes telling him how hot he looked. His dapper day lasted only until lunch period, when one fawning admirer spilled fruit punch all over him—and the rental. The tux shop didn't make him pay to clean it, but they did rescind the prom discount.

The second tux had been for the prom itself, which Roman happily handed over a good chunk of his lawnmowing savings to rent because it would of course be his "best night *ever*." But his date had decided before 9 p.m. that she was in love with the class president, and the class president's girlfriend decided she was in love with one of the catering waitresses, and Roman, the most popular jock in school, suddenly wasn't in love at all.

Roman had worn the third tux to his older brother's wedding five years ago, but he'd worn jeans and a cotton button-down shirt to the courthouse a year after that, to stand beside Tony as he asked a judge for a divorce. Tony's wife didn't feel the need to show up.

Roman now examined his head-to-toe reflection in the mirrored wall, scanning his body before he saw his own scowl. He tried to relax his jaw, his lips. He took a deep breath and blew it out.

The tux was an inanimate object, and it likely didn't intend to send Roman down Unfortunate Memory Lane. Roman's slightly older, softer body filled it out a little differently than his teenage athlete's body had, but it wasn't bad. Roman's dark, wavy hair was still abundant, but his face was fuller. He attempted a smile, but it looked strange hovering over the negative foreshadowing of the tux.

Then, behind his left elbow, he saw her.

He didn't turn; instead, he brought his hands up to straighten the bow tie that didn't need straightening, while he watched her in the mirror.

Juliana Capuano.

It was her; he was sure of it.

Her face had been the preoccupation of his junior and senior year. She floated down the hallways like she didn't walk on the sticky, squeaky high school floor the rest of the students walked on.

He was voted Most Popular and Class Clown in their senior yearbook. But neither of those labels made a boy worthy of the Most Brilliant Girl, the Girl Most Likely to Be a Billionaire.

And he'd never managed to say a word to her before they all graduated and went their own ways. Not one word.

Her light brown hair was pulled back into a low twist, accentuating her long neck. She still moved as slowly, as gracefully, as she had back then, studying everyone carefully through her glasses as if engaging in a lifelong anthropological study of the people around her.

Roman paused and also looked at the people around him, the few milling in the hallway, with more heading out to the outdoor ceremony setup. *I don't know anyone here* was his first thought, followed immediately by, *no, wait, I know* everyone *here*. This wedding predated their tenth high school reunion, which was at the end of the month, and today was the first glimpse in a decade of so many of his old classmates together in one place.

He turned back to the mirror and startled to find Juliana now standing beside him, watching his reflection. She still wore glasses, but these glasses weren't the big round ones she had back then, with wire frames. These had brown squarish frames; they were edgier. Sexier.

"Hi," she said.

Just hi.

He swallowed hard.

"Hi," he said.

They gazed at each other's reflections for a while. Her dress was very ruffly and very pink. Very bridesmaidy.

"Can you believe a wedding on Labor Day weekend?" she asked.

He turned away from his own stupid face to look at her lovely live one. "Um ... yeah," he said. "It was a great idea."

"What?" she scoffed. "What do you mean, great idea? Who holds a wedding on a holiday weekend?"

"It's convenient. A lot of people have Labor Day off, so it's easy to travel to an out-of-town wedding, and stay an extra day before having to go home."

"Don't you think," Juliana said, "that people would rather use their federal holiday to relax in their preferred way? To lie in bed and read, or go to the beach, or whatever they love to do? Instead, they're stuck going to a wedding, and it's just more work. Especially the bridesmaids." She swept her hand in front of him, top to bottom. "And the groomsmen."

"Wow. Have you told the bride how you feel?"

"Absolutely *not*," Juliana said. "And I won't, because it's her day, and she deserves for it to be perfect."

"So you decided to tell me instead?"

"I was in need of a confidant. I thought you could relate, seeing as how we have similar responsibilities."

"I don't think we do," Roman said. "You undoubtedly have far more responsibilities than me. As a groomsman, all I'm obligated to do is to participate in a bachelor party we'll all regret, put on a penguin suit, and make sure the groom shows up at the altar. As a bridesmaid, I suspect you have a lot of other things to worry about. Makeup, hair, wearing a dress you likely hate, a bridal shower, input on flowers and colors and tablecloths, emotional support, and … making sure the bride shows up at the altar." He put his hands in his pockets. "This day is full of obligation for you. I can't blame you in the slightest for feeling deprived of your holiday weekend."

"I appreciate your understanding."

"I appreciate your trust in making me your confidant."

She smiled.

Had she ever smiled directly at him before? No. He would have remembered this feeling of wanting to fall to the floor and open his arms wide, satisfied that life had now given him everything.

She leaned closer; her coconutty perfume made him dizzy. "*Was* the bachelor party a regrettable one?"

"Yes, in that I don't remember a good deal of it."

"Too drunk?"

"Too food poisoned."

"What? No!"

"Didn't Lacey tell you?"

"Lacey and I aren't as … close as we once were."

"But you're her bridesmaid."

"She has eight bridesmaids. To be honest, I suspect I wouldn't have made it on a shorter list. But I think she wanted there to be a Seasalter High School nostalgia theme."

"I'm sorry."

"For what?"

"You don't seem entirely thrilled to be here."

"Are you?" She cocked her head slightly. "You've been loitering outside the ballroom for a few minutes now, checking your reflection every now and then. You seem as though you're avoiding something."

Busted. He wasn't a … big fan of weddings. Or marriage in general. He had mixed feelings about being surrounded by classmates he hadn't seen in ten years.

But Juliana Capuano wasn't merely a classmate in his memory. She was an immortal, a demigoddess.

He remembered it was his turn to speak. "*You're* not avoiding something?"

"Oh, I am," she said. "I live in New York now, so because of my distance and schedule, I missed all the things you mentioned: the shower, the choosing of floral arrangements. I haven't seen any of the other bridesmaids in ten years."

"They're not your friends anymore?"

She winced, as if his word choice hurt. "I wouldn't put it that exact way. That implies a falling out of some kind, and there was none of that. I lost touch over the years and, yeah … I guess we're not friends anymore and now it feels … awkward."

"I know what you mean."

Juliana's mood was shifting, and he didn't want her to decide talking to him was a bummer, so he changed the subject. "You live in New York, you said?"

"Yes."

The class valedictorian could be anything in New York. A high-profile attorney, an editor at a publishing house, a financial analyst. Before he got a chance to ask, though, she said, "You have no idea who I am, do you?"

Roman's bottom jaw fell.

Every time he'd walked into the cafeteria, he'd looked for her, sitting with her little group, her brown hair tumbling around her face, the strands brushing an open textbook. When he'd strutted with his friends down the hallways, loudly owning everything, he'd glanced left and right to see if she stood at a locker, chatting with another girl, or if she was walking briskly toward the lab as she checked the watch on her slender wrist. He'd thought of her as he lay alone in bed at night, wondering what time she went to sleep, or if she read half the night, or if she listened to the radio while identifying constellations out her window.

It had been ten years since she gave the valedictory speech at their commencement, and she'd long ago ceased to be his preoccupation. When his old baseball buddy, Jake Prescott, called him a few months ago and said he was marrying Lacey Adams from high school, Roman had a fleeting thought of Juliana, but he never thought he'd be standing in front of her here, talking to her like she was even an acquaintance.

She misinterpreted his hesitance. "I knew you wouldn't remember me from Seasalter High. Guys like you—"

"Juliana Capuano," Roman said.

She blinked in surprise, her blink almost anime-large behind the lenses of her glasses. He gave her a moment to recover. "Well done," she finally said, "Roman Montgomery. And I go by Ana now."

"And what do you mean, guys like me?"

"Popular guys. Jock guys. Guys that girls fell over their own feet for."

"Not you, as I recall."

"No," she said. "Not me."

They were silent for a second.

"We're ten years away from high school," he said, "and getting further every day. No more cliques."

"Right."

"We can talk to whomever we want."

She nodded.

"You're the one who chose to talk to me," he pointed out. "I was keeping busy by admiring myself, and suddenly you were telling me your gripes about Labor Day. Which I'm still not sure I agree with."

"No need to agree," Ana said. "Healthy debate livens up a conversation." She thought a moment. "And a relationship, for that matter."

Of course, Ana was oblivious to the fact that she'd uttered the one R word that wasn't in his common vocabulary. Or in his long-term plans.

But there was no reason to muck up the vibe again with downer talk.

He laughed. "You don't want a guy who thinks you're right all the time?" He stopped laughing and cleared his throat. "Sorry, that was assuming you don't already have a guy. Or girl."

"It would be a guy, and no. I'm single. Another reason I wasn't much joyfully anticipating this event. I used to be the Mathletes champion, and now I'm forced to fill in a zero where the problem explicitly says I need to have plus-one."

"If it makes you feel any better," he said, "I wasn't very good at math, so I leaned over and copied your zero for my own test."

"You don't have a date?" She frowned. "You've had a date to every event since sixth grade."

"Keeping track of my social calendar, were you?" Was she?

"Of course not. But I bet I'm not wrong."

"No," he admitted, "you're not wrong."

"Well," Ana said, "I suppose I can hang out with you while all the couples are doing the Chicken Dance. We can rate their performances."

"What are your standards for a superior Chicken Dance?"

"Enthusiasm. If the elbows are flapping in perfect time, if the butt wiggling is seductive."

"I refuse to judge Jake's grandma's butt wiggling. Please don't make me."

"Wow, that's not very open-minded of you. Older women are super hot."

"If she catches me checking her out," Roman said, "I'm blaming you."

"That's fine. I can take it."

Ana grinned. Roman's heart thumped erratically.

"This is unexpected," he said, then realized his inner monologue had become dialogue without his conscious consent.

"Yes, it is. You've proven yourself surprisingly adept at banter."

"I suspect I ought to take that as an insult, but I can't be bothered."

"Don't. It's a genuine compliment. You haven't even brought up the banal small-talk topic of the weather." She glanced around at the few people who'd wandered in to take a peek at the elaborately decorated tables in the ballroom before the ceremony outside. "To be honest, I almost didn't talk to you."

"Why did you?"

She paused, as if trying to decide how honest she wanted to be. "You seem different now."

From across the room, all she'd had to go on was his looks.

Before he could hurt his own heart with silent criticism, she added, "You look … more serious. Stronger. You look like someone who's seen some shit but can handle it."

He didn't care if she was a little bit right and a little bit wrong. He cared that that was what she saw—the positive version of what he was.

"How are you different now?" Roman asked.

She thought a moment. "I've seen some shit."

Roman chuckled. "And you can handle it?"

"I'm—"

"Juliana! Juli!"

A woman in an identical dress rushed Ana and hugged her before Roman could even identify her. Their taffeta gowns made a scratchy sound sliding against one other as she rocked Ana side to side like a bizarre wind-up doll. Ana's arms remained at her side, since her upper arms were pinned in the embrace. She peered at Roman over the woman's shoulder and made a face between surprise and horror.

Roman took a step back in case this new woman was a serial hugger.

"It's been forever!" the woman squealed. "I've missed you."

"I—I might have missed you too," Ana said. "But you came at me so fast and wearing so much froof that I don't even know who you are."

The woman laughed, rocked Ana one more time to each side, and took two steps back to show her face.

"Sarai," Ana said, and initiated a second, shorter hug. "It's been—a very long time."

"Yes," Sarai said. "I was sad when it didn't seem we'd hear from you again."

Ana didn't seem to quite know what to say.

"And," Sarai added, "I'll have you know, it's been a real struggle since high school to excel without your greatness to chase."

Sarai Thornton was the salutatorian, number two to Juliana Capuano's forever number one. Roman remembered that wild, curly auburn hair always near Ana at an awards dais or a podium or a stage or a cafeteria table.

"I can't believe we lost track of each other," Sarai said. "We are going to have a very long talk at the reception, so I can find out what you've been up to and if I've managed to keep up with your success, even from a distance."

If Roman hadn't been watching Ana's face very carefully, he'd have missed that barest moment when her expression iced over.

"Sure," she said to Sarai as Sarai stood back and gazed at her, hands on her shoulders. "I'm sorry, I was—is Lacey missing me?"

Sarai waved her hand dismissively. "Between her posse of bridesmaids, her mother, her grandmother, the photographer, and the frightfully efficient wedding planner, she doesn't even notice that either of us is missing."

Sarai turned to Roman and squinted at him. "I know you." Then her eyes went wide. "Roman Montgomery! Damn."

Roman tried to smile. "Damn, what?"

"Just damn, it's been a long time since Seasalter High." She glanced at Ana, then back at him, and then something seemed to click in her brain. "Oh! Um, okay. Well, you two keep—doing whatever, and Juli, maybe come to the bridal suite in about fifteen?" She checked her phone. "Forty-five minutes until showtime."

She squeezed Ana's arm again, pulled up her poofy skirt with one fist, and rushed off.

"She's more beautiful than ever," Ana said, "so this is not a knock on her at all but I'm going to ask you seriously—does this dress look unfortunate on me also?"

"I'm afraid so."

Ana shook her head slowly. "This is my nightmare."

"The bridesmaid's anthem," Roman said, satisfied when she giggled. "Want to take a look outside? Before it all starts?"

Though he held out a gallant elbow, he was surprised when she took it. Her hand was warm on his arm.

They strolled together to the open doorway and gazed upon the garden-wedding scene. White folding chairs, a pristine white runner up the aisle, an arch of flowers in shades of pink—an assortment Roman couldn't identify except for the roses. The seats were about half filled with chatting guests, dressed in sundresses and linen suits.

The friendly air between Roman and Ana turned awkward as they stared at the place where the bride and groom would stand to pledge undying love.

He took a breath. "It certainly is a beautiful day. No rain in the forecast for the whole weekend."

Ana laughed, and just like that, the tension was broken. "There it is. Small-talk poison."

"Aw, come on, it's not that bad. People have the weather in common. It's as good a place to start as any. When you don't have high school memories to fall back on."

"Fair enough," Ana said, "though I'll expect you to—"

"Sorry," Sarai said, having materialized on Ana's other side. "Would you excuse us, Roman?"

Ana flashed him an apologetic smile and let Sarai lead her a few feet away.

Roman watched the women bend their heads together as Sarai whispered urgently to her.

Ana didn't answer with words, but with a puzzled look. Sarai motioned for her to follow.

Ana did, giving Roman the same baffled expression and a tiny, one-shoulder shrug.

Must be some bridal emergency. Doing up back straps of a dress? Mediating with a mother-in-law?

Roman considered heading in to see what was happening with Jake, though it was likely absolutely nothing. He'd left Jake and the other wedding-party men lounging in the groom's suite, watching English football on the large flatscreen as if it were any morning at home.

He turned and nearly ran into Mark in his own tux. "Watch out, buddy."

"Sorry, Roman," Mark said. "But you gotta get back to the room."

"Okay." Roman ran a hand over his hair. "Pictures?"

"N-no, not exactly," Mark said. "Let's go."

Roman allowed Mark to hustle him back inside, past the ballroom and down a hallway to the left. "Is something wrong?"

"Yeah," Mark said.

"Like, call-a-doctor wrong?"

"No, not like that," Mark said. "Just … Jake's freaking out."

Roman relaxed, though their pace didn't slow. "That's normal, just nerves. He'll be fine."

"This is … really not normal," Mark said as he opened the door to reveal Jake slouched on the floor in the corner, heedless of the tux's wrinkling, tugging at his floppy brown hair. The other men were pacing around, staring at each other helplessly.

"What's happening here?" Roman asked everyone.

But before the question had completely left his mouth, he knew.

And it was why he had vowed years ago, standing next to his distraught brother in court, never to put himself in this position. Ever.

"Oh, buddy," he said, and went to sit beside Jake.

Tuxedos: 4. Roman: 0.

CHAPTER 2

Ana hurried after Sarai, who was moving at an impressive clip despite her four-inch heels.

Sarai had said into her ear, "*We have a problem. We need help.*"

It was strange for Ana to be part of the "we" again, after years of isolating herself into an "I."

But instead of dwelling on the word "we," Ana concentrated on the word "problem." They assumed Juliana Capuano was still good at solving problems. If she could show them they were right, it might give her a boost in their estimation. Maybe then, when they inevitably learned that Ana was a big failure in every facet of her life, she could still maintain a shred of dignity.

They rushed past the ballroom and turned right to run down a smaller hallway.

All right, Ana told herself. Whatever this was—a broken heel, a fight between cousins, an appetizer shortage—she would have answers. She would help.

Sarai and Ana crashed into the bridal suite.

Lacey sat on a fluffy, tuffet-like mushroom of a seat, her face in her hands, crying.

Three bridesmaids had their arms wrapped around her, murmuring. One bridesmaid was pacing. One bridesmaid was tapping urgently on her phone, and the last one sat in her own chair, wringing her hands.

Ana had used "out of state" and "working" as an excuse to skip most of the bridesmaid events. She had almost tried to use it as an excuse to turn down being a bridesmaid in the first place, but Lacey had sounded so genuinely excited to talk to her on the phone after so long and to ask her to be a part of her day that Ana didn't have the heart. She'd seen Lacey when she came for the dress fitting—on a different day than everyone else. But she'd made the excuse that she couldn't drive to Rhode Island until early this morning, and so she'd gotten out of the group hair and makeup festivities, doing her own French twist and usual makeup in a Connecticut rest-stop bathroom. It wasn't that she was particularly introverted or antisocial; it was that this particular group of smart, accomplished women intimidated her.

Because she used to be their queen, their most likely to succeed.

Not their most likely to crash-land and burn.

Due to her avoidance tactics, now was the first moment she was seeing all these women for this wedding. Two were Lacey's sisters, but the other five were in all Ana's yearbooks, all her photo albums, all her teenage memories. She recognized faces, but she also recognized this was not the time for reunion conversation.

As if no time had elapsed, they all looked at her now the way they used to—like Ana would have the answer.

She went to the bride and knelt at her feet. "Lacey?"

Lacey lifted her face, red and splotchy and unbridal. "Jul—Juli," she hiccupped.

Ana took her hand, wet with tears. "What happened?"

"Nothing *h-happened*," Lacey said.

When she said nothing else, Ana said gently, "I'm missing some information here."

"He didn't cheat on me," Lacey said.

Again, she didn't elaborate, so Ana said, "Well, that's good."

"No, it's not," Lacey said. "He didn't cheat on me, he didn't steal money, he wasn't disrespectful. He didn't do any of the things I needed him to do."

Ana glanced at Sarai, who shrugged with wide eyes.

"Why did you need Jake to do something bad, honey?" Ana asked.

"Well, I didn't want him to, not really. But if he did, I could call it off, and no one would blame me. Because now if I call it off, it will make *me* the bad guy."

"You're ... you're calling it off?" Ana asked. "The wedding?"

"I-I-I—think so."

"Why?"

"I just can't do this," Lacey said. "I can't. I can't."

"Is it possible," Ana said, "that this is just jitters? And you didn't expect jitters because you love Jake, and it's throwing you off?"

Lacey shook her head a few times, harder with each repetition. "No. No. I can't do this."

"You have to do this," Lacey's sister Mara said. "This is a three-hundred-and-fifty-person wedding with a sixteen-member bridal party. Mom and Dad will—"

"That doesn't matter, Mara," Sarai snapped. "This is Lacey's future. If she can't do it, she can't do it."

"This isn't your business, Sarai," Mara said calmly.

"This four-hundred-dollar pink dress makes it my business," Sarai countered.

Ana took hold of Lacey's wrist. "Come with me," she whispered.

She walked Lacey into the quiet adjoining room, nodding at Sarai to close the door. When she and Lacey were alone, she said, "I don't require explanations. You're not obligated to defend yourself to me, to your sisters, to anyone else. But you're using the word 'can't.' "

"Because I can't," Lacey repeated. "I can't do it."

"I understand. But the Lacey I knew for so long didn't use the word 'can't.' If she did, she wouldn't have been the lead in every school musical, and she wouldn't have won 'Rhode Island's Got Talent.' And she wouldn't be a Broadway actress now, in the big show everyone's talking about."

Lacey's smile was watery.

"The truth is, you *can* get married today. It's not a matter of can or can't," Ana said. "Now, let's pretend the word 'can't' doesn't exist, because for you, it doesn't. If the word 'can't' doesn't exist, are you getting married today?"

Lacey furrowed her brow.

"You don't have to tell me your thoughts or reasons," Ana said. "Just tell me if you are or you aren't."

Lacey was silent a moment, staring at the thick light blue carpet.

As Lacey considered, guilt tied itself into a thick, elaborate knot and settled itself at the bottom of Ana's stomach. Lacey had been a good friend—smiling, brilliant, fun, helpful—from when they met in first grade through the summer after high school graduation. If Ana had not retreated into her private nightmare, if she had asked for help or at least just stayed in touch, she could have been here for Lacey before the wedding. Maybe Lacey wouldn't be so emotionally torn up in her perfect wedding dress. Ana might have been able to support her through whatever was happening.

When Ana stopped telling Sarai and Lacey and the others about her life, they continued to reach out for a while, then eventually stopped calling and texting and emailing to tell her about their lives. The long friendships had faded and withered. Along with all Ana's dreams for herself.

At the time, Ana had told herself that her friends didn't need someone like her; what she'd become would only drag them down. She didn't know if she'd been completely wrong, because that assessment still felt correct, but longtime friends deserved better than what Ana had been able to give.

Lacey looked up at Ana. Her tears had stopped and her voice was firm when she said, "I'm not getting married today."

Ana nodded. "All right. Then it's the correct decision for you to not get married today, and everyone else will have to deal with it."

Lacey nodded. "Jake will hate me for this."

"I don't know what Jake will do, but you have to do what's right for you."

Lacey kept nodding.

"Let's tell the others," Ana said, "and figure out what comes next." She turned to the door.

Lacey grabbed her arm. "Wait."

Ana turned back around.

"Will you tell Jake?"

Ana blinked. "You want me to tell him?"

"Yes."

"Um, he hasn't seen me since high school. Isn't it best if one of your sisters tells him, or your mother?" Or *anyone* else?

"My sisters and my mother are going to be upset about this for various reasons," Lacey said, carelessly wiping beneath her eyes with her hand and smearing eyeliner. "At me, mostly. At him, probably. But you came in here, calm and in control, as always."

Oh, the irony at being considered the calm, logical one in the room once again.

"All you have to do is tell Jake the wedding's off, but make sure you tell him it's not him at all, it's me, and I'm really sorry but I'll talk to him later, and there are a lot of reasons but I love him and—"

Ana held up a hand. "I don't want to have a conversation about the future of your relationship on your behalf. That wouldn't be best for either of you. I'll just tell him that for your own reasons, the wedding is off for now, and you'll talk to him soon."

"Y-yes," Lacey said, then cleared her throat. "Yes, that's best."

"Someone needs to tell the guests," Ana said.

"Maybe Allison? The wedding planner?"

"Sure, that sounds right. Where is she?"

"Running around. Carrying a clipboard."

Doing a job. Just like Ana would. "All right. Let's go. Oh … Lacey, I meant to tell you. I go by Ana now."

Lacey nodded. "I like that for you."

That small approval, the first Ana had gotten in so long, filled her heart.

She led Lacey into the room filled with bridesmaids. Lacey's mother and a clipboard-waving Allison were now also there.

"Did you talk sense into her?" Lacey's mother demanded of Ana.

"This wasn't Jul—Ana's call," Lacey said. "It's mine, and the wedding is off."

There was a sudden silence, then pandemonium.

Lacey's sisters and mother were all talking at once, with the Seasalter High alum sharing their shock amongst themselves.

Ana edged toward the door.

I don't want to do this.

Ugh, I really don't want to do this.

I'm going to screw this up.

No, Ana contradicted herself. *I'm not going to screw this up, because there's nothing to screw up. I have a task, and it's not personal, and I'm going to complete it. I owe it to Lacey. I owe her years of not being there. I can do this one thing to help now.*

She kept moving to the door in the flurry of pink taffeta.

"Juli?" Sarai asked.

Juli, her high school nickname, was a long-ago identity. In college and in law school, she had been Juliana because it was more mature. On her hospital bracelet, she had been Juliana because that's how it was listed on her health insurance. At work, she was now Ana … but it didn't matter what she was at work, because work didn't matter.

"I'm going by Ana now."

"Oh, sorry."

"Don't be sorry. Listen, Lacey asked me to be the messenger."

"Oh, no," Sarai said.

"Yeah. I'm just going to do it quickly. Like ripping off a bandage … that Jake didn't know he had on."

"Do you need help?"

Ana glanced around. She wanted to say yes, but she had to do this for Lacey. "No, it's probably better for Jake if it's only me, so he doesn't feel ambushed."

"Good thinking." Sarai smiled. "Hey, are you in town for the rest of the weekend?"

"Until tomorrow."

"Are you staying at your parents'?"

Ana's parents didn't even know she was in Seasalter this weekend. It wasn't that she didn't want to see Mom and Dad. Part of her did, but a bigger part of her wouldn't be able to stand the awkwardness. They would take her out to dinner, and Mom would talk about her graduate students, and Dad would talk about interesting patient cases, and Ana would listen, but her silence about her own unimportant and uninfluential life would be embarrassing for all three of them.

"No," she said. "I'm staying at this inn that just opened. Looks beautiful online."

Sarai appeared for a moment as if she wanted to ask why Ana wouldn't spend the time with her family but thought better of it. "Give me your phone."

Ana handed it to her, and Sarai tapped a few keys. "Here's my number. Call me tonight, and we can make plans for dinner or brunch or something. This"—she gestured around the room at all the women who weren't paying attention to them—"needs to be discussed and analyzed."

"I've got to go," Ana murmured. "I need to take care of this."

Sarai rubbed her shoulder affectionately, and before Ana left the room, she caught herself thinking she didn't deserve Sarai's kindness.

She walked down to the main hallway where the ballroom was and glanced at the open glass doors at the other end of the hall. The outdoor seats were nearly filled to capacity, with others standing and chatting.

Ana felt sick.

But she shouldn't.

This was not her problem. Lacey and Jake were having the problem, and she was just here to support Lacey in what she needed. She should have participated in the pre-wedding bridesmaid formalities. She saw that now, and she needed to make up for that and for her years of hiding.

But her palms were cold and clammy, while her chest and stomach were hot inside.

She took a deep breath and took one step toward the hallway to the groom's suite when she saw someone walking in her direction. Someone also walking with purpose and urgency, as if—

"Roman," she said, and they stood facing one another, the bright sun from outside shining down the hallway onto their faces.

"Ana," he said. "I need to get a message to Lacey from Jake."

"You—what?"

"I'm sorry," he said, "but it can't wait."

He made as if to step around her, but he stopped in his tracks when she said, "Lacey sent me. With a message for the groom."

Roman turned, and they stared at one another.

That face. Ana's friends had swooned over that cut jawline and those deep brown eyes and that shaggy dark hair for their entire high school experience. Ana had shrugged it all off; there was no use making a fool out of herself for a handsome, popular jock who would never glance in a nerd's direction.

She'd only partly told him the truth before as to why she'd decided to talk to him earlier. He seemed different now, and she was curious. But she'd also secretly thought that if she could get the attention of the Seasalter High golden boy at this wedding, keep him at her side, maybe that would be enough to hold off questions about her life. All present would assume her worthy, if Roman had deemed her to be.

He'd turned out to be a surprise.

This new situation was another surprise.

"Pardon me for saying so," Roman said, "but I think what I have to say to Lacey might be more crucial, so you might want to hold off on whatever you need to tell Jake."

"I very, very much beg to differ," Ana said. "In fact, I'm one hundred percent certain that my message is the ultimate game-changer this morning."

He tilted his head.

She opened her mouth slightly.

"Are you saying what it sounds like you're saying?" he asked.

"Are—are you?"

She tilted her head.

He opened his mouth slightly.

"Let's say it at the same time," Ana said.

"Count of three?"

She nodded.

"One," he said, "two ... three."

"The wedding's off," they said at the same time.

Both pairs of eyes widened. Then they both looked to their right and left, worried they might have been overheard.

"The wedding's *off*?" they both scream-whispered.

"No," Ana said. "No way. Lacey is calling off this wedding."

"*Jake's* calling off the wedding," Roman said.

"He can't do that."

"Why not?"

"Because *Lacey* is calling it off."

They stared at one another.

"Why are you angry?" Roman asked.

"I'm not. You are."

"No, I'm not."

"Well, Lacey's not angry," Ana clarified. "She feels really bad."

"So does Jake. He doesn't want to hurt her."

"Did he tell you why he's not going through with it?"

"No. He wasn't feeling very articulate."

"Lacey didn't tell me why either," she said, "though I told her she doesn't owe me an explanation."

"Right. They only owe each other explanations."

He looked out at the guests in their seats, checking their phones and watches. "Jake told me to ask the wedding planner to tell everyone."

"Yes, Lacey told me the wedding planner would do it."

Suddenly, Allison with the clipboard slammed out of the bridal suite, stormed down the hallway muttering curses, pushed past them, and went down the fourth hallway that led to the parking lot. They heard the door crash open, then click shut.

"Was that the wedding planner?" Roman asked.

Ana nodded.

Roman dragged his hand over his face. Ana would have done the same if it wouldn't have smeared her eyeshadow down her cheek.

"Lacey and Jake are both aware it's off, then," he said. "But someone needs to tell everyone else."

"I—I can't do it."

"Why not?"

"Because—*because*," she said, her heart pounding. "*Look* at everyone."

She couldn't disappoint a huge crowd of people all at once.

She'd disappointed enough people for a lifetime.

Not that any of this today was her doing, but still.

"I understand," Roman said. "But one of us needs to man up."

"What a sexist expression."

"I'll woman up, then," Roman said.

"I'll come with you. But—you do the talking."

"All right."

But they lingered. Maybe Roman wasn't that brave. Or maybe her anxiety wasn't that unreasonable.

"Let's go," he said. "The sooner we do it, the sooner you can toss that dress in a secondhand bin."

"Don't tell Lacey that's what convinced me."

They both walked briskly to the doors.

A hush fell over the many, many gathered guests as Roman and Ana walked down the aisle together, despite the fact that they walked at a fire-drill pace that was not at all in keeping with the sweet classical tune of the string quartet.

The officiant wasn't at the front yet, so it was only Ana and Roman who turned and faced the crowd. The quartet conductor quieted the musicians with a one-handed flourish.

"Good morning," Roman said. "Thank you all for coming today. I'm—I'm afraid we have some news."

Hands fanning with programs stilled. Whispering people sat up tall. It seemed even the birds ceased singing, and the leaves in the trees decided not to rustle.

"There isn't going to be a wedding today," Roman said.

A moment of stunned silence.

Then, a big collective gasp.

"What?" "What?" "No wedding?" "Is this a joke?"

A few guests in the groom's half of chairs stood and peered behind them, as if expecting Jake to swoop in and convince everyone this was a prank. Several guests on the bride's side of the setup whipped out their phones, no doubt checking for a clarification text from Lacey. Guests on both sides murmured and whispered and widened their eyes.

As moment passed after moment, the well-dressed, coiffed guests began to realize what they had heard wasn't a joke or a mistake. One question, the one on everyone's minds, began in the back and gathered up power as it rolled ahead, a wave cresting at the front row.

"Why?"

"Why?"

"Why?"

Ana and Roman exchanged a look. Lacey and Jake hadn't even explained to one another yet.

"This is all we know at this time," Roman said, as if leading a press conference.

But it didn't stop.

"Tell us why!"

"We bought gifts!"

"We have a right to know!"

"We gave up our holiday weekend!"

"What did I tell you?" Ana said into Roman's ear. "A wedding on a holiday weekend is never a good idea."

"Why is the wedding off?" everyone demanded.

It was discouraging that no one got up to check on Lacey or Jake. Everyone was most upset for their own inconvenience.

"We have to tell them something," Roman said quietly.

Ana nodded and pushed up her glasses.

Roman lifted his chin and opened his mouth, waiting for a break in the verbal outrage before saying, "It's been decided—"

"By who?" someone shouted.

Whom, Ana silently corrected.

"The groom has decided—" Roman started again.

The bride's side of the assembly erupted with shocked tsks.

"Well, no," Ana said. "No," she repeated, louder. "The *bride* has decided to, ah, postpone the wedding."

The groom's half of the crowd put hands over mouths and shook their heads.

"Wait, *who* called it off?" one woman asked. "You two aren't making sense."

"The bride," Ana said at the same time Roman said, "The groom."

"And that's all we know," Roman said with some finality.

"Well, we came here for a wedding," called a man who looked familiar to Ana—another Seasalter High alum, it seemed. "How about you two?"

Ana put on a polite smile and shook her head at the joke.

"Why not?" a woman called from the back. "We were about to see a Seasalter High jock marry a nerd anyway. You guys are perfect substitutes."

"No!" Roman said, and Ana winced at the fervor with which he declined.

She could contribute her own.

"No *way*," she said. "That wouldn't happen."

"Never," Roman said.

"Not in a million years," Ana said.

"When pigs fly first class."

"And not even then."

She turned her head to level a glare at Roman, but he was already aiming one at her.

"Right," she said.

"Thank you, everyone," Roman said, "and we apologize on behalf of—of—"

"Everyone," Ana finished.

Guests began to stand, bickering, blaming, texting, sighing.

Roman offered an arm to help Ana down the two steps, and she didn't want to take it but she did. They walked down the aisle even faster than before.

The string quartet quietly played an upbeat tune.

If Ana had hoped coming back inside would shelter them from the fallout, she was wrong. Lacey and Jake were in a faceoff at the end of the hallway.

"*You're* dumping *me*?" they screamed at the same time.

"Uh-oh," Ana said.

"How *dare* you say you're not going to marry me?" Lacey yelled. "Do you have any idea how much this wedding cost?"

"I sure do have an idea, since your parents tell me every chance they get!" Jake shouted back. "And how dare *you* call it off?"

"I thought you said Lacey felt bad about her decision, that she wasn't angry," Roman said.

"She wasn't. But that was before she learned the groom was calling it off. And didn't you say Jake felt sorry also?"

"Guess finding out the bride was bailing changed all that."

Guests were gathering at the glass doors, wanting to see the fireworks but unwilling to walk in on them. Ana wanted to be classy enough to walk away, but sadly, she was as riveted by the unfolding scene as everyone else was.

"By the way," she said to Roman. "You didn't have to sound *so* much out there like marrying me would be equivalent to being thrown into the ocean on a zero-degree winter day."

"Me?" Roman asked. "You were behaving as if marrying me would be worse than summer traffic on the Seasalter Drawbridge."

Lacey splashed something at Jake, possibly champagne. Jake looked down at his soaked tux, his face going cherry red.

"Aaaand … that's the point of no return," Roman said.

"It's not you personally," Ana said, her eyes on the unfolding scene. "It's marriage itself. No offense meant."

"None taken. And same. How could one have a sugary dream of marriage, particularly after witnessing this?"

Guests, giving up on decorum, began to spill into the hallway to spectate. Lacey's divorced parents were alternating hissing at one another and arguing with an indignant couple whom Ana assumed were Jake's parents.

"Marriages end like this often," Roman said. "But not usually this early."

"I don't disagree."

Jake's groomsmen had emerged from their suite to stand behind Jake, literally and figuratively. Lacey's bridesmaids were lined up at her back as well. One of the groomsmen stepped forward and said something, and that something was clearly not the most conciliatory thing he could have said, because it provoked an angry retort from a bridesmaid.

"I don't want to be a part of this street fight," Ana said.

"Neither do I," Roman said.

A few men in stern suits emerged from a side office and ordered everyone out of the building, warning that they'd call police.

"Should I make a run for it?" Roman wondered aloud. "Is it every man for himself? Or am I obligated to get arrested with the groom? This isn't in my handbook."

Ana lifted a brow.

"No need to call police!" Lacey shrieked. "I am *out* of here!"

"Not before *I* am!" Jake said.

Sarai caught Ana's eye, and Ana muttered a curse under her breath as Sarai ran over.

"We're going all to Lacey's hotel room," she said.

"Of course," Ana said. "Whatever she needs."

Sarai glared at Roman for a solid three seconds before walking away.

"What was *that* for?" Roman asked. "The heck did I do?"

"You're guilty by association," Ana said. "You'd better go, before one of your boys notices you consorting with the enemy side."

Roman took a deep breath and looked at her—really looked at her. Ana felt her cheeks turning pink under his scrutiny.

"This wedding," he said, "which should have been as boring and routine and nondescript chicken dinner as any other wedding, was nothing like I'd thought it would be."

"No kidding."

"But of all the surprising elements, you are—"

"Montgomery!" a groomsman called. Ana squinted at him. Liam something. His locker had been in the same hallway as hers, and he was now bulldozing his way over to them. "We're going to Jake's parents'."

Just as in high school, he didn't glance at the nerd girl beside his friend, instead grabbing Roman's arm and steering him toward the other men.

Roman looked back at her, his expression apologetic, and she gave him a tight-lipped smile that she wasn't even sure he saw before he vanished into the mayhem.

Ana sighed and jogged—the best she could in a gown and heels—over to the bridesmaids, and joined them in escorting the tearful bride to the parking lot.

CHAPTER 3

Selene began a slow walk around the farmhouse, trying to see each lamp, each chair, each bed as if for the first time.

Trying to see everything the way guests would.

Because today, the first guests would.

She had only surveyed the common sitting area and the dining room before she conceded it was an impossible task.

She knew every ultra-plush bath towel, every embroidered curtain sash, every bar of artisan soap. Each detail had been pondered, debated, and finally selected and placed.

Selene had to trust she—they—had chosen correctly.

"It looks beautiful," Dan said into her ear, his lips close.

She closed her eyes and turned her head toward his memory, but he dissolved and floated away before she could smell his shirt, or feel his breath on her skin.

"I can't do this alone," she whispered.

It wasn't the first time she'd said it. She'd said it to her mirror reflection a year ago, before she left for her husband's funeral. She'd said it to the air when she watched her daughter leave for her new life in Arizona, so far from Rhode Island. She'd said it when the planned opening date of the Moonrise Inn came and went, and she simply couldn't pull out of the grief to bring Dan's dream to life.

This was his dream—an inn by the ocean. Selene didn't really know what a dream like that felt like, and she didn't really understand the drive to make it come true.

She was an advice columnist, dedicated to the practical and to the pragmatic. Dan was the daydreamer, the stargazer, the rainbow wisher, the myth maker. A man of the moon.

"The Moonrise Inn," he'd said when this house came up for sale, and he proposed buying it. "I can do this. We can do this."

"I don't know how to run an inn," she'd said.

"We'll learn," he'd said.

They bought the house, sold theirs, and moved in upstairs. They renovated, cleared, cleaned, decorated, prepared. They readied for a Memorial Day opening weekend that never happened.

She couldn't leave her bed after he died, never mind open the inn. Dust gathered thick on the new, plush blue sofa and on the repainted bookcase.

A year later, Selene—with bills piling up and the savings gone into the inn—faced a choice.

Sell or open.

She closed her eyes.

"Your name is Selene?" he'd said the night they met. "The Greek moon goddess? She fell in love with a mortal, as you know."

"Oh." She'd been taken aback at a man's easy use of the word *love*. "No, I don't know. And I don't think my parents knew the myth. They liked the name, I suppose."

"I love mythology," he'd said, "and the moon—the moon is an eternal myth in the sky for us to experience. Every night."

"That's—a magical thing to say."

"Selene fell in love with Endymion."

"A mortal, you said?"

"Yes, she visited him every night. She came down to Earth in her moon chariot to be with him while he slept."

"Doesn't sound very convenient."

"She asked Jupiter to grant Endymion immortality—eternal sleep—to preserve his beauty. And so she could visit him every night forever."

"That's devotion. Also … a little weird."

"She bore him fifty daughters."

"Well, don't get any ideas, Endymion."

She and Dan had gotten one idea, though, and they named her Luna.

And the moon goddess and Endymion were together forever.

But Selene had thought forever would be longer than twenty-five years.

Several guests were arriving today to stay the long Labor Day weekend.

Yes, the inn's opening weekend was the last weekend of tourist season. Not a brilliant startup strategy, Selene was aware, but this was the earliest she could manage to open without help. She couldn't afford help. Not yet. And Luna—Luna didn't want to help. When her father had died, she couldn't bear to have any more to do with his dream of the inn's success.

Salt air blew in on a warm wind through the open windows. In the silence, Selene could hear the rush of waves on the beach two blocks away. She wondered if she'd be able to hear it when this inn was full of people.

She looked at the crystal crescent moon hanging in the main window, at the pillow embroidered with the night sky, at the grinning full moon on the light switch cover. Even if she removed every sparkling, smiling moon decoration in this inn, the real moon still hung in the sky, immortal. Some nights, it burned through her heart. Some nights, it was a calming blanket. Every night, it was a reminder that she was facing her second big career—and the second half of her life—alone.

She sat on the celestial blue sofa and hugged a pillow to her chest.

"I can't do this," she whispered one more time, probably the last time she'd have the luxury of free time to say it.

"Yes, you can," all the moons in the room said to her in Dan's voice.

She stood and patted the pillow back into place. She lit a stick of fragrant incense, unlocked the front door of the Moonrise Inn, and was about to head to the kitchen to prepare a few pitchers of cucumber water when her cell phone rang.

She picked it up. "Hello?"

"Um, hello. Is this the Moonrise Inn?"

Selene shook her head. What a way to start. She cleared her throat. "Yes. Moonrise Inn, can I help you?"

"Yes, I'd like to make a reservation," the man said.

Selene's other expected guests this weekend had made online reservations, so this phone call was her first real interaction with a potential customer. Her heart pounded hard while she tried to maintain a steady, professional tone.

"Of course. What date would you like to arrive?"

"Would today be okay?"

* * *

It was hard enough to walk in a puffy pink concoction of a dress; trying to navigate steps in that dress while juggling two weekend bags was even more challenging.

"Oh!" Ana heard from inside, and a woman opened the door with a bit of a flourish.

"Welcome!" the woman said. Ana dropped her two bags on the floor.

Her thoughts, which were swirling into a mental tornado when she walked into the inn, suddenly settled peacefully in this deep-blue, celestial-themed sitting room. It smelled mystical and magical, like patchouli and saltwater and starlight.

Ana's shoulders drooped as she let out a breath she'd been holding for hours.

The woman gestured to the ceiling, the floor, and then the pretty blue room at large. "This is the Moonrise Inn," she said. "I'm Selene. I'm … um, I'm very glad you're here. I'm happy to host you. I'm … happy you're here."

The smile on Selene's face was genuine but seemed awkwardly placed, as if it were usually tucked in a private drawer and rarely on open display. Her blond hair was pulled into a claw clip at the back of her neck, with wild wispy ends sprouting out the top. Tortoiseshell reading glasses sat on her head like a librarian's tiara. Her frame was thin, and her hands didn't seem to be able to stay still. She wore cutoff denim shorts, and the tan legs extending from the frayed hems were as shapely as an athletic college student's, though the smallest little lines around her mouth and eyes put her about thirty years past a typical college degree.

"I'm Ana Capuano. I have a reservation for tonight?"

Selene took a deep breath. "Yes, Ana. Of course. This is our—my—opening day. So forgive me for being a little … not very good at this."

"You're doing great," Ana said. Anxiety was familiar, and the fact that it wasn't coming from herself was refreshing. "Listen, I was just at an almost-wedding."

"I was about to say, you seem, ah, unusually dressed for a Labor Day weekend getaway." She tilted her head. "An almost-wedding?"

"Yes. The bride called it off, and the groom called it off, and when they each found out the other was calling it off, chaos reigned. Then I had the pleasure of having to inform the guests."

"Oh, no." Selene placed a comforting hand on Ana's shoulder. "That's terrible."

Ana resisted the weird urge to step closer to Selene for a motherly embrace. "Then I spent a solid three hours in the bride's hotel room. I don't want to seem insensitive," she hurried to add. "I'm not. I can't imagine—well, I can't imagine getting married at all, so I can't imagine this happening on my wedding day. But I'm ... well, I'm really tired. I finally had to tell them I needed to check in."

"You sound like a very supportive friend."

Ugh. If Ana was anything, it wasn't that. She'd been a nonexistent friend for so many years, and today she'd been an uncomfortable acquaintance, at best.

Just another thing she'd failed at in life.

She shrugged one shoulder, and Selene, perhaps intuiting that her guest didn't want to talk about the unusual events of her day, said, "How about I show you to your room, so you can settle in? Maybe change out of your dress?"

Ana nodded gratefully.

Selene picked up one of Ana's bags and nodded at her to follow her. "You're on the main floor just this way. The other guests are arriving later today."

They stopped at the one guest room that opened to the main sitting room. A cute wooden sign hung on the door, proclaiming it the Stardust Suite. Selene fiddled with a ring of keys, selecting the correct one and pushing the door open. The afternoon light flooded over the regal, canopied queen bed and its rose-colored bedspread. On a large framed print, a pink moonrise hung over a dark field of flowers. A carved trunk with a white cushion on top sat at the foot of the bed. There was an adjoining room with a flatscreen TV, a small cream-colored sofa, a standing wardrobe, and a writing desk. Both rooms had soft, thick rose carpet. The room smelled pristine and unused. The glass on the picture window was so clean, it seemed there was no glass at all.

"So beautiful," Ana said. "And spacious."

She dropped her bag on the bed as Selene glided from window to window, opening each to let in the fresh sea air. Ana closed her eyes. "I can smell the beach."

Selene smiled and pointed out the window beside the bed. "Two blocks that way."

This would be good. A little time away, a little space, a little beach air. She didn't have to leave first thing tomorrow in the morning, after all. She wasn't scheduled to work until Monday evening. Maybe she could linger a bit, read a book, get a little peace before leaving …

As Selene puttered, Ana went to the quaint bathroom with blue starry wallpaper, fragrant soap, and a small window with a golden full moon in stained glass. She took off her glasses and set them on the sink, rubbing her forefinger over the dent they made in the bridge of her nose. She pulled her makeup bag from her purse, spritzed rose water on her face, and carefully applied mauve lip gloss. She began to pull the bobby pins out of her light-brown hair, and every two or three pins removed dropped a lock of hair. Finally, it was all down except for one section, but she couldn't find the pins.

She put her glasses on and stepped out of the bathroom. "Can I ask an odd favor? I can't find the last couple of pins in my hair, and—"

Selene laughed. "Sit on the bed."

Ana obeyed, and Selene combed her fingers softly and surely through her hair with practiced fingers.

"Do you have a daughter?" Ana asked.

"Yes," Selene said. "One daughter. Luna."

"That's a pretty name."

"My husband is—was—a fan of the night sky."

"Oh! Moonrise Inn. Of course." Ana noticed the past tense when it came to Selene's husband but didn't want to intrude by asking about it. "You seem like you've taken pins out of hair before," Ana said.

"Good deduction," Selene smiled. "Though Luna was never as patient with me as you are. But that's the way of mothers and daughters."

Ana felt one, then another, pin slide gently out of her hair, feeling it tumble down. "There we go," Selene said as Ana shook her head like a cat.

Not *there you go*, but *there we go*, like they were a team here, like they were doing this together. No one had been on Ana's team in a long time. But today—twice. Here, with Selene, and this morning, with Roman.

For a few moments there, it had felt like Juliana Capuano and Roman Montgomery were teammates, a united front, a—couple.

Unexpected, and—nice.

"Here are your keys," Selene said, handing them to her. "The larger one is for the front door, which I lock around 10 p.m."

"All right."

"Do you need any restaurant suggestions?"

Ana shook her head.

"Well, there's a folder on the desk there with lots of suggestions with addresses and phone numbers. Some places may require reservations since it's the holiday weekend. Are you meeting friends or family?"

"No. I grew up in Seasalter, so I'm familiar with the area, though maybe not with newer places like this inn or some restaurants."

"Oh!" Selene said. "Maybe we can chat later, and you can tell me about any interesting or cool places that only locals would know. I grew up on Long Island, and my husband and I lived in the Providence area until we bought this place about two and a half years ago, so I don't know as much as he—did. And I haven't had a lot of time to explore."

Again, Ana noticed the past tense, and now understood that Selene had lost her husband very recently. But again, she felt too awkward to ask about it. "I might know a few places, but I was not a kid anyone would call cool, so I might not be very helpful. I was sort of a nose-in-a-book type. But I'll try my best."

"No pressure. Are your parents here?"

"My parents do live here," Ana said, "but I wasn't planning on ..." She let her voice trail off, realizing that she sounded kind of awful.

But Selene didn't even blink a judgmental eye. "I understand. Families are complicated. You're allowed to do what you need to do to keep yourself happy and sane."

Tears sprang to Ana's eyes. "Thank you." Being granted permission felt like a relief. "It—it sounds like you lost your husband recently?"

Selene bit her lip and nodded. "Yes," she said after a moment. "Dan." She blinked quickly, took a deep breath, and smiled. "This was his favorite room. He would have been happy to meet you, its very first guest. He also would have talked your ear off, demanding to know the details of this wedding debacle."

"Debacle is the right word," Ana said. "It only firmed my resolve to never do it myself."

"Get married?"

"Marriage, relationship. It's all ..." Ana waved her hand vaguely. "Not a goal of mine anymore."

"Fair enough. It doesn't have to be."

Ana nodded, satisfied that Selene affirmed her feelings but also hoping Selene wouldn't ask her what her goal was instead, because she didn't have an answer for that.

She used to. But she hadn't for a while now, and might never again.

She didn't need to have a goal anyway, did she? Wasn't it enough to just live through each day with as little stress as possible?

They both heard the front door open.

"I still have one guest who hasn't checked in yet," Selene said. "That's probably him now. My cell phone number is in the packet on the desk, so if you need something and can't find me, just text me."

"I will. Thank you again."

"Consider some beach therapy."

Selene slipped out of the room, and Ana heard her say, "Hello! Welcome to the Moonrise Inn."

Then she heard a masculine voice respond—a strangely familiar voice.

Ana set about unpacking her bag and changing hurriedly into denim shorts and a red T-shirt, and when she was done, she heard the two still talking in the sitting room.

She turned the knob silently and cracked her room door open an inch.

Then she turned her head and pressed it against the doorframe so she could look out with one eyeball.

She saw a leg, ending in a highly polished black dress shoe. A large burgundy duffel bag sat on the ground.

Unable to see anymore, Ana tried to somehow squint her ears. She heard words: "wedding," "groom," "stay in town."

Oh, this was ridiculous. She was a guest here. She could simply walk out and see who was it was.

Because she knew who it was.

Pocketing the key, she stepped out and pulled the door shut behind her just as Selene led tuxedoed Roman Montgomery down the hallway.

"Unless there's a hashtag trend of cancelling Seasalter weddings at the zero hour," Selene said, "I have a feeling you two know each other."

Roman's eyes widened a bit. "You."

Ana smirked. "You."

"You're staying here?"

"*You're* staying here?"

He seemed as though he was trying not to laugh. "Are you going out?"

"Maybe."

"Wait for me," he said. "Selene's showing me my room, and then I'll change and come with you."

"How do you know I'm going anywhere you'll want to go?"

"Are you going to a canceled wedding reception with the bridesmaids and groomsmen brawling like the Sharks and the Jets?"

"It wasn't my plan, no."

His voice got slightly deeper and a little quieter, as if about to reveal a delicious secret. "Then I definitely want to come with you."

Heat pooled in Ana's belly, and energy tingled between her legs. She fought the urge to bite her lip or cross her thighs, not wanting Roman to see how his one sentence affected her. She glanced at Selene, who was rifling through keys on a ring, oblivious.

Ana realized Roman was waiting for her acquiescence. "Sure. Yes."

Selene found the key to his room—next door to Ana's Stardust Suite.

They went in, and Ana wandered to the sitting room.

Again, despite everything happening today, this room hyp-
notized her. Sheer white curtains blew into the room with the
salt air. The curtains were covered with a white-on-white cur-
sive print, and the breeze brought the poetry to life. Several
peaceful plants dwelled on a tabletop and in a corner planter
stand. A small but intricate framed needlepoint of a moon and
stars hung on the light blue wall, offering its nighttime mystery
even in the middle of the sunny summer day.

This was a room that gracefully held dreams.

Maybe even dreamless Ana could create one again if she sat
in here long enough.

Her phone buzzed in her pocket, and she slid it out. She
glanced at the ID, then slipped out to the porch to answer it.

"Sarai," she said. "How's it going?"

Sarai, Ana, and the bridesmaids not related to Lacey had
spent a couple of hours with Lacey in her hotel room, alternating between wiping her tears and shouting "yeahs!" as Lacey
called Jake every noncomplimentary adjective she could think
of.

"Well," Sarai said. "Lacey just called me crying. This is hard
for her."

"Of course it is. It's going to be for a while."

"Well, yes, that's why I'm calling. She really needs support,
and all her friends are going back home tomorrow or Monday,"
Sarai said. "I can't leave her alone. I'm going to stay in town for
a while to be with her."

"What about Lacey's family?" Ana asked, intending for
it to come out diplomatically but realizing it sounded more
pass-the-buck.

If Sarai noticed, she didn't call her out on it. "Her mother
and her sisters are only contributing to the problem. They're
all screaming at her for wasting money, at each other for not

noticing sooner that something was wrong. They're not exactly Team Lacey."

"I'm sorry." Ana was sorry. Because she knew firsthand that if you were in crisis and your family didn't or wouldn't understand, you were really alone. Worse than alone, because at least if you were alone, you didn't have anyone exacerbating the issue. "Are you … are you calling to see if I'll stay?"

"Yes. I'm going to take some time off. Kate is trying to rearrange her schedule and see if she can take clients remotely. But everyone else needs to get home."

Of eight bridesmaids, only one could stay, and one was a maybe? Lacey had just lost the person she'd intended to have as a life partner. She didn't deserve to watch her bridesmaids flee like fluffy pink-frocked rats off a sinking wedding ship.

"You're the last one I called," Sarai admitted, "because you were too busy to come to bridesmaid things, and I assume your schedule is tight, but—"

"I'll stay," Ana interrupted. Then, when she realized it was truly what she wanted to do, she repeated more strongly, "I'll stay."

"Oh, Ana, that would be amazing. Lacey will be so happy. She's missed you so … Are you sure?"

"Of course. What are … bridesmaids for?" Ana felt guilty for not saying the word "friend," but she felt as if she had to earn that title back.

And she would earn it back.

This was something broken that Ana might really be able to repair: her friendships. She could be there for Lacey, be a part of the group again.

"Thank you," Sarai said. "This means so much."

"Um." Ana needed to mentally strategize now that she'd committed. She was supposed to work Monday. And this one-night inn stay was already taking a chunk of her meager savings, one that it would take her lowly per-hour wage several months to build back up. "No problem," she said, with more confidence than her situation warranted. "I have to call work, and I have to check with this inn to see if I can stay a few more nights." She wondered how much room she had on her credit card after the bridesmaid-dress charge. "How long are you staying?"

"I'm going to plan on a week."

There was no way on this green Earth that Ana's boss was going to go for that. "I'll stay a week also."

"Lacey's going to be so happy. And I'm glad too, because that will give us some time to catch up. I want to hear about everything you've been doing."

Sarai thought that she wanted to hear it. But on the off chance Ana told her anything that had happened, Sarai would be as surprised—and disappointed—as Ana's parents.

Almost as much as Ana was in herself.

But she couldn't think about how to handle that right now. Lacey needed her, and she was finally going to be there for her. She told Sarai she'd call her later and clicked off, immediately tapping on her bank's app to check her balance. She scowled at the pitiful numbers.

"Hey."

She whirled around. "Roman."

He stepped out onto the porch, now in knee-length khaki shorts and a dark purple tee. "Sorry. I didn't mean to sneak up on you."

"You didn't. I was just—there's a lot happening."

"Anything you want to share?"

There were three large wicker rockers on the porch with cushions swirling with colors. He gestured to one of the chairs.

She sat, and he sat in the one beside her. She pushed off with her toe, and the chair creaked forward and back soothingly.

She leaned her head back and closed her eyes for a moment, rocking side by side with a man whose presence was a warm croissant of comfort. She pretended for a few moments to be a far older woman, who knew the also-older man next to her so well that they didn't need to talk. They only needed to rock in sync, sharing the air they breathed, sharing an existence.

It was surprisingly easy to imagine Roman that way. In the future-fantasy, she reached over and took his hand. She wondered if he was imagining something similar. But she kept her real-life palms down on the arm rests, wrapping her thumbs and pinkies around.

She melted into the present moment, allowing her eyes to flutter shut.

The salt breeze on her skin, the hot late-afternoon sun, the distant surf. All the sounds of Ana's childhood—her happy, ambitious childhood. She relaxed into it for a moment, grateful that Roman didn't push her to speak. It was probably why she finally did.

"I was talking to Sarai." She opened her eyes. "She's staying in town for a week to help Lacey cope. Kate might too. So I'm going to stay."

"Good."

She looked at Roman, his chiseled chin pointed to the sky as he talked to her with his own eyes closed, undoubtedly soaking in his own childhood memories of Seasalter.

"Is it awkward for you, staying to help?" he asked.

"Why would you say that?"

"You told me earlier that you aren't as close to your friends as you once were."

"I did say that," she remembered. "Maybe it will be a little awkward, but it's the right thing to do. I can help."

"Good," he repeated.

She sighed. "I do have to call my boss and ask for time off, however."

"I'm sure your boss will understand personal time, an emergency."

"I hope so. I should just call now and get it over with."

"Your workplace is open on Labor Day weekend?"

It was depressing to consider what glamorous job Roman undoubtedly thought she had.

"Yes. It's … it's twenty-four hours."

Roman stood. "I'll go wait in the front room, give you some privacy. What are our plans after that?"

"Just a walk into town, I suppose."

"Sounds great."

"It does?"

Roman paused. "A walk into town with Juliana Capuano is, quite honestly, the only way I'd like to spend the day."

Ana didn't know what expression was on her face, and she didn't know what expression she wanted it to be. She searched her brain for a witty response, but her few thoughts rattled around the space like in an empty can. "All right," she finally said.

He walked into the inn, and she sat very still for a moment.

Roman Montgomery had been the "it" boy of Seasalter High. He clearly thought she'd made something of herself—probably because she felt comfortable and confident talking to him. Which surprised her beyond belief, because she didn't open up to anyone, ever. She couldn't bear talking to her parents. She'd held her old friends at arm's length for years. She hadn't made any new real friends since college. She'd gravitated to Roman Montgomery at the wedding, surmising that his popularity would be an effective shield, but she'd strung more sentences together in conversation with him than she had in the last year in total.

It ... meant something.

But it was fleeting. Because once he found out she wasn't anything he thought she was, that she'd collapsed under pressure before meeting a single real-world expectation, he would probably decide spending the day with her was a waste of time.

Besides, Lacey wouldn't love it if she knew Ana was hanging around with one of Jake's best friends right now.

Ana might as well enjoy the time with Roman while it lasted. Which wouldn't be for much longer.

CHAPTER 4

R oman took a seat on the blue sofa, not expecting it to feel so much like sitting on a cloud.

Selene bustled into the room, carrying a pile of folded cloth napkins. "Hi! Do you need me for something?"

"No, I'm waiting for Ana. She's making a call."

"Ah." She smiled at him, then lifted her chin toward the small breakfast room. "It's this way to cookies, if you're interested."

"I'm always interested in cookies."

"Don't know too many people who aren't."

He followed her to the breakfast room.

"Have a seat anywhere," she said, dropping the napkins on one of the tables. "Let me grab them. They just came out of the oven."

"What kind of cookies?" Roman asked, realizing he sounded like an eight-year-old.

But Selene grinned. "Chocolate chip, and peanut butter."

"Do I have to choose?"

"What kind of monster do you take me for?" she asked with a wink, and left for the kitchen.

The small breakfast room was already set for the morning. There were colorful placemats, cloth napkins, and a little bud vase filled with prettiness on each table. There was a bay window overlooking a large green yard, and a beautiful oak tree towered over the yard, keeping most of it in the shade.

He eyeballed the intricate crown moldings in the high corners of the room and open window doors, white wood with slats. The little knobs were gleaming gold. As a new-ish real estate agent, he was still training himself to examine all the sweetest little interior details of a house so he could point them out with sincere enthusiasm to prospective buyers. This inn had beautiful details, from the sitting room to his bedroom to this kitchen. He was also training himself to find imperfections, but he'd found none here so far, not even when he squinted at the walls and the floorboards.

Every detail was tended to.

Selene came back in and set a plate in front of him. Two cookies, one peanut butter and one chocolate chip, so large they each hung over the edge of the plate.

"Can I live here?" Roman asked, and Selene patted his shoulder.

"You can stay as long as you want." She sat and began to fold napkins.

"Well, like I said when I called earlier, it's going to be a week, at least," Roman said, breaking off a piece of the peanut-butter cookie and holding it under his nose. "My plan was to go home tonight, but now that this all happened, the groom—um, ex-groom?—asked a few of us to stay for moral support."

"Were you surprised? Or did you sort of suspect something might be off about this wedding?"

Roman chewed thoughtfully. "I didn't see this coming particularly, no," he said. "Though half of all marriages end in divorce, right? It's foolish to assume every wedding is happily ever after. Maybe happily for a while. This one wasn't even happily to the altar."

"Kind of a pessimistic attitude to marriage you got there," Selene said, but the smile remained on her face, softening her observation.

"I prefer to think of it as realistic."

Selene nodded slowly. "Marriage isn't for everyone," she admitted. "And all relationships aren't the right one. It's probably a good thing your friend figured it out before going through with making it legal."

Roman watched her work. "Do you need help?"

"Aw, thanks for asking, hon, but sometimes I need the busy-work. Folding quiets my mind."

"There was one surprise today, though," Roman said.

"What was that?"

They both looked up at the sound of the front door opening.

"Here it comes," Roman said quietly as Ana walked in.

"Shall we go?" she asked, and though Roman had only interacted with her cumulatively about an hour out of his lifetime, he knew false cheerfulness when he heard it.

"Sure." He broke the chocolate-chip cookie in half and offered it to Ana as he stood.

"That's what I need," Ana said, taking a huge bite.

"Thanks, Selene," Roman said.

"You two have fun. Text me if you need anything. Or if you get lost."

Roman and Ana both chuckled. "We grew up here," Ana reminded her.

"You can get lost anywhere," Selene said. "Even the places you think you know."

As they walked outside, Roman asked, "Did that feel like some sort of sage Mr. Yoda Miyagi advice?"

"Yes." Ana finished the cookie. "She's like a placid lake that's deceptively very deep."

They walked down the small side street that was the Moonrise Inn's address, Oceanview Road, up to Broad Street. Every few steps, Roman stole a glance down at her. She was about five-foot-eight to his six feet, so he didn't have to look down very far. Her jaw was tight, a little muscle under her ear twitching, as if she were actively squeezing her back teeth together and releasing, squeezing and releasing.

The easy camaraderie that had been between them while wearing a tux and a bridesmaid dress was gone now, replaced with the kind of uncomfortable silence that he'd been afraid he'd get from her if he'd actually talked to her in high school. "Food?" Roman asked.

Ana was silent for about ten seconds, then said, "I want a burrito. I want a super burrito that is stuffed with so much rice and beans and sour cream and cheese and salsa and chicken that about halfway through, I consider taking the rest home, but I plow through anyway and have a bloated stomach until lunch tomorrow."

"That's very specific."

"Thank you."

"And very doable."

"I thought so."

"And I very much appreciate you not saying, 'Yeah, I could eat, what do you want?' and making me come up with options."

"I'm very decisive."

"Clearly."

"Especially when it comes to food. I know what I want when I want it."

Roman was ashamed to replay her last sentence in his mind, imagining her hovering over his prone body as she said it, her hair tickling his face.

But only slightly ashamed.

They passed the local bookstore, and Ana peered in. "Oh, that thriller looks good. I've read everything by that author."

"Want to go in and grab it? You might have some time to read this week."

"Good point, but I don't want to sp—carry it around all day."

It sounded as if she was about to say she didn't want to spend money on a book, but that wouldn't make sense. Whatever Ana Capuano did for a living would certainly be enough to splurge in a bookstore if she wanted.

"Did it go okay with your boss?" he asked.

"Oh, he fired me."

Roman laughed, then peered at her, then choked back his laughter so quickly he nearly coughed. "You're not kidding?"

"No." Her voice was flat. "I'm unemployed."

"For asking for a few days off?"

"Yes."

"Are—are you okay?"

"It's not like I—" She stopped, speaking and walking. She leaned against the outer wall of the diner so as not to block the sidewalk, congested with Labor Day tourists. "I'm curious, Roman Montgomery. What is it you think I do?"

"Do?" Roman asked stupidly.

"Yes, what do you think my career is?"

"I've never been very good at pop quizzes," he said. "They struck fear in my heart that if I failed, I would go on academic probation and not be able to play ball."

"This quiz has no consequence," Ana assured him.

"Are you a doctor?" Would a doctor be fired for taking a few days off? Probably not. "No. Are you an engineer?"

"That might have been cool, but no."

"Law?"

She laughed at that, and the laugh looked like it hurt her. "Nope, definitely not law."

"I give up."

"Well, up until about fifteen minutes ago, I sold hot dogs."

Hot dogs? Was that some kind of code for—something on Wall Street, maybe? Sold hot dogs on the trading floor? "I don't follow."

"Not just hot dogs," she added. "All kinds of fried snacks. Gum. Sports drinks. Newspapers. Bad coffee."

Roman blinked.

"I work—worked—at Conveenience," Ana finally said.

"The deliberately misspelled chain of corner stores?"

"My secret hunch is that it's not at all deliberate."

Roman thought for a moment. "Are you in corporate?"

"No, in an apron behind the counter."

Roman said nothing for a moment.

"Didn't expect that, did you?"

"I didn't," Roman confessed. "But ... there's nothing wrong or bad about working at a convenience store. It's something we all need and use."

"Of course," she said. "But if you were the valedictorian and queen of the nerds in high school, and your IQ score got you into Mensa when you were twelve, there are certain—expectations."

"It's your life. You don't need to live up to anyone's expectations."

"I agree. The problem is, they were also my expectations." She pointed across the street at Taco Tuesday. "Is that where we're going? It's not Joe's Burritos anymore."

"Taco Tuesday is catchier. Plus, Joe was not a young guy when we were in high school. He's probably retired."

"Let's go."

They waited for a break in the traffic, then jogged together across the street, weaving between parked cars at the curb. Roman held the door open for her, and she smiled as she walked in ahead of him.

Was this a date? He was sure a Broad Street stroll could easily be explained as two guests at the same inn walking side by side in the same direction, but once food was happening at a table between them, that was a date, right?

He should be embarrassed at the thrill that went through him at the prospect of having burritos with Ana. But that emotion was overtaken by something else—a contentment. A feeling of finally experiencing something he'd been too afraid to set in motion when he was young.

It was between lunch and dinner times, so Taco Tuesday had only a few diners and no customers in front of them. Ana was already at the counter, ordering her burrito. She wasn't kidding about how hungry she was; it took her a full minute to explain all the extras she wanted. When Roman stepped up to the counter, the two men behind the counter called, "Heeeeeeey, Roman Montgomery!"

Roman laughed. "I haven't been in here in a few years."

"It's not as if we get out much," Darryl said, stirring the rice with vigor.

"Clearly," Roman said. "How's Joe?"

"Retired."

"I figured as much."

"Sold us the place," Kyle, at the register, said. "Both of us. He's in South Carolina now, emails us pictures of the beach. Like we don't got a beach right here."

"Down there he gets to go every day," Roman pointed out. "He's done with Rhode Island winters."

"Lucky bastard." Darryl turned his attention back to the refried beans.

Roman ordered his own burrito and asked for two margaritas, glancing at Ana as he did. She nodded her approval.

"You look good, buddy," Kyle said.

"Ah, you're a liar," Roman said. "I certainly don't look like I used to."

"No one looks like they did in high school," Kyle said, holding out his hand for Roman's debit card. "And I didn't say you look the same. I said you look good." Ana tried to hand him her card too, and he told her, "Your money's no good here. Let your boyfriend take care of you."

"He's not—"

"It's good to see you," Kyle interrupted her, handing Roman's card back and clapping him on the shoulder. "Seasalter High baseball never recovered from you graduating."

Darryl slid the burritos across the counter and winked at Ana. "Some extra chips for you. Don't share them with him."

Ana grinned. "Thanks. I won't."

"That's the spirit."

Roman let Ana lead them to a small corner booth in the back. Exactly the table he'd have picked, if this were a date.

"You're a celebrity," Ana said, rolling her eyes. "For your information, if we stopped at the library, I assure you they'd roll out the red carpet for me. That was where I was the popular girl."

"I don't doubt it." He pointed. "That's Kyle and Darryl. You didn't come to Joe's?"

"I did, but apparently I didn't make the impression you did. People didn't really notice me back then."

Was she kidding? Noticing Ana was his part-time job back then. "The team always came here after games."

"Thanks for lunch," Ana said. "But you didn't have to buy. I'm sure—I'm sure I'll get another job soon."

"I'm sure you will too. Believe me, that's not a pity burrito."

"Pity burrito," she repeated, and took the biggest bite he'd ever seen a human take of anything. The way she closed her eyes in pleasure at what was happening in her mouth tightened his groin. "That would be a great concept for a restaurant," she said after swallowing.

"What do you mean?" He licked the salt off the rim of the margarita glass and took a sip. Perfect.

"Like, a mood restaurant. Comfort food is a thing, right? So maybe a menu that pairs up foods with emotions. 'Pity Burrito, to buy your friend who just got fired.'"

"I get it. Like, 'I'm So Over It Mac and Cheese, for when you're done with the world.'"

"Yes! 'Breakup Sundae, because what's two thousand calories when your heart's been ripped out and squashed?' "

"Or 'Pat on the Back Pizza, because you deserve it for doing the thing.' "

"You are tremendous at this," Ana said.

Roman couldn't help beaming at her praise. He wasn't used to rushing to keep up with conversation and he was pleased with his own ability. Maybe he'd needed her to discover he had it in him. "Not sure what food I'd pair with 'just got fired because my jilted friend needs me.' "

"I don't either. Not hot dogs, though."

"Agreed."

"Lacey wasn't jilted, by the way. Jake was."

"Whatever you say."

She scowled at him, but it didn't have much bite behind it.

"I'm really sorry about your job," Roman said.

Ana half shrugged. "I'll survive. I have two roommates at my apartment in Staten Island. One roommate was between jobs for two months, and we all pulled it together until she found a new one. I'm not too worried."

Her tone didn't match the confidence of her words, but Roman didn't say that.

"Meanwhile," she said, "the most important thing now for me is Lacey. I have a chance to—" She stopped, and he noticed her eyes were wet. He wanted to take her hand or give her a napkin, but something told him she didn't want her tears called out.

"I understand," Roman said. "I'm going to support Jake the same way."

"You are?"

"Yes. He asked me to stay a few more days also. A week sounds about right. So that's my goal, too."

"I haven't … I haven't been a very good friend," Ana said. "Not since law sch—"

She cut herself off and glanced at him before turning her attention to her plate again.

So she did go to law school.

Something happened that she didn't want to talk about. But he wouldn't push. He wasn't sure if it was selfishness at not wanting to spoil this date / not date, or sensitivity to her secrets, but it was at least partly the latter.

"I don't want to get into it," she finally said, "but suffice it to say that it was my fault that my friendships faded into nostalgia. I allowed myself to forget how important those women have been to me, and it would … *mean* a lot to me to get something right. To rebuild myself as a better person, at least in this one way."

"You're doing it. You're here for Lacey now," he told her. "This is when it counts. When someone is down and out, that's when you have the chance to prove what kind of friend you are."

"Exactly," she said, seemingly relieved that he didn't take this conversation down the law school path. "Lacey deserves so much more."

"So does Jake. My older brother, Tony, got a divorce four years ago, and it was the worst thing to ever happen to him other than our father—" He stopped himself there, because he could keep things to himself also if Ana could. "And I wasn't there for him either. I thought I was. I was really busy at the time, living in Boston and working in an insurance office and coaching Little League, and wrapped up in my own life. Tony called me every week to talk, so I thought I was being supportive, and though he sounded sad, I never came back here to see him in person because he told me not to. I allowed him to put me first, and I shouldn't have."

"That's what older brothers do," Ana said. "I assume. I'm an only child."

"I did come home to go to court with him to finalize the divorce, and it wasn't until I saw him—with so much new gray in his hair and dark circles under his eyes and pale skin and permanent frown—that I realized how hurt he was, how I'd missed the chance to support him the way I should have."

"That's terrible. I'm so sorry. How is he now?"

"He's better. I come to Seasalter every two or three months now to visit him and Mom, and they're both ... managing."

"Is he in a new relationship?"

"No." He couldn't even imagine it for Tony, not after that huge mess.

"You live in Boston?"

"Yes."

"You're in insurance?"

"For a while but it wasn't my thing. I've been giving a few different careers a trial run because I want to love what I do. I recently started working as a real estate agent, and it's the closest thing to ideal I've found. I'm still learning, but I think I'll stick with it a while because I really do like meeting people, finding out what their dreams are, seeing if I can find the right place for them."

For their stability. Roman's job allowed him the satisfaction of offering the opportunity of stability, in the form of a house, to others. Others who would do a better job at making a life and a home with a partner than he would.

"You are talking about it like you love it." Ana took a long sip of her margarita, not meeting his eyes. "That's a sign you're on the right track."

"I think so."

"You're—you're staying at the Moonrise Inn for the week?"

"Yeah. My mom is still in the house I grew up in, but it's in the middle of some major renovation. I don't think my old room is quite intact anymore. And even if it were, I don't think waking up at six every morning for the contractors to start drilling and hammering would be ideal."

"Ah."

"My brother has a one-bedroom down on Prince Street, but he has limited space. I don't want to sleep on his pullout sofa for a week."

"That would be unpleasant."

"I'll definitely mooch some dinners at Mom's. You're welcome to join us."

"It's very nice of you to offer, but—"

"Don't say no yet. Wait a few days and see if you crave some homemade ravioli."

"Okay," she said. "Thank you. My parents—don't know I'm in town."

"Yeah. I got the impression you're kind of a lone wolf, so I'm not surprised."

She nodded and used a plastic fork to scoop up burrito filling that fell onto her plate. "It's a little strange how I talk to you. As if we're … close. For all intents and purposes, I just met you today, even though I knew who you were before."

Roman hoped it was because she trusted him, or had decided he was worthy of her deeper thoughts, or both. "We're friends."

"Just like that?"

"Well, not *just* like that. We went through an ordeal this morning. We're connected now."

He mentally reprimanded himself for saying something so bold, but she only smiled. He watched her scoop the last of the rice and beans. He loved that she ate voraciously, without apology.

"We probably shouldn't be hanging out like this," Roman said. "Or talking. This is crossing enemy lines."

She opened her mouth, closed it to think a moment, then opened it again. "I'm not sure if you're joking or not, but to be honest, Lacey said at the hotel today that—" She stopped herself.

"Come on. You can't not tell me now."

"No, it wouldn't be right."

"Tell me, and I'll tell you what Jake said, and then we'll be even and keep it all between us. You did say you wanted a confidant."

Ana sighed. "She said Jake is—well, I'll redact her particular adjective-and-noun combination for the sake of privacy—and that all his friends are—again, I'll censor myself. My point is, you are a minion to Jake's supervillain. As her bridesmaid, I was obligated to agree that you are a pack of vile trolls. Sorry. It's not personal to you."

"Yet, vile troll feels kind of personal to me."

"It's not. At least, not for me. I admit that if this were yesterday, my heart would have been more in it. But since getting to know your human side, I was slightly less enthusiastic in my denouncement of you and your boys."

"I won't tell Jake. I promised you I would confess something also," Roman said, putting down the last bite of his burrito and lacing his fingers together earnestly. "Jake called Lacey and all her friends a bunch of harpies and witches who transform at night into bloodsucking insects of Satan."

"That's quite a paranormal mashup."

"I was forced to agree. And for the record, I want to say I don't believe a word of it."

"You'll find out, won't you?" Ana said. "We are staying at the same inn. If you see a creepy spider or beetle in your room, you'd better think twice before squashing me. I mean, it."

Roman fought the urge to lean over the table, take her face into his hands, and kiss her until Taco Tuesday collapsed into dust around them.

Then he wondered why he should fight the urge. She was grinning. She seemed happy to be here. Happy to be with him. He could—

His phone buzzed.

"Pardon me," he said, and glanced at his phone.

I miss you. Let me know when you'd like to visit your mother. xx

He felt a twinge of the guilt he always felt when his mother said she missed him. He'd seen what missing his father did to her, and though her text was lighthearted, his responsibility weighed on him as much as it always did.

He looked at Ana, and reality came crashing down on his skull.

He couldn't kiss her.

He wasn't the man for anyone, least of all her.

A woman like Ana Capuano deserved a man who would know how to never break her heart. And Roman was not that man. He knew nothing.

They were on opposite sides of the Wedding War, but he had no business pursuing anything with her either way.

Except friendship.

"I appreciate your commitment to confidential talk," Ana said, "but we need to limit our contact with one another from here on out."

"Why?"

"You know why. You just said it. You need to be here for Jake. I need to be here for Lacey. Our friendships are the priority."

"You're not wrong," he acknowledged, wishing she were.

"And though it's traitorous, I have enjoyed this."

"What?"

He was aware he was making her articulate it, but she didn't seem to mind. "Having burritos with you. Chatting. You're the one bearable thing that's happened today."

"Just bearable, huh? Not exactly a ringing endorsement of me."

"More than bearable," Ana admitted. "Happy?"

Delirious. "It'll do."

"If you tell Jake or any of your other bonehead friends that I said you're bearable, I'll call you a liar."

"I won't say that, but they're not boneheads."

"Sorry."

"No offense taken. Emotions are high."

They studied one another for a few moments before Ana opened her purse, withdrew a little blue cloth, removed her glasses, and wiped the lenses. Roman hid a smile at the little red dent the glasses had imprinted on the bridge of her nose. She squinted a bit at what she was doing, hinting at how bad her uncorrected vision was.

It was a small intimacy, unsmudging her glasses in front of him, and he wasn't prepared for the way his heart expanded in his chest, pushing against his sternum.

She slid her glasses back on and looked at him, startling back. "Whoa."

"What?"

"I didn't realize how unfortunate-looking you actually are. Thank God I cleaned my lenses, or I might have continued to think you were hot."

"Was that what you thought?"

"Doesn't matter what I used to think. I've seen the light, and now I can barely stand to look at you. Good thing, because it's going to make staying away from you far easier."

She winked and he grinned despite the truth: Staying away from Ana was going to be impossible. "This is it, then?" he asked, his grin fading. "Forever?"

Disappointment flitted across her face. "Unless Lacey and Jake work it out."

"You think they'll work it out?"

"I have no idea," she said. "I'm still not even sure why either of them called it off. This afternoon didn't involve any real talking. It was mostly just tears and swearing and eating the wedding cake."

"*You* got the cake?"

"Sure did. It was delicious."

Roman sighed. "I don't know what's going on either but I'm sure we'll find out."

Ana stood and started to gather their plates and wrappings and empty cups.

"Leave it," Kyle called. "I'll get it."

"Don't be silly," she said. Roman carried the dishes and glasses to the counter as Ana dutifully separated the recyclables from the trash and threw them into their respective receptacles.

"She's a sweet one," Darryl murmured, taking the plates from Roman. "Pretty too."

"She's the smartest woman in every room she's in," Roman said.

Darryl raised his eyebrows.

Roman and Ana stepped outside into the slanted late-afternoon sun. "Well, Roman Montgomery," Ana said. "This is goodbye."

She put out her hand, and he hesitated for one moment, certain that if he touched her, it wouldn't be goodbye. It would never be goodbye.

Jake's anguished face rose in his memory, followed by Tony's.

Roman put out his hand and took hers, softening his natural grip the way he did when he shook a woman's hand, but she squeezed so hard, one of their joints cracked.

"Impressive grip," he remarked. "Make sure you shake hands exactly like this at your next hot-dog job interview. You'll definitely land it."

She looked him right in the eye, her face serious. He opened his mouth to pull his foot out of it and apologize, but she laughed. And laughed and laughed, until he joined in. They doubled over. He propped his hands on his knees, and she grabbed his upper arm as they laughed out every moment of tension this day had brought them.

When the peals subsided, she wiped her eye with her bare forearm. "I think that is the first time I've ever allowed myself to laugh at … everything."

"You're allowed to. That's the best place to start over."

She stood tall and let her shoulders relax. "Bye, Roman."

"Bye, Ana."

She turned and began walking in the direction of the Moonrise Inn.

So did he, about four steps behind her.

After half a block, she stopped and allowed him to catch up.

"I suppose it would be goofy for us to just not walk together," she said.

"It would."

They lapsed into a companionable silence. A curly-haired child ran toward, then between them with a scoop of chocolate ice cream balancing precariously on the rim of a sugar cone. An older couple in practically identical khaki shorts strolled around them, their arms encircling each other's waists, pastel sweatshirts tied around their shoulders. Restaurants' outdoor tables were starting to fill with people enjoying a late-summer mojito or an indulgent plate of loaded nachos. Seagulls hovered overhead as if suspended on marionette strings, crying their indignance at everything.

"At least," Roman said, "we're back home."

Ana nodded, the faintest smile on her face.

They turned onto Oceanview and walked half a block in the shade of rustling leaves to the Moonrise Inn.

Roman allowed himself a moment of satisfaction at walking up the porch steps and into the gorgeous house at the end of a harrowing day with the most beautiful woman in the world.

It wasn't in his future, so he might as well appreciate it in the present.

"I'm in the Stardust Suite," Ana said. "Right here."

"I'm next to you, in the Sea of Tranquility."

"It's not going to be tranquil. I snore."

"The walls probably aren't that thin."

"My roommates have informed me that my snores would penetrate a stone fortress."

"I look forward to finding out," he said.

Now that it really was a sort of goodbye, he didn't know what else to say. He supposed Ana didn't either, because she just put her key in the door, offered a small smile, went inside, and closed the door.

It would be creepy to stand outside her door. So instead, he stood outside his room door. For a long time.

CHAPTER 5

After a few hours of lounging on the comfortable sofa and watching TV, Ana still wasn't tired enough to go to bed. It was only eight thirty, anyway.

It was a good thing she never got Roman's phone number, because she was tempted to text him and say—anything, really. She felt she could say anything to him, and he would understand.

But it wasn't simply the craving of companionship.

It was craving, period.

Roman Montgomery had been every Seasalter High girl's obsession, but Ana had been far too driven to particularly care for boys. Ana was far more attracted to him now, to the body that she could easily gaze upon after he'd changed into shorts and a T-shirt before they went out. The teen-athlete muscles had softened, and he seemed like an easy chair she could relax into after sex, rather than a bag of hard rocks.

Sex?

She couldn't remember when the word had last crossed her mind, or when the desire had last crossed her body, but both had happened today with this man, several times. When he took her hand, she'd nearly yanked him toward her to kiss him, to see if she could taste margarita salt on his expressive lips.

Ana couldn't help wishing she'd done something to regret. Just once, before she'd fled into the Stardust Suite for hours of television in her underwear. But repairing her relationships with Lacey and Sarai and Kate was the first opportunity she'd had in a long time to return to a little bit of what she used to be, and now that she'd made her mind up to do it, Roman was merely a distraction.

A devastatingly handsome, funny, and charming distraction. But a distraction, nonetheless.

Ana hated air conditioning, so she'd opened all the windows in both rooms of her little suite to let in the sea breeze. She was on the ground floor, but the hedges were tall around the property, so Labor Day vacationers wouldn't see her in her room. Normally, she wouldn't have booked a suite, but she loved the photos of it online, and it was only for one night—she'd assumed. If she were going to sleep away from home for the first time since the hospital, she would allow herself to spend a few extra dollars for the comfort.

Now, jobless, she'd need to pay for a week in this room. Not that her miserable job would have been enough to afford this.

Luckily, she had room on her credit card since she wasn't much of a spender on anything. And maybe she could ask Selene to switch her to a smaller room when the Labor Day guests checked out.

And if she couldn't, well, Ana could consider the expense her penance for letting her friendships crumble into dust.

Not that this inn felt like any sort of punishment, with that peaceful sitting room and homemade cookies on two plates in the breakfast room and the hottest man she'd ever met in the room next door.

Ana abruptly pushed herself off the sofa and went into the bedroom, putting on the shorts and T-shirt she'd removed earlier. Then she returned to the TV room and slid the sofa back about six inches, giving her a little more floor room.

In her recovery from her breakdown, Ana had discovered that physically working out eased her anxiety immensely, for the hour or so that she exercised and sometimes even for the rest of the day following it. In New York, even the least expensive gyms weren't in Ana's meager budget, so she trained in front of the television, with YouTube fitness videos and a padded mat and free weights that she kept in the living room. When the videos began to bore her, she created her own programs, combining high-intensity dance intervals, dumbbell work, and proprioceptive stretching in adventurous and unique patterns to keep it fun and beneficial. She found herself researching functional movement and complementary muscle groups. She completed an online, go-at-your-own-pace fitness certification course. She filled a couple of spiral notebooks and a notes app on her phone with plans and put together playlists of music she loved.

She moved around the floor now, careful not to make too much noise. She didn't have any dumbbells with her, but she'd tossed a resistance band in her duffel, so she used that for part of her workout. She listened to a playlist of songs that complemented her stronger moves and encouraged her to sweat, and songs that were slower and more languid, offering an opportunity to sink into stretches.

Forty-five minutes later, her body was achy and gooey, but her mind hadn't quite gone as quiet as she'd hoped. She slid the sofa back into place, and after allowing her sweat to evaporate a bit, she slid the key into one pocket and her phone in the other, then paused at the door, her hand on the doorknob.

Ana was an in-for-the-night kind of person. She didn't leave the house spontaneously once her day was over. Being at home was a comfort for her. When she was at the hospital, the staff had checked her whereabouts every fifteen minutes, and instead of being annoyed by it, she liked it. She might be reading in bed, or sitting in the common room watching a sitcom, or playing cards, and each time she spotted the staff member checking on her, she'd wave and smile. It was their job, but it instilled in her a sense of security. In the five years since, she'd had no one to do that for her; she could do that for herself, though, and did.

But here she was in a hotel, already breaking her routine. Might as well go out. The town was familiar ground, after all.

She opened the door, trying to be silent but cringing when it squeaked. She glanced at the Sea of Tranquility, noticing the light was still on under the door. She was embarrassed to already know that Roman hadn't left the room, because she'd been watching the TV on low, listening for his door. She wasn't sure why.

She locked her room and walked through the sitting room, illuminated by soft candlelight. She left the inn, letting the door swing shut behind her.

She walked through the little garden in the not-quite darkness. Tall sunflowers waved to her as she headed down the slate walkway through little white stones. She opened the gate to the street, and gulls shrieked a companionable song to her as she headed to the beach.

The street was lined with farm-style houses in different colors. The sky-blue Moonrise Inn with its black shutters and trim was the largest house on the short block, though two other houses sported inn and B&B signs. Though she hadn't grown up on this particular street, it was representative of the style of the entire small town.

Ana came to the final intersection, crossed, and walked up the steps to traverse a little wooden bridge over the dunes. Finally, she came to the boardwalk and settled herself on the first bench she saw. Wind whipped her hair around her face as she gazed at the ocean. It sparkled under the moon, which would be full in a few days, Ana guessed.

She turned in her seat and watched the boardwalk for a few minutes. She crossed one arm over her chest for protection against the cooling breeze. One cyclist zipped past her, and several people jogged at different paces in both directions. Then she turned back around and looked at the beach again. The sand was clean and white and, as she knew from years of playing in it, very soft, and the tide was coming in.

The beach was a little more lively than it would ordinarily be at this hour; the holiday had spurred vacationers to put on windbreakers and remain in the summer bliss, some with music coming out of speakers.

Ana lived in New York City now, but despite the urban sprawl, she wasn't far from the ocean. She would never be able to live far inland. The beach was eternal peace.

She closed her eyes and listened to the waves crash, the thumping Latin beats, the spinning of bike chains. She heard Lacey giggling as she pointed at a cute boy in swim trunks, and Sarai humming along with a pop song, and Kate screaming as the cold saltwater hit her ankles.

We're back home, Roman said in her ear.

Ana felt the sting of tears. She didn't know why, but instead of trying to figure it out, she considered how human tears were salty, as if they all had their own oceans inside.

She stood, grasped the metal railing of the boardwalk, and leaned toward the horizon for a moment, inhaling. Then she walked back to the inn.

When she pushed open the door, she startled to find Roman sitting on the blue sofa in the sitting room. He hadn't turned on a lamp; instead, he lounged in the candlelight and the light from his phone screen as he tapped away. But as soon as he looked up, he stood. "Hey."

He wore dark sweatpants—in the dim light, she couldn't tell if they were black or navy or green—and a white T-shirt with a small hole in the hem.

"You didn't have to get all dressed up for me," Ana said. Because if she didn't say that, she might have said what she was really thinking, which was in direct opposition to their agreement to stop spending time together.

"Noted," he said. "Next time I'll go for something less formal than what I sleep in."

Ana was glad for the primitive lighting concept so he didn't see her blush, now knowing she was seeing him in what he wore to bed.

"Can't sleep?" she asked.

"It's a little early for me to sleep. I'll be honest. I heard your door open and then I heard the front door open, so I thought I'd come out here and ... well ..."

"Were you waiting up for me?"

"I wanted to make sure you got back okay from wherever you went," he finished.

"I walked down to the beach," she said.

"I can tell."

"How?"

"Your hair is kind of ... beachy now."

She lifted a hand and tried to run her fingers through, but beachy meant knotty, and that was what she found. She gave up trying to comb through it and looked around so she didn't have to meet his eyes in candlelight.

"Oh." She pointed at the two bottom shelves in a tall bookcase. "Board games."

"Really?" He stood, walked around the coffee table, and crouched down into the dark corner. Ana flipped on a small lamp on a side table; the bulb was warm. The poetry curtains danced.

"This is an old favorite," he said, pulling out a board game. "Want to play?"

"Roman Montgomery plays board games?" Ana couldn't help asking. "Thought that was strictly nerd territory."

"Tony and my mother loved board games. We played a lot, especially after …"

Ana waited a breath. "After what?"

"After my dad was … gone. Playing board games gave our evenings and weekends some structure, and something to think about instead of thinking about him. Board games are … comforting, I guess."

Ana waited a few moments, but Roman began to set up the game board and didn't elaborate. She didn't ask if his father had died or left; best to let him tell her such an intimate detail in his own time.

Eventually she said, "But we decided to not … hang out."

His face brightened. "I've been thinking about that. We're staying in the same inn, so it would be senseless to just walk around each other and not talk. The Moonrise Inn can be a neutral ground. If we want to talk or play board games, we can. It's not like it's … a big thing."

"Right," Ana said slowly. "It's just convenience."

"I'll casually not mention to my friends that you're here, and you can do the same."

Ana thought for a moment. Roman held up the game box and raised his eyebrows hopefully.

"Sure, set it up," she said.

They sat on the floor and set up the game on the coffee table. Roman pressed the bubble in the center to roll the dice, and winced as it made a pop.

"All the other guest rooms are upstairs, I think," Ana said. "Besides, it's only about nine o'clock. I think we can make a little noise. And I love that noise."

"So do I."

They popped the dice and moved their pieces around, and for the first time since dropping out of law school and checking into the hospital, Ana wished she had something she could bring to a relationship: accomplishment, money, ambition. Anything of value.

She popped the dice bubble and shrugged off the feeling as she counted spaces on the board. No use dwelling on something that couldn't happen anyway. The Wedding War had closed the book on that.

CHAPTER 6

The next morning, when the guests had all eaten breakfast and left for whatever their days held, Selene collapsed onto the blue sofa and dropped her head back.

Was it even possible to take a nap?

No one had requested made beds or new towels yet, so she was off the hook for one thing, but she still had thousands of other chores to prioritize and do.

Should she have hired some help before she was certain she'd be able to afford it?

Probably, but the worry of not being able to do everything alone would be replaced with the worry that she'd discover too late that she couldn't pay someone. Best to wait and see what the books yielded. After this weekend, it would quiet down.

Was everyone having fun?

The Raines couple in Supernova told her they loved the pancakes. Breakfast was always the one meal Selene didn't manage to make a mess of, but still, she was pleased at the compliment. She was surprised that the lovebirds in Milky Way were even able to eat, they were so enamored with one another. The woman, Terri, told Selene it was still a new relationship, and their first getaway weekend together.

Her two first-floor guests were the most interesting, though: Ana and Roman. Former classmates who seemed to not know each other very well. But last night, Selene had crept down the stairs silently to grab a towel for herself, and she saw Ana and Roman playing a board game. They kept a respectful distance between them on the floor, the way newer friends would. But they didn't notice Selene at all; the sparks between them were so strong, Selene had glanced in the corner to make sure the fire extinguisher was in its proper place.

Selene wondered if an unexpected zero-hour broken engagement could sprout something more real and lasting, and if it could be happening here.

There's magic here, Dan reminded her now.

The front door opened, and Selene lifted her head, standing quickly when she realized it wasn't a current guest. It was a man she'd never seen before—perhaps he wanted to book a room.

"Welcome to the Moonrise Inn," Selene said, the words rolling off her tongue more easily than they had the first time she'd said them. She'd gotten used to the phrase after saying it several times yesterday. "Can I help you?"

He said nothing, just studied the room. Selene glanced around as well, suddenly worried something was out of place, but everything was where it should be. The thin smoke of airy incense carried around the room and out the open window.

She looked back at him. He was tall, maybe about six foot three, and he was casual in jeans, a gray T-shirt, and sneakers. His salt-and-pepper hair was just long enough to hang over the tops of his ears and to flop over his forehead. His eyes were a startling and unexpected dark green.

"Can I help you?" she repeated in the same friendly tone.

She waited, but still he said nothing. A muscle near his jaw twitched.

Every time Selene sat in this room, it brought her peace. She'd noticed when Ana checked in, her shoulders relaxed in this room. Claudine Raines had said yesterday that this room had made her want to close her eyes, sit in the corner, and meditate. So Selene wasn't sure what about this room could possibly be making this stranger angry.

After another solid minute of watching the seething man take in the room, Selene said, "Tea?"

The man looked at her then, and blinked, as if waking from a daze. "What?"

"It seems you plan on staying a while," Selene said. "Offering you tea seems like the polite thing to do. And maybe my polite thing will inspire you to do something polite in return, like say hello." She kept her voice cheerful, kept the smile on her face.

He narrowed his eyes into green slits. "Are you the owner?"

"Yes, I'm Selene. And you are—?"

"You were supposed to open a while ago. But you didn't."

"No. We didn't."

"But now you're open."

Selene raised her brows. "Excellent observation. Do you need a room?"

He laughed, but it was humorless. "You standing here, in *this* house, and asking *me* if I need a room is about as crazy as it gets."

Selene put a hand on her back pocket to assure herself she had her phone if she needed help.

"I'm not sure what else to offer," she said. "This is an inn, so we have rooms. Though not this weekend. We're booked through tomorrow."

"I don't care. I don't want a room."

Selene crossed her arms. "Listen. I'm perfectly happy to help anyone coming into my place of business. Until you talk to me with disrespect. Then, surprise—I'm a lot less willing to assist you. You don't strike me as someone not in control of his faculties, so you obviously want something. Please say it."

"Why did you take so long to open?" he demanded. "You bought this place, and an open date was posted. There were renovations—then nothing. Everything was closed up tight. Until now. I just want to know what's going on, and what your intentions are."

Selene pulled in her chin, not even trying to hide her incredulous expression. "Why do you care? What's your interest in our business?"

"Who's 'we'?"

"What?"

"You keep saying 'we' and 'our.' Is there another owner? Your husband? Where is he?"

A flash of hot red bloomed behind Selene's vision, and she waited for it to clear before she said evenly, "Yes, the other owner is my husband. And he's dead."

"Oh." He looked genuinely stricken. "I'm … oh, God, I'm sorry."

"I said 'we' for twenty-five years," Selene added. "It's a hard habit to break, especially when I'm not particularly interested in breaking it."

"Of course not. I'm—I'm really sorry. I had no idea."

"I don't know how you could have." Selene swallowed the tears that threatened to rise from her throat and into her eyes. "And honestly, how dare you? What is your problem?"

"I—"

"Answer me," Selene said. "Who are you to think you can come in here asking rude and weird questions and demanding anything from me? More simply, who are you?"

He lifted his hands to her, palms up.

"This is my house."

★ ★ ★

Selene handed the man a mug of tea, and she gestured for him to sit in the white armchair. He moved a blue pillow aside and sat as she sat on the sofa across from him with her own tea.

"Talk," she said. "Start with your name."

"My name is Owen Cardiff. I—I'm sorry. What was your name again?"

"Selene Bellamy."

"Pretty name."

Selene cocked her head and waited.

"I grew up in this house," Owen said. "My older brother, my younger sister, and I were all raised here until we went to college."

Selene nodded slowly. "You do realize that growing up here doesn't mean it's your house now."

"My father grew up here," he continued, "and his father grew up here. My great-grandfather was the original owner. My room was the third floor, first door on the left."

"The smallest room."

"Yeah," he said, a ghost of a smile on his face. "All my birthdays until I was eighteen. Every Christmas. Every important day and every unimportant day was … here."

"I understand. This place was your home."

"It's supposed to be my home now."

"I suppose that's the part I don't understand."

"My mother died fifteen years ago."

"Oh, I'm so sorry. She was young."

"Yes," he said, his voice fading on the word. But it got stronger again when he said, "I was surprised when Dad got married again three years later."

"Not everyone wants to be alone forever," Selene said. She would be, but that wasn't anything to say to Owen.

"Yeah, well … the woman he married wasn't exactly fond of me."

"Let me guess. You made as good a first impression with her as you did with me."

"I'm sorry, I—"

"No, I'm sorry. Please, go on."

"I did make a bad first impression," he admitted. "Dad hadn't even told us he was dating anyone before he announced he was engaged. I made my confusion and my disappointment and my shock fully known when I finally met her at their engagement party. To everyone."

Selene raised her brows.

"Not my finest moment, I confess. Nor my most mature."

"No, but eventually forgivable, I'd say, under the circumstances." She almost took a sip of tea but she wasn't really thirsty. The warm cup was all she really needed right now; some comfort in this baffling conversation.

"She never forgave me. Anyway, they were married for about nine years, then Dad also died."

Selene shook her head in sympathy.

"Dad always intended this house to go to me," he said. "We talked about it a few times. My brother's in California and my sister is in Maine, and neither of them wanted to come back to Rhode Island, so it was agreed that this house would be mine. But ... at some point, Dad changed the will so everything was left to his wife, to split as she saw fit."

"Why?"

"I don't know. She was his wife. I suppose they discussed it, and he wanted to take care of her, and that was that. I'm sure he wanted to tell me, but he never got the chance."

"I think I can guess this one, too. She didn't give you the house."

"No. But when she didn't want to live here anymore, she decided to sell it. I told her I would buy it. She led me to believe it was a done deal."

"But?"

"But then she sold it out from under me."

"To me and Dan."

"Yes."

"I didn't know there was any dispute. And I'm sure Dan didn't."

"No, he couldn't have known. But I—I was angry."

"I imagine so. That's a lot of loss in just a few years."

He brushed a hand over his thigh, as if sweeping away lint, but Selene didn't see any. "All I wanted to do was come home."

Selene sighed. "We had a tight schedule, but we were on track to open the inn quickly. But ..."

"Your husband," Owen said quietly.

"Yes, and I couldn't—" Selene swallowed. "It took me a while. I'm sorry you had to wait so long to be able to walk in the door again."

"I'm sorry I put you in a position to apologize. It's not your fault."

Neither said anything for a while, looking around each other politely. Eventually, they locked gazes.

"I hope," Selene finally said, "you're not here to try to make some kind of deal."

"I'll make any offer you need."

"We just renovated."

"I see that."

"My enthusiastic husband convinced me to make a higher offer than we should have. And already it's worth more than that. You have access to that kind of money?"

"I'm not a rich man," Owen said. "But I'm a fair one."

"Then as a fair man, you'll understand when I say thank you, but no, thank you."

"You're running this place alone? No help?"

Selene stood and held out her hand for his mug. He gave it to her and his fingers touched hers; they were surprisingly warm. "Thanks for stopping by, Owen. And you're welcome to stop by any time and visit your former home."

"I didn't mean to insult you," he said. "I meant that you could just take the money and walk away."

Selene looked at the crescent moon etched into the base of the table lamp. It seemed to wink its own cheerful eye at her. *We can do this.*

Owen apparently took her silence as consideration. "Do you have hospitality experience?"

"No, I don't have any experience. I'm a writer. I was a writer."

"So wha—"

"You think I'm in over my head."

"Are you?"

"Yes," she said simply. "I am. And I know that I could take your money and walk away, and that would make my life a lot easier. But it's not what I will do."

Suddenly everything went very ... still.

As if the house stopped breathing.

"What just happened?" she murmured, then realized the little fan by the kitchen door had stopped whirring. And the little digital clock on the table by the front door had gone dark.

"The power went out," she said. "Will you see yourself out? I need to take care of this."

"Of course." Owen moved to the door. "It was nice to meet you, Selene."

She held up her hand behind her in a wave, then rushed down the hallway and opened the door to the basement. She flicked the light switch, then shook her head at herself when no light went on. She powered up the flashlight on her phone and clattered down the stairs.

Strange. No storm, no high wind today. Probably just a fuse.

She stepped around some boxes and made her way to the fuse box. She squinted at the stickers labeling the different switches.

"Selene?" she heard from the top of the stairs. "Do you need help?"

"I'm fine, Owen," she called back, then thought better of it. With his help, she wouldn't have to run up and down the stairs. "Hey, wait, is the power back yet?"

"No."

"Is it all the rooms?"

"Yes."

Selene went back to the fuse box and flipped switches in frustration. "How about now?"

"Still no."

She cursed under her breath. "Are the other houses on the block out?"

"Hang on."

After a moment, he said, "No, I can see the traffic light on the corner headed to town and it's on. And the house across the street still has a porch light on from last night."

Selene had no idea what to do. She knew well the house they'd lived in for most of their marriage, but this house—Dan dealt with the contractors.

Dan did everything.

She banged a fist against her thigh in frustration before trudging up the stairs. Without power, she couldn't vacuum, she couldn't keep the coffeepot running, she couldn't even turn on a bathroom light—and neither could anyone else. After all the renovations, she and Dan had decided to wait a few months until colder weather to buy a generator. Then the winter had come and gone, and a new one was just a few months off.

Owen was at the top of the stairs. "Thanks," Selene said to him as she walked past him back to the front room. "If you'll excuse me, I'm going to call the electric company and take care of this."

"Wait."

She ignored him and searched for the number to the power company. Speaking of power, her phone battery was also low. As she pressed the last digit, the fan whirred to life. The clock on the front table blinked 12:00.

"Oh," she said, and Owen stood up from where he had been kneeling behind the armchair.

"Wha—did you just do something?" Selene asked.

He nodded to something near his feet. She kneeled on the chair and hung over the back of it to look at the outlet.

"That outlet," he said. "It's some kind of magic. Whatever's plugged into that. You have a nightlight there, so I just flicked it on and off again."

"Are you kidding?"

"Yeah, it's crazy."

Selene met his green gaze.

"I'm telling you," he said, "I know this house. Every quirk. Every crack. Everything."

"Well. Thank you."

"It's the least I can do. Are you sure you won't consider—"

"I'm sure," she said firmly. "But I meant what I said. You're welcome to stop by any time and visit the house. That's the best I can do."

He pressed his lips together in a thin line, and eventually nodded. He walked to the front door and put his hand on the door frame. He rested it there for a moment, as if absorbing—or offering—energy. Then he patted the frame once before leaving.

He didn't look back.

CHAPTER 7

"I don't know about this," Ana said, looking around the threadbare lobby of Monster Rage, a new business on the northern border of Seasalter. The secondhand sofas were mismatched, one gold velveteen and one faded purple brocade, and there were no windows in this warehouse space.

"What's to know?" Sarai asked. "We're going to break stuff."

"I have rage," Lacey said. "I need to let it out."

"Speaking as an actual therapist," Kate said, pushing a lock of silky black hair behind an ear, "this doesn't take the place of, say, actual therapy."

Kate was a family therapist with a thriving private practice in Boston. Her savvy and entertaining use of social media and her brilliant media networking skills had turned her into a hot influencer for mental health awareness and a darling of the Korean-American professional community.

Ana might never have known, had she not often searched phrases like "how to stop a panic attack" and "can anxiety ever be cured" and one day, Kate Yoon popped up, advising Ana how to cope. Ana was deeply jealous of Kate's success but couldn't help watching her twice-weekly videos. They really were informative, fun, accessible, and kind.

"My therapist is on speed dial right now," Lacey said. "Don't you worry about that. I just—I just have to get this anger out of my body somehow. I can only eat so much sugar. My cousin texted me and told me about this place."

"I'm all for it," Sarai said. "I don't have any real rage currently, but it's probably fun to break stuff. What about you,

Ana?" she asked. "Do you have any rage simmering under that cool and collected façade?"

"You have no idea," Ana said. Sarai paused, then chuckled a bit uncomfortably, clearly unsure if any subtext was lurking in Ana's deadpan delivery.

It wasn't subtext; Ana had made sure so far that her high school friends didn't have any real idea of what Ana's life was like. She didn't need their pity, their exchanged looks of helplessness, their caring platitudes. It would only make Ana feel worse about herself, if that were even possible.

A tall, thin man came in. "Hello, ladies. Ready to smash things?"

They all nodded. He fitted each of them with a helmet and a thick pair of gloves and handed them each a pair of goggles, instructing them to put them on. Ana carefully arranged them over her glasses. She had woken up at dawn to a late-night text from Lacey asking her to wear jeans and a long-sleeved shirt, and she'd put on the only ones she'd brought to Seasalter. She wondered again what she would do for clothing for the next few days. Hopefully Selene had a washer and dryer.

The man led them all into a room cluttered with bottles, ancient computer monitors, and old television sets. Mismatched plates and tea sets were stacked on crates.

"That's the smash zone," the man said, indicating a roped-off area of the room. "Only one of you can be in there smashing things at a time."

They all nodded. Despite her earlier warning, Kate glanced around eagerly, like she couldn't wait to demolish something.

The man gestured to a wall. "There are your smash implements. Baseball bats, crowbars."

Sarai's eyes widened behind the goggles.

It was all junk, but Ana had a twinge of guilt. Ever since she was a kid, she'd been so careful with her phones, her laptops, her collection of porcelain dolls; wanting to keep everything pristine and scratch-free. This went against everything she was. The thin thread of anxiety began to wind itself around her lungs.

Maybe she should beg out. She could meet them later—

"People like to smash to music," the man said. "I'll pipe it in for you if you want. Any preferences? Death metal is a popular choice."

"Your call," Sarai said to Lacey.

Lacey narrowed her eyes. "No, not death metal. I want classical music. Pretty music. Wedding music. Can you do that?"

He raised his eyebrows. "That's a first. But sure, you're the boss. You have thirty minutes. Feel free to scream. I can't hear anything out there. You probably won't get hurt, but if you do, press that red button on the wall there, and I'll come get you."

He left the windowless room, closing the metal door behind him.

Lacey turned in a small circle, assessing. Kate, Sarai, and Ana let her take the lead.

"It doesn't even seem that intimidating," Lacey said. "Once you've destroyed an engagement and a wedding, breaking TVs is almost a step back."

"Try it," Sarai encouraged. "See how it makes you feel."

Lacey grabbed four bottles of various shapes and color, and placed one on a table in the smash zone. She selected a fierce-looking crowbar and stood with it resting on her shoulder, considering the bottle. A string harmony began to play softly through the speakers in the ceiling, and one tear escaped from her goggles and slid down her cheek.

Ana was about to ask Lacey if she was okay when, without warning, Lacey swung the iron like an action hero and smashed the bottle. The other three women flinched, covering their heads instinctively before realizing they were far enough away.

"Yeah!" Sarai shouted.

Lacey lined the other three bottles up, fire in her eyes. She swung the iron again, this time with a Xena-like war cry. All three bottles exploded.

Sarai and Kate jumped up and down. "Woo! You got this!" they yelled. The adrenaline was contagious, and after a moment, Ana also found herself cheering.

Lacey pushed an old television set to the middle of the floor and began beating on it, shouting with abandon every time the crowbar came down on the mangled monitor. The screen smashed, wires sprang out the back of it, but each time she connected with it, her friends whooped and hollered.

A dot-matrix printer and two ugly vases later, Lacey held up her arms like a victorious warrior princess. All four of them screamed in shared rage.

"My turn," Sarai said, and Lacey handed her the crowbar.

Yesterday, Sarai had showed Ana pictures of her lovely townhouse and adorable Labradoodle and told Ana about her fulfilling work as a pediatric resident. Now, Sarai demolished a file cabinet, dent by massive dent. Ana could see fury on Sarai's face, even covered with safety equipment.

Sarai flung the crowbar on the ground with a final yell, and it bounced with a clang on the concrete. Kate glanced at Ana, and Ana nodded at the smash zone. Kate, the mild-mannered internet therapist, picked up the crowbar and destroyed an ancient two-tape-deck stereo system with no hesitation.

"Ana," Sarai said.

Ana turned away from the mesmerizing spectacle of Kate pulling knobs off the stereo and flinging them against the wall. Lacey stepped closer to them to hear Sarai also.

"I don't know what happened to you," Sarai said. "You don't have to tell us. But we're all so glad you're here."

"Yes." Lacey squeezed her arm.

"And you don't have to tell us but … you can," Sarai said. "We'll all understand."

"And even if we don't, you can trust us," Lacey added.

Icy, fearful fingers wrapped around Ana's heart.

"This … none of this is about me," Ana said. "This is Lacey's time."

"You did see the worst of my life yesterday," Lacey said. "But … we all have stuff."

Kate lowered her voice conspiratorially. "We absolutely do. I'll tell you stuff that will make you wonder how I can possibly be a therapist. I have my own therapist."

"So do I," Ana said with a small smile.

"Good. Everyone should," Kate said. "And everyone should have friends, too."

She held the crowbar out to Ana.

Ana waved off the weapon and moved to the smash zone.

She turned in a small circle. Her trepidation at breaking things had faded while watching the others do it, and she wanted to make sure what she chose would satisfy her—

Then she saw it.

A rickety, cracked three-shelf bookcase. It was unsalvageable, with two shelves broken and peeled paint. It listed to one side.

Ana put one hand on each side of it and walked it, side after side, out to the middle of the smash zone. She imagined it full of thick, intimidating law textbooks. Secondhand books full of other students' highlights and margin notes, because new texts were far too expensive.

She went to the weaponry wall and surveyed her choices, her gaze landing on an aluminum baseball bat. She picked it up.

Had she ever seen Roman play for Seasalter High? He had been an all-around athlete, but baseball had been his real talent, his real passion. She hadn't gone to any games but might she have seen him practicing on the diamonds in the field behind the school? She couldn't remember exactly.

Not the way she could remember his smile in the soft light of the Moonrise Inn's sitting room last night when she won the board game and pointed at him in a sore-winner manner. Not the way she could remember the warmth of his arm in the tuxedo jacket when he'd escorted her out to the altar. Not the way she could remember how he matched her in conversation, wit for wit, and his almost-surprised eyebrows at being able to do so.

She closed her eyes and saw his face again. Not the teenage Roman; this Roman, the remarkably funny and sweet and sexy man he'd become.

With her eyes still closed, she said loudly, "When I was at Columbia Law, in my second year, I was so overwhelmed."

The other women didn't answer, but the charged silence told her they were listening.

"I had three papers due in one week and I was so far behind. I never fell behind, not at high school, not at Yale. But I was burned out and lost and depressed and I didn't know how to dig myself out."

She clenched her back teeth so hard, she thought they might explode like one of Lacey's bottles. "I—I had a breakdown. They took me to the hospital."

She opened her eyes, heaved the bat over her head, and smashed the top of the bookcase. It cracked loudly all the way across.

She imagined the textbooks, filled with her dreams of success and accomplishment, falling out and scattering across the floor around her feet. "I was in the hospital for two weeks. I got on medication, I got a therapist, I did everything I could to come back." She pounded the top of the bookcase again, and this time the top shelf broke in two, wood splinters jutting up.

"I got back to school, and I stood outside my first class with my books and my bag, and I couldn't go in. Finally, the professor closed the door, and I just stood in the hallway until class was over."

She swung the bat around like a Major League slugger, and the bookcase fell onto its side. She loomed over it like a deranged assailant, holding the bat aloft again. "I dropped out of law school. My parents were upset. Concerned, then angry. They told me I had to figure out what I wanted."

She brought the bat down again and again, watching the two other shelves split apart. "The thing is ... I discovered I want nothing. I work jobs I don't care about. I don't have any real friends in New York. I don't *do* anything. And I'm so ashamed of all of it, but I'm most ashamed that I don't care anymore. I don't *want* to care anymore."

Roman's face surfaced in her mind again, and her tears fell freely. "I don't want to care," she said to him, and smashed the bookcase over and over until suddenly she was on her knees and the bat was rolling away and she was crying, and her friends were holding her, rocking her, comforting her the way she hadn't allowed anyone to for a long, long time.

"You do care," Lacey said into her ear. "Even if you don't want to, you do. You're here because you care about me."

"I do," Ana said through her sniffles. "I won't let you down ever again. I promise."

She scrunched her eyes shut and willed Roman's face away from her mind.

★ ★ ★

Of all the places Roman could have suspected Jake would want to drink away his troubles, Jasmine Pink's Tea Shoppe would have been the absolute last.

Jasmine's predated Roman's existence. It was a mainstay of Seasalter tourism; the buses that came from Boston and Providence full of retired ladies who wanted to enjoy the salt air while they shopped for cozy mysteries and kitchen towels always crowded into Jasmine's for a delicately flowered cup of brewed looseleaf oolong or green tea.

When Mark and Jake and Pete and Roman walked in, the little bell above the door tinkled and all the ladies at tables turned and widened their eyes at the bulky bulls who'd lumbered into their china shop.

Roman was about to apologize for intruding on their quaint afternoon when a woman behind the counter cried, "Jakey! You brought friends!"

"I did, Delilah," Jake said as the at least eighty-year-young woman hustled into the main shop and hugged him like he was a long-lost son, her mostly gray head pressed into his ribcage. Her arms didn't even go all the way around him, and she rubbed her hands up and down the sides of his back in a motherly way.

"I'm so sorry, honey," she said.

"For … you heard?" Jake asked.

"Seasalter isn't that big. People talk."

Mark rolled his eyes at Roman. "People should mind their own business," he muttered.

A muscle under Jake's eye twitched. Then he closed his eyes for a moment longer than a regular blink and opened them again. "I need your lavender chamomile."

"Perfect," Delilah said. "Exactly what I would have prescribed. Sit anywhere you like."

Roman glanced around. There were three tables free, but each looked constructed for a dolls' tea party. He was afraid if he sat in one of these chairs, it would splinter and squeak and collapse under him in a pile of kindling.

But Jake walked smoothly over to the table closest to the little fireplace, dragged out a chair, and sat with no issue. Mark, Roman, and Pete all glanced at one another before they did the same. Once seated, Roman rocked from one buttock to another, impressed with the strength of the small chair.

"And you, Jake's friends?" Delilah asked. "Out-of-towners?"

"No," Mark said. He pointed a thumb at Pete. "He and I live here. We all grew up here."

Delilah squinted at each of them in turn. Roman squirmed under her cafeteria-monitorlike scrutiny. "Why don't I know any of you?"

"We ... ah ..." Roman started, desperately searching his brain for diplomatic language.

"I understand," Delilah said. "Manly men. Not tea shop frequenters."

"That's right," Mark said, seemingly relieved she understood without explanation.

"Who are your mothers?"

They said nothing for a moment.

"Out with it," she said.

"Kim Crane," Mark said.

"Kim is absolutely lovely. A fan of my mint tea. So you're Mark."

"Yes," Mark said, surprised.

Delilah turned to the next young man.

"Georgina Strauss," Pete said.

"She was in yesterday! She's more of a coffee girl, but she comes in for the sugar doughnuts."

"I love those doughnuts."

"I bet you do, Pete. What about you?" she asked Roman.

"Theresa Montgomery."

Delilah laid a hand on her heart. "Theresa! She introduced me to your brother Tony once, so you must be Roman. Theresa is an angel walking this earth as a favor to the rest of us. And I don't say that capriciously. How is she? I haven't seen her in a while."

Roman felt a stab of worry. "Does she come in often?"

"Not too often, but often enough that I realize I haven't seen her. If you see her—"

"I will."

"I'll give you some doughnuts for her."

"Thanks," Roman said absently. With the Wedding War raging, he'd forgotten it was nearly the anniversary of Dad leaving. Fourteen? No, fifteen years.

Ugh. The worry was quickly replaced by its more insidious emotional cousin, guilt.

The first few years were hard, but after a while, they blended in with the rest of time, so some years he didn't even remember until October that another year had come and gone. But fifteen years was a milestone number. He hoped Mom wasn't moving into a bad place.

He'd go to see her tonight.

"Here's how it works here at Jasmine's." Delilah rubbed her hands together. "You tell me how you're feeling, and I prescribe a tea for you."

"Like medicine?" Pete, now a pharmacist, perked up at the word "prescribe."

"I can't legally say that," she said, but then lowered her voice and muttered, "Yes."

The men exchanged glances.

"Come on," Delilah said. "We all have feelings. Even men. I've heard it all before."

"I'm a little angry," Mark admitted. "Maybe more than a little. At Lacey, for hurting my friend."

Roman opened his mouth to say that Jake had intended the same outcome, that neither of them wanted to hurt the other, but Jake was not ready to hear that now. Neither was Mark, apparently.

"Rose," Delilah said. Mark wrinkled his nose. "Trust me," she assured him. He nodded.

"Pete," she said. "What's happening?"

"I'm … nervous. Worried."

"Why, honey?" she asked.

"It's just my natural state. I run kind of hot on the anxiety spectrum."

She cocked her head. "Ginger, with peppermint."

"You're anxious, buddy?" Roman asked.

"I can't believe I just admitted that," Pete said. "It's all the flowers in here or something."

"Roman?"

"Um," he said.

She studied his face as he realized he didn't want to reveal his feelings. There were just too many of them, between Jake and his mother—and Ana. He didn't want to lie either, partly because he was a crappy liar, and partly because he suspected Delilah could smell a lie a mile off.

"You know what?" She smiled. "I think I know exactly what you need. Any allergies or tastes you hate?"

"No, and not particularly."

"Then I'll just bring you the prescription."

He nodded, and with a last pat on Jake's shoulder, she walked away.

Roman leaned back in his seat, then jolted back up when he heard the tiniest creak. He still didn't fully trust these tiny chairs. Mark's phone chimed, and he squinted at the text message that came in. "Ah, crap. My wife's telling me she thinks our kid's got an ear infection again. She's going to urgent care."

Pete glanced at his watch. "Pharmacy's open until five tonight. You've got time. Tell her to have them call in the scrip. I'll go there with you after tea, make sure they fill it today."

"Thanks, buddy."

"Teamwork," Pete said, high-fiving Mark.

Mark was the only one of them married—though Jake would have joined that club yesterday—and he was the owner of a fast-food burger franchise just outside town, off I-95. He'd put a manager in charge for a few days, but Roman couldn't help noticing him glancing at his phone more often than usual, making sure there was nothing he had to handle himself.

"Also, did you just say 'after tea'?" Mark asked, sliding his phone in his pocket after one last read. "Who *are* we suddenly?"

"I'm not gonna lie, Jake," Pete said, "but I kind of thought we'd be headed to a strip club. Or ax throwing. Or somewhere to watch a game."

"Nah," Jake said. "This is my place now. Once I was walking on the main drag and a thunderstorm cracked open over my head, and since I was right out front, I hopped in here to stay dry. Delilah gave me a cup of chai tea, and it was like nothing I'd ever put in my mouth before."

"That's what she said," Pete said.

Roman shook his head with a smirk, and wondered if long-time female friends regressed to teenage talk as much as male friends did when they got together.

"I like it." Mark sat back and put his hands behind his head. "Nice change of pace. Even though all the women in here are watching us like toddlers about to break something."

"You can't blame them," Roman said.

"I don't."

Roman had awakened this morning a little past nine—late for him, but he'd been up pretty late playing games with Ana, then when they went to their rooms, he'd lain wide-eyed and keyed up in his bed while he thought of her in her own bed in the next room. He wondered about all the things he could say to her in the morning. He wondered if she'd like to eat breakfast with him. And after he'd finally woke and showered and dressed, he'd paused before knocking on her door, wondering if she was tired of him.

There was no answer, and as he devoured Selene's pancakes, she'd mentioned that Ana had gotten up with the metaphorical chickens and was out the door before any other guest had stirred.

He wasn't so insecure as to think that Ana had run out early to avoid him.

All right, maybe he was that insecure, but he'd also had the kind of fun with her last night that didn't tend to be one-sided. He would assume that like he had for Jake, Ana had woken up early this morning to spend time with Lacey and her other friends. He'd had a more leisurely morning, reading a thriller he found on Selene's shelves until he got Jake's call to meet in town in front of the tea shop. He hadn't thought the tea shop would be their ultimate destination.

Roman realized he'd tuned out for a few seconds, so he refocused on the little tea table. Pete and Mark were huddled over their phones, going over last night's Major League scores. Jake was studying Roman carefully. "What?" Roman asked, scooting his chair closer.

"I'm—" Jake started softly, then cut himself off. "I'm—"

"You don't have to tell me," Roman said.

"But I do. I didn't expect to lose Lacey. Things don't always go the way you imagine. And it's not right to not tell people the truth about how you feel. And I feel lucky you decided to stay a few days. I—I needed my friends."

Jake's eyes shone bright with tears he didn't allow to fall.

Roman wondered how many tears his mother didn't allow to fall in front of him, and how many tears Tony had let fall without Roman there beside him.

"You're not alone," Roman said. "I'll make sure of it."

Jake pressed his lips together and nodded. "I've never been so … betrayed."

Delilah came back to the table, expertly managing a large tray. She set each cup down, reminding them of the flavor and offering them a little pink-edged explanatory card. The aromas mixed in the air around them all, an intoxicating kind of magic.

She set Roman's cup down last, and furtively pressed the card into his hand like a CIA spy. Finally, she put a plate of sugar doughnuts in the center of the table.

Pete dug into the doughnuts immediately, while Mark read his card, lifted his cup with one pinkie extended, sniffed the tea, and took a delicate sip. Jake and Delilah both nodded, approving, and Delilah left to take care of two new customers who'd just walked in.

"This," Mark said, "is extremely civilized."

Pete's expression was wary as he lifted his teacup, and his slurp was unrefined, but his eyebrows raised in surprise. "Wow. It's … kind of delicious."

Roman held the card in his palm and read:

Chocolate-Dipped Strawberry Tea. The sweetness of romance is all around you.

He glanced at Delilah, but she was bustling about, not paying attention.

He lifted the cup to his lips and breathed in as he'd seen Mark do. The light fruity strawberry scent was Ana's laugh, and the smell of thick chocolate was—forbidden.

They sat with their tea and doughnuts for about twenty minutes. Then the little bell above the door tinkled again, and Jake, facing the entrance, gripped the edge of the table with white knuckles.

In walked Lacey, Kate, Sarai, and Ana.

They were smiling, giggling, relaxed, but as soon as Lacey saw the table of men, she stopped in her tracks.

Sensing a disturbance, the few ladies at scattered tables sat up to watch the something that was clearly about to happen.

Even Delilah stopped moving about, calmly waiting.

"What are you doing here?" Lacey finally asked.

"What does it look like?" Jake took a remarkably calm sip of tea. "What are you doing here?"

Lacey looked like she wanted to smash Jake's teacup, then chew the glass shards. "What kind of question is that?"

A reasonable question when she'd asked it, apparently, but Roman didn't want to say that. He didn't want to say anything. A near-rumble at an almost-wedding reception had been bad enough. A confrontation at a tea shop midday on a holiday weekend would be no better.

Ana shrank back a tiny bit, not meeting Roman's—or anyone's—eyes.

"I can't believe you have the nerve to show your face any-where," Lacey said, "after *leaving* me at the altar!"

The tea customers gasped. One gray-haired woman fanned herself with her tea card while leaning forward, still not wanting to miss a word.

"I didn't have the chance to do that, did I?" Jake said. "Since you decided to leave *me* at the altar."

The gasps got louder. "What did he say?" one lady asked.

"They dumped each other," her companion said. "At the same time."

"Seems like they did the right thing," the first lady said, "if they have so much anger."

"What tea is that?" Lacey asked.

"Lavender chamomile," Jake said.

Lacey stomped her foot. "That's what I was going to have! I can't believe you."

"You're a jerk, Jake," Sarai said. "And I think you should all leave."

"*You* should leave," Mark said. "This shop was peaceful until you walked in."

"My *life* was peaceful until Lacey walked in," Jake said.

Lacey gasped theatrically ... which, as a Broadway actress, she was very good at. Hand splayed on her chest and everything. All the patrons in the shop gasped along with her.

Ana pushed in front of Lacey, her face flushed, her jaw set. Roman's admiration of her as a warrior was short-lived; her warrior sights were on his friend.

"You." She pointed at Jake. "How *could* you? You're not even—"

"Good enough?" Jake interjected. "That's it, isn't it? I'm not good enough for her."

"Um." Ana shook her head. "I wasn't going to—"

"How could *he*?" Roman stood and walked around the table as if shielding Jake from sticks and stones. "How could *you*, Lacey? You don't even know—"

"How to be married?" Lacey cut in. "Because my parents are divorced and I have no firsthand experience of what a loving marriage should be?"

"I ..." Roman's voice trailed off. "That's not what I—"

"That's enough," Delilah said loudly. "Jasmine Pink's Tea Shoppe is a respite within the respite of Seasalter itself. I understand that you're hurt, but you can't have it out here. I would love it if you all came back another time for a friendly tea, but today ... no. Everyone out, please."

Roman and Ana, on the front lines now, stared at one another with equal parts sympathy and bafflement.

"Let's go," Lacey finally said. "Sorry, Delilah."

"Don't worry about it," Delilah said. "Just go take care of yourself."

Lacey left with the other women in tow. Ana was last, lingering with her hand on the open door as if she wanted to say something to Roman, but appeared to think better of it and left. The men stood. Jake raked a hand through his hair and shook his head. They waited until the women were likely a block or two away, then they left, the door tinkling cheerfully as they stepped onto the street.

"That nerd was out of line," Pete said. "Way out."

"Who?" Roman asked, knowing fully well who. They walked to the end of the block, turned left, and headed for the beach in silent agreement.

"Juli," Jake said.

"She goes by Ana now," Roman said, ignoring Mark when he quirked an eyebrow at that.

"Ana, Juli, I don't care," Jake said. "Can you believe she said I wasn't good enough for Lacey?"

"I ... did she say that?" Roman asked.

"She just earned herself the second slot on my enemy list right now. Right under Lacey."

Roman wasn't sure what to say.

Jake stopped in his tracks. "You know why?"

"Disrespect," Pete said. Roman turned his head so Pete couldn't see, and rolled his eyes.

"No," Jake said. "It's because she's right. I'm *not* good enough for Lacey, and that's why I couldn't marry her."

★ ★ ★

"I cannot *even* with Roman Montgomery!" Lacey said as they headed for the Seasalter Town Diner on the other end of the main drag. Tea would have been nice, but carb-loading pan-cakes after the Monster Rage smash room was probably the better move anyway. "I could hit *him* with a baseball bat."

"Roman?" Ana asked. "Why are you mad at him?"

"For saying I don't know how to have a good marriage, because I didn't have role models growing up."

"Roman said that?" Ana asked.

"Why did that make you so angry, Lacey?" Kate asked in her professional therapist's voice.

"Because, damn him," Lacey said with a sniffle, "it's true. I *don't* know how to be a good partner, and that's why I couldn't marry Jake."

CHAPTER 8

Ana was sitting on the blue sofa in the Moonrise sitting room in the midafternoon, a game of solitaire spread before her, when Roman walked in.

She didn't look up. She knew it was him even when she heard his sneakers on the wooden porch steps. She was fully aware of him every time he was near: the minty smell of his shampoo and the brightness of his smile and the freckles on his forearms.

She was also aware that it was inconvenient and bad timing and Hatfields vs. McCoys and everything else that dooms a relationship.

The door closed behind him, and she felt him hesitate before he said, "Hi."

"Hi," she murmured, keeping her eyes on her card game.

"Can I sit?"

Ana shrugged one shoulder, allowing him to extract any response he preferred. He came around the coffee table and sat on the other end of the sofa. Ana moved the seven of diamonds into place.

"Who's winning?" he asked.

Ana leaned her elbow on her thigh and looked at him, shaking her head sadly. "No one."

"Yeah. It's not fun."

They sat in silence for a moment.

"I'm not going to lie," Ana said. "I can't help thinking I'm being disloyal to Lacey by talking to you."

"Same. To Jake. He's pretty mad at you."

"Yeah, Lacey's not president of your fan club right now either."

"I guess we both hit a nerve."

"I didn't mean to," Ana said. "He said that thing about not being good enough for Lacey as if it—" She stopped, putting two and two together. "As if that were *actually* the reason. Oh, man."

"I'm going to hazard a guess that Lacey's mad because she thinks I said she doesn't know how to have a good marriage."

"I'm not confirming or denying."

"You don't have to," Roman said. "We're not betraying confidences. They said it themselves in front of all of us."

"So Jake thinks he's not good enough for Lacey, and that's why he called it off." It was a solid punch to Ana's own heart, because she understood it too well.

"And ... Lacey thinks she wouldn't be a good partner because of her own parents' history," Roman said slowly.

They both fell silent, lost in thought.

"Jake has a solid point," Ana said. "If he feels he's not bringing enough to the table, maybe he shouldn't get married." Or be in a relationship. Or fall in love.

"He's bringing plenty to the table," Roman protested.

"You don't know that. You don't know what's happening between them. She's a brilliant, accomplished woman. There are not many who could be her professional equal."

Roman didn't argue, and Ana realized she was hoping he'd argue, that he'd say it didn't matter what Jake did for a living or what he'd accomplished, that he had plenty to offer.

"What about Lacey?" Roman said. "If she doesn't feel like she can hold up her end of a marriage, then she shouldn't be in one."

"No, it's not reasonable. What happened to her parents won't necessarily happen to her."

"There's a pretty good chance."

Ana thought about the way Lacey flinched every time her parents came to see her in a show and ended up bickering in the high school hallway while she clutched her congratulatory bouquets. She lived in their bad marriage all through their formative years. So Ana said nothing.

Roman's shoulders slumped a bit, and if they hadn't been talking about others, she'd have interpreted it as some kind of disappointment. Maybe it was fatigue. This was a long week already, and they were only on day two.

"I'm going to my mom's for dinner," Roman said. "Care to join me?"

"Nah. I need to find Selene and ask her if I can do some laundry tonight. I only brought enough clean clothes to stay a couple of nights, and I can't exactly afford to buy new clothes without a job." Even with that lousy job, she didn't have extra money to spend.

"Even more reason to come by," Roman said. "I'm guessing my mom is around your size or a little bigger, so I'm sure she has some shirts and shorts you can borrow."

"Oh, I couldn't impose—"

"It's not imposing. I'm going to tell her about this weekend, and that will include you, and I'll probably mention you had to stay an unplanned week, and she'll ask if you have enough clothes, and she'll send me back with three bags anyway. So you might as well come with me and choose them yourself, and also get a free meal."

"You're going to tell your mom about me?" Ana asked.

Roman paused, the slightest of blushes creeping up his neck. "Yeah," he said softly.

Ana was sure her blush matched his.

"You'll have to duck down as we drive out of Seasalter," Roman said. "And I wish I was kidding. If Jake saw—"

"If Lacey saw—"

"It's silly," Roman said. "It's not like we're having an affair."

The word *affair* in his voice pushed a flash of images through Ana's brain: Roman pressing her up against a wall, kissing her, one hand tangled in her hair, one hand sliding down the front of her shorts, both of them covered in a sheen of sweat, breathing dirty words in each other's ears, licking, biting …

"No," Ana said, a little too forcefully, but she needed to shatter her fantasies. "It's not an affair."

"It hurts no one for you and I to spend time together."

The phrase *you and I* sounded … good. "In their current emotional state, they'll think so," Ana said.

"We won't tell them."

Ana sighed. Nothing could happen with Roman anyway. Ana wasn't good enough for anyone at this point in her life. It was just a dinner she wouldn't have to pay for, and some clothes she also wouldn't have to pay for.

"No, we definitely won't tell them," she finally said. "All right. And we'll take separate cars in case Lacey needs me and I have to leave."

"Fair enough."

★ ★ ★

Ana followed Roman's cute red Jeep in her embarrassingly old Subaru to his mother's house. She eyed the sidewalks now and then, but of course she didn't see any of her friends among the Labor Day weekend tourists. Roman had given her his phone number in case she got lost, if that was even possible—not only did she know Seasalter's every street, but he drove hilariously slowly, waving at her every eighth of a mile or so, so he wouldn't lose her. She waved back every time with a smirk.

Theresa Montgomery lived in a modest white Cape house in the western, inland part of Seasalter. Gorgeous blooms cheerfully filled window boxes in the front. One side of the house was covered in scaffolding and plastic, renovations on hold for the holiday.

A man was mowing the lawn, and when Roman pulled into the driveway, the man waved at him. Ana parked at the curb, and when she got out, the man eyed her curiously and shut off the mower. He and Roman hugged warmly with several back pats, and when they separated, Ana was struck by their resemblance: same dark hair, same athletic build, same cocky grin. But this man's eyes were bright blue beach glass.

"Tony, this is Ana Capuano," Roman said. "We went to high school together. Ana, this is my brother, Tony."

"I think I remember seeing you in the halls when I was a freshman," Ana said.

"Yeah, I was three years ahead of you twerps," Tony said. "You're here for the wedding that never was?"

Ana nodded. "Yeah, this is a first."

"Probably for the best," Tony said. "I can tell you firsthand that divorce isn't a blast."

"I'm sorry," Ana said.

Tony waved it off with a grimace. "Eh. Go inside and see Ma. I'm just finishing up out here. Nice to meet you, Ana."

"You too." She followed Roman inside.

The house smelled like simmering tomato sauce, and opera blared from the kitchen—Ana recognized *Don Giovanni*. She followed Roman through the darker living room into the brightly lit kitchen. "Hey, Ma," Roman said.

Theresa spun around from the stove. "Roman!" She hugged her arms around his waist, her hand still clutching a wooden spoon. She closed her eyes for a moment, relishing her son's embrace, then opened her eyes and gasped when she saw Ana.

Theresa had long, thick, layered dark hair and any gray strands that might have been visible weren't, likely thanks to salon color visits. Her lips were dark pink, slick with recently applied gloss, and the air around her was a faint, sweet freesia. She was in dark denim shorts and a navy T-shirt, and her tanned legs ended in bare, French-pedicured feet.

"Hi," Ana said loudly, to be heard over Pavarotti. "I hope Roman told you I was coming."

"Of course he did." Theresa released her son and turned down the volume. "But I just now realized I recognize you from Seasalter High School. You're the smart girl, the one who gave the beautiful graduation speech."

Ana wanted to say "yes" to having been the one to give the speech but she was unsure she could say yes without also agreeing she was "the smart girl" when that wasn't quite true anymore. So she just made a sort of agreeable noise.

Theresa clasped her hand, not noticing or caring that Ana didn't respond like a human. "I have antipasto for you to nibble. Roman, I didn't know you two were friends at school."

"We weren't," Ana said. "I wasn't cool enough."

"You were too cool, you mean," Roman said. "You said it yourself, Ma. Ana is the smart girl. I hung around with athletes. Completely different cliques."

Theresa handed Ana the antipasto platter, enough for eight people rather than four. "My friend group wasn't a clique," Ana said, carrying the tray to the table and spearing a slice of prosciutto and a slice of mozzarella with a toothpick. "We were outside all the cliques."

"I'm sure you thought so then," Roman said. "We all thought we weren't in cliques, that other people formed groups and we were different. But we weren't. Why do you think you and I never talked?"

"Because you were too popular, and I was a dork."

"Or," Roman postulated, popping a black olive in his mouth, "because you were too smart and I ... wasn't."

"You make it sound like you even once considered talking to me."

Roman didn't answer; just fixed her with an unsettling gaze.

She cocked her head and squinted one eye, studying him back. He *had* known her name right away at the wedding. Was it even possible that teenage Roman Montgomery had—

No. No way.

Theresa stirred the simmering pot on the stove, and Ana closed her eyes for a moment and breathed it in. The oregano and tomato blend was ... familiar. Ana's grandmother had made sauce from scratch every Sunday for dinner, and though she'd passed when Ana was in college, the scent reminded Ana of sitting at the table—set with the "good" dishes and crowded with her parents and her cousins—laughing and eating, and being normal. While they ate, there were no expectations to live up to. Just existing and enjoying was enough.

"You're lost in thought, hon," Theresa said, and Ana thought she was talking to her son before she realized she was addressing her.

"I was remembering my grandmother's hands—they always smelled faintly like garlic, even if she wasn't cooking. I miss that."

Theresa smiled softly, and Tony crashed in from outside, heading over to the kitchen sink to wash his hands. "Lawn looks good, Ma. I trimmed the hedges also."

"You didn't have to do that," Theresa said.

"If I didn't, who would? This layabout?" He nodded at Roman with a grin, drying his hands with a small towel.

Ana didn't grow up with siblings, but her friends did, and she recognized sibling teasing when she saw it, so she was surprised that Roman didn't smile. "I'm sorry," he said quickly. "Jake's going through it, and he needs me, and—"

"I'm kidding," Tony said. "I live five blocks away. You're visiting from Boston. You're not here to do yard work."

"I'm saying if you need me to—"

"We don't. Ma's fine."

"I'm fine," Theresa echoed.

Roman nodded but didn't seem entirely convinced.

"I hope you like ravioli, Ana," Theresa said.

"Listen to how she says this," Roman said. "Ma, you're going to make Ana think you bought ravioli frozen from the supermarket. What she means to say, Ana, is she hopes you like ravioli she made herself in this kitchen."

"I'm a little worried now," Ana said, "that you're about to ruin all supermarket ravioli for me forever."

"Sorry, not sorry," Theresa said.

"I hope you didn't go to too much trouble," Ana said.

"No way," Theresa said. "I haven't had a chance to really cook a big meal in weeks, and I miss doing it. The office is closed for the long weekend, and I was excited when I realized I'd have both these goons at home for a change. I thought I made too much, but then Roman texted you were coming and with a last name like Capuano, I fully expect you to have an Italian appetite. Here." She handed Ana two bottles of red wine.

"But what will you all drink?" Ana asked.

"I like this girl," Theresa said to Roman. "I'm keeping her."

"She's got an appetite, all right. You should have seen the size of the burrito she put away yesterday," Roman said.

Ana pretended to be embarrassed. "Hey! I had a rough"— week? year? life?—"day."

"So I hear," Theresa said. "I went to the butcher for the sausage this morning, and I heard four people arguing about the canceled wedding."

"Arguing?" Tony asked.

"Yes, two people said Lacey is a cold-hearted soul who dumped lovesick Jake, and two said no, that Jake, who's basically a player, dumped poor innocent Lacey."

"Neither is true," Ana said.

"And, at the same time, both are true," Roman countered. "The dumping parts. Not the rest."

"Then," Theresa said, "I had to run out to the Four Corners Market about ninety minutes ago for an onion because I was out, and a couple of people there said a gang fight nearly broke out at Jasmine Pink's today over the wedding. Can you even believe that?"

Roman and Ana glanced at one another, but not furtively enough.

"That was you?" Theresa asked.

"In my defense," Roman said, "I was calmly drinking tea with the men when Lacey and her Amazons stormed in."

Ana pressed her lips together and shook her head at him. "Wow."

Theresa began to drop the ravioli in a now-boiling pot of water. "It's not easy," she said so quietly, Ana had to step closer to hear her. "I hope both of them are okay."

Ana saw Tony and Roman exchange a concerned look, but she didn't know how to interpret it.

"How're you doing, Ma?" Roman asked.

Theresa frowned as she sprinkled something into the pot, then sniffed the steam, nodding before stirring some more. "Fine. Didn't I say 'fine' already in this conversation?"

"I'm just making sure."

"Making sure your hearing is okay?" Theresa quipped.

Roman shifted uncomfortably and glanced at his brother, who was suddenly studying his phone with a worried look. Then Tony began tapping with purpose, in what seemed like a very long text.

Ana decided to give them a few minutes of privacy. Roman was clearly trying to find out something about his mother, and maybe she wasn't answering because Ana was present.

"Restroom?" she asked, and Tony pointed her through the living room and down the hall.

After washing up, Ana stopped in the hallway to look at all the pictures on the wall. There were so many—including several of the Roman she remembered but never really knew: in a pin-striped baseball uniform leaning on his bat and grinning; poised in navy swim trunks on a diving board, flexing for the camera before making a splash; in red cap and gown, one arm around Tony and one around his mother. Ana found herself looking over their shoulders at the sea of graduation outfits, knowing she was also there, in white cap and gown and golden honor society sash.

She turned away from the wall's photo history to peer into the room behind her—the master bedroom with a perfectly made bed, complete with dust ruffle; a low dresser with a mirror tray covered in trinket boxes and paperback romances; and a taller, more masculine bureau with a mahogany box designed to house a man's watch and money clip and cuff links. A large wedding photo with an elaborate silver frame sat on one edge of the dresser—Roman's parents. A smaller wooden photo frame graced the opposite edge, and Ana didn't want to step into the room, but she could see it was Theresa, smiling in her husband's one-armed embrace as he gazed fondly down at her and she watched their two small boys playing with a black dog on the green grass of the lawn she'd just seen Tony mowing.

Ana's gaze wandered around the room. A man's dark-green robe hung on a peg next to a woman's tattered yellow robe on the wall outside the adjoining bath.

Ana knit her brows, then spun to inspect the hallway photo wall again, but found herself face to face with Roman.

"Um," she said, clearly caught eyeballing his mother's bedroom.

"Hi," he said with a small unbothered smile.

"Hi. I'm sorry. I'm positive this looks like I was snooping."

"Nah. It's on the way back from the bathroom. I peek in people's rooms, too, when I'm in a house for the first time. Well, I do it more now that I'm a real estate agent. But there's nothing wrong with glancing around. You're a guest."

"Your father," Ana said.

Roman's smile remained, but the positive emotion drained out of it. He raised his brows though, an invitation for her to continue to say whatever she was about to say.

"I don't remember ever seeing you with him," she said. "At school events. I must have assumed your parents are divorced, because if he had died when you were young, that's something kids find out and talk about, and I don't recall that. I thought you said last night he's gone but … he still lives here?"

"No. He left us almost exactly fifteen years ago."

"That's why there are no photos of him out here," Ana said.

"There used to be. But I … when I was about thirteen, I smashed my fist through the glass of one photo he was in, a picture of him and me and Tony. I was walking past and I realized it bugged me to walk past it every day and that day, I couldn't anymore. After that, Mom hid all the pictures of him away somewhere. Except the ones in her room. Which I have no right to tell her to remove."

"Some of his things are—"

"I know," he said. "Still there. I don't know if it's grief or hope or denial. It's been all three at various times over the years, but I don't know what it is today. He … ripped her heart out. She is a great mother without him, but she just hasn't let go. I don't … understand how he could hurt her that way. I don't *forgive* how he could hurt her that way."

"He hurt you and Tony too."

"Yeah, but we were kids, and we were resilient, and we adapted. I was never really angry at him for me. I was angry at him because of the way my mother cried for months. Years. She was an adult who'd chosen this man who'd promised to be with her for life. She believed him." He sighed. "We never saw him again after he left, but I will say for him that he never missed a support payment, spousal or child."

"At least, that."

He sighed. "I hate to say that sometimes, I wished he did. Having less money would have made Mom's life very hard, but every time a payment came, I could see in Mom's face that it was not only a reminder that he had gone, but a catalyst of hope that maybe he still cared enough to one day return. That was somehow worse."

"A constant tearing of a scab that kept trying to heal," Ana said.

"Yes." Roman's jaw softened at her interpretation.

"That's why you kept asking your mom tonight if she was okay."

"Oh," Roman said. "I was trying to be subtle."

"Yeah, you weren't."

Neither of them said anything for a moment.

"I meant for this dinner to be a break for us from all the tension," he finally said. "But I'm afraid this is a bummer of a conversation."

"Life doesn't get breaks. You just find moments within that life that are—peaceful. Beautiful. Memorable." She nodded over his shoulder. "Like all those moments on the wall."

She locked eyes with him. There was a hum in her ears, a current that ran through all the nerve endings in her body, lighting them up on its way to her panties, where it pooled, warm and alive. A thousand restless moths fluttered in her stomach.

"Like this moment," Roman said.

Her brain tried to save her. *You're not good enough*, it reminded her, as it always, always did.

She would have listened. She would have smiled politely and stepped away, breaking the current.

But Roman licked his lips.

Shut up, she told her brain. It was only a moment in life, after all.

She slid both her hands into Roman's hair and pressed her lips to his.

She softened her lips, dragging them from one corner of his mouth to the other. She poked the tip of her tongue out and traced the seam of his lips, and when they didn't open, she nipped his bottom lip, then sucked in his top lip—playing, exploring.

He didn't move but he could have leaned away, breaking the kiss, and he didn't. A tiny noise emerged from his throat as she continued to taste him. He was taking, and she was happy to give if that's how he wanted it in this moment.

Then he wrapped his arms around her, drew her against his chest, and opened his mouth, plunging his tongue inside to tangle with hers. He spun her around, away from the bedroom door, and walked her into the opposite wall. A corner of a photo frame poked into the skin of her neck, and she wrapped one leg around his thighs, buckling his knees and pulling him even closer until she could feel his hardness through his shorts. She lifted her hips into it, and they both groaned.

Perspiration beaded on her chest above her bra as they both deepened the kiss, desperate to be closer than basic physics would allow.

"Roman!" Theresa called from the kitchen, and Roman quickly stepped back. The sudden lack of him on her body was as if she'd stepped into a freezer case.

"Yeah?" he called, his eyes not leaving Ana's. She watched a few things pass over his face, and they weren't things she wanted to see after being kissed like that. The guilt could be for making out in his mother's hallway, but it wasn't accompanied by the sheepish grin of satisfaction or a wink of rebelliousness; rather, there was the furrowed brow of confusion, and the slight wince of regret.

"Dinner's ready!"

Only a moment.

Maybe she didn't deserve more than that, but she had none of her own regret; just a vow to not repeat it.

She angled her head toward the kitchen and headed down the hallway without waiting for him.

CHAPTER 9

*J*uliana Capuano had kissed him.
Juliana Capuano *had* kissed him.
Juliana Capuano had *kissed* him.
Juliana Capuano had kissed *him*.
No part of that sentence was fathomable.

He tried to follow everything being said at dinner but he couldn't, because his lips were buzzing and his brain was short-circuited and sparking. Luckily, Ma and Tony absolutely adored her, and Ana smiled and laughed all through dinner and dessert, which went on well over two hours with second and third helpings. After the meal, Ma led Ana to her room to put together a bag of clothes that Ana could borrow for the week.

"I really appreciate this," Roman heard Ana say as they went down the hallway together.

"Well," Tony said when he and his brother were left alone at the table together. "Can't say I expected this tonight."

"Shut up."

Tony chuckled, but glanced at his phone again and frowned.

"What's going on with you?" Roman asked. "You've been checking your phone every five seconds."

Tony sighed and put the cell facedown on the table. "I've been talking to Phoebe."

"Your ex-wife's friend?"

"Shh." Tony glanced at the doorway.

"Can't say I expected *this* tonight," Roman said.

"Ha ha." Tony shook his head. "We ran into each other a couple of weeks ago in Newport, and she texted me first after that. I don't know."

"You don't know what?"

"I like her," he said. "But she's friends with Meredith, and it could get messy."

"Meredith left you."

"Thanks for the reminder."

"What I mean is, she got over your marriage before you did. Why should it bother her?"

"I shouldn't care if it does, right?"

"No, you should care, but I'm not convinced she would be bothered."

"I want to ask Phoebe out," Tony said. "Should I?"

"You're asking me?" Roman was still reeling from Ana's lips on his, and even if he weren't, he knew as little as his brother did about how to navigate relationships. They were their father's sons, after all. What did they know?

"Please," Tony said. "I need advice."

Roman still harbored guilt in his heart about not being around when Tony was struggling at the end of his marriage. He didn't feel like he could deny his brother help now that Tony was asking. "Maybe you could tell her the truth," he said slowly. "Tell Phoebe that you're interested in her, but you're worried about how Meredith will feel. See what she says to that."

"Put the ball in her court. Good idea." Tony picked up the phone and started furiously tapping.

"You could wait five minutes," Roman said.

"Nah. I've been waffling for days. It's time to make a move."

Roman shrugged as Ana and his mother returned to the room, Ana lugging two recyclable supermarket bags.

"Your mom has my exact taste in clothes," Ana said. "It was almost like shopping in my own closet."

"Ready to go?" Roman asked.

"Yup."

His mother wrapped her arms around Ana and rocked her as she hugged her. Tony also hugged Ana, telling her he'd insist that Roman bring her around again soon.

Tony then hugged Roman, and as he slapped him on the back, said in his ear, "Phoebe said she'll talk to Meredith. Thanks, man. You're a genius."

When his familiar front door closed—the door Roman had stood in front of for first-day-of-kindergarten pictures and pre-prom pictures—the silence between him and Ana was even louder than the evening peepers and crickets. The sky was almost fully dark, still pink and purple at the edge of the horizon, peeking through the lush leaves of neighborhood trees.

Ma had maintained a cheerful demeanor all through dinner, but the anniversary of her heartbreak was here. Roman was sure she was hurting inside.

Roman's concern was forgotten, though, when his lips were on Ana's, when his fingers were splayed on her waist, when he was pressing her against the wall, finally holding her in his reality.

Until he'd stepped back and remembered he was standing in the hallway of the home where he and Tony had learned nothing about marriage except how to ruin it.

Ana had studied Roman's face. It was highly unlikely she was a mind reader, but he had a feeling she'd read something before they went back to his mom and brother and ate dinner.

Now, he walked her to her car. "Thanks," she said, poking her tongue into her cheek. "I wasn't sure I'd get all the way to the curb safely."

"You're welcome. Who knows what these bushes are hiding? Could be a toddler on a Big Wheel. Could be a squirrel who needs a week's worth of my mom's clothes. You can't be too careful."

Her smile through her—embarrassment? awkwardness? regret?—was still gratifying.

"I'll see you back at the inn," she said.

"You up for some games? I noticed Selene has a trivia game in a 'Rad '80s' edition."

Her brows lifted and her eyes widened with interest, but in a split second, she seemed to remember something. He knew full well what.

"I'm kind of tired," she said. "Let me see how I feel when we get back."

He nodded and went to his car. She waited until he pulled out of the driveway before she followed, so he interpreted that as her wanting to drive home "together."

Roman peered in his rearview mirror at Ana carefully following him. Even though she undoubtedly knew the way in her own hometown back to the inn, he stopped at red lights he could have easily passed while yellow, so he could stay with her.

He only made it to the end of his street before the phone clanged through the Jeep's speakers.

"Hey, bud," Roman said. "How're you holding up?"

"Not good," Jake said. "Roman, I miss her. Even after what happened. Is that bad? I'm weak. I'm a weak, pathetic soul."

"Don't say that. You love Lacey."

"I hate her."

"Okay."

"I mean, right? I hate her?"

"Uh ... you tell me."

"I ... don't know."

An idea burst like a kernel of popcorn in the warm microwave of Roman's brain. "You need to talk to her," Roman said, because it was clear that Jake was asking his advice, and he'd given successful relationship advice to Tony a few minutes ago. Maybe he was on an unusual roll.

"I ..." Jake started, and faltered. "I have no clue what to say to her."

"Is not talking to her getting you anywhere good?"

"Not really," Jake admitted.

"That's right, buddy. Up until yesterday, she was the person you talked to about everything that bothered you. You took some time away, but now you both have to confront what's happening here." Roman warmed to his own words, his confidence building.

"But you don't realize how smart she is. That's the whole problem here. She's brilliant and talented and she's on Broadway, and I sell cars in a showroom."

"There's nothing wrong with that, buddy."

"Not in general, but I'm no match for her."

"Did she ever say that?"

"No, but how can that be enough for her in the long run?"

"You need to tell her that's what you're thinking about."

"We never argued much before," Jake said. "Frankly, I'm a little too scared to ever argue with her. She can argue anyone in circles because she knows so much."

"You're not meeting her to argue. You're meeting to talk."

"She's better at it than me."

"I think it's safe to say that if there's any subject where you have a little bit more expertise than her, it's the subject of you. You know you better than anyone, even her. All you have to do is tell her how you feel, and listen to how she feels, and see if you can get to a place where you can help each other understand what happened and how to resolve it."

"What if we can't?"

"Then instead of wondering, you'll be sure, and you can do whatever you need to do."

"What if—what if we can?"

"Then you work together," Roman said. "It takes diligence and desire to change."

Jake paused. "But ... you're not in a relationship."

Roman swallowed. No, he wasn't. Mainly because he had no idea how. What Jake was politely asking was, who was Roman to offer this kind of advice?

"Do you remember Charlie Ramos?"

Jake half laughed. "Sure, I do. That kid that transferred from Providence junior year. Made me nuts."

"He made all of us on the team nuts. He walked around the locker room, tossing out insults, snapping us with wet towels, making up nicknames we hated. We couldn't stand him. But his batting average—"

"Don't even remind me. I'm still jealous."

"He was a valuable part of the team, but we could hardly stand him. Until Mark told him flat out one day that he needed to stop riding everyone, that no one liked it."

"Yeah ..." Jake thought a moment. "He apologized."

"He did. He didn't realize that it was what his old team did, but that our team was different, and he needed to learn to read the room and adjust."

"And he did."

"He did. When he transferred again, I was sad about it. And not just because he was a good player. But—we had to talk to him to get him to understand. He wasn't going to read our minds. Lacey—man, she is smart. Still, she can't read your mind." Roman braked at a stop sign and watched two little girls drag a red wagon full of half-dressed Barbie dolls along the crosswalk, their mothers walking slowly behind. He waved at Ana in the rearview mirror, and she saluted back. "Communication's not just a romantic relationship thing," Roman said. "It's a human thing. Right?"

He wasn't sure if he was asking himself or Jake, but Jake answered. "Right."

"So ... you want to talk to Lacey?"

"I do," Jake said weakly.

"I'll arrange it. On ... neutral ground."

"Now?"

"No, not now," Roman said. "Give yourself time to really think about what you want to say, and prepare yourself to listen to what she has to say. Tomorrow night. Okay?"

"Oh ... okay."

Jake's voice was thin and resigned. Roman remembered Jake in the locker room in high school, yelling motivational quotes at the baseball team—which he never could get right, so they were always things like, "There's no I in win!" or "You gotta pull those punches!"—but he spouted the nonsense with such vigor and confidence that every boy was cheering and hyped up by the time they ran onto the diamond.

Before this weekend, Roman had never heard Jake sound—like this.

"This is good," Roman said, taking up the motivational mantle. "You're stepping up to the plate. That's what a real man does."

Jake's breath was shaky, and a little watery. "Thanks, buddy. I trust you."

Roman realized when they hung up that Jake had assumed Roman would know how to find Lacey. In his current emotional state, he wasn't considering details.

Luckily, Roman knew exactly what to do.

Suddenly, his phone rang on the Jeep's speakers. Unknown number. He was about to ignore it when he glanced in the rearview mirror again and saw Ana waving her cell phone.

"Do you have any idea," he answered, "how much cell phones distract drivers?"

"I do, but as you are driving us back to the inn at approximately four miles an hour, I feel relatively safe."

He snorted.

"Plus," she added, "I saw your lips moving. So either you were singing with the radio or you were just on the phone."

"Jake called me."

"Ah, interesting. Lacey left a voice message while we were eating. And a couple of texts. I think she misses Jake."

"How can you tell?"

"Mainly because her text says, 'I miss Jake.' " She cut herself off, and Roman glanced in his mirror to see her chewing her bottom lip. "I shouldn't have told you that."

"Maybe not, but in this instance, I'm glad you did. I was just talking to Jake and he misses Lacey also."

"Really?"

"Yeah."

He pulled into the gravelly driveway of the Moonrise Inn. There were only two parking spots left, so he took the one farthest from the front door, leaving the better space for Ana's car. She smoothly pulled in and got out, taking the bag of clothes out with her.

They each held their phone to their ear.

"Your mom's the best," she said to him into the phone, walking toward him. "I couldn't thank her enough."

"You didn't need to," Roman said, not clicking off the phone until she was at his side and did the same. "I'm sure when you walked into her massive closet, you noticed that the woman loves her clothes. She even has a wall with pegs where she hangs her necklaces and earrings. She won't even miss what she lent you."

Ana nodded, and they fell silent again, that oppressive silence that hung over two people who were ignoring something monumental between them. Two people who both wanted to say something but couldn't. Two people who were equally desperate for the other person to bring up the subject—and terrified that they would.

He didn't want her to think he'd forget about the kiss. That kiss was branded onto his brain matter. It would be the memory he would sink into in peace when it came time for him to leave this life.

It just couldn't happen again.

Ana stopped midstride on the walkway to the front porch and turned to him. The twinkle lights hanging over the patio sparkled in her eyes, in her hair.

Please don't make me say it can't happen again.

"Lacey," she said.

Roman blinked.

"What should we do?" she continued.

Right. They had a task at hand. Nothing like an important task to avoid an uncomfortable conversation.

"I have a plan," Roman said.

"Oooh. I like that, 'I have a plan.' I've always wanted to be present when someone says they have a plan."

"I proposed to Jake that he should talk to Lacey."

"Talking," Ana said. "Such a simple concept, yet it took this long for someone to come up with it."

Roman smirked. "You're just jealous you didn't think of it first, Miss Mensa."

Ana cocked her head and nodded. "Maybe. How much convincing did it take?"

"Minimal."

"Huh. That's a positive sign."

"Agreed. I suggested tomorrow night, so he could think for a while first."

"Good idea. I have a feeling from Lacey's tone in her messages that she'd acquiesce to a summit. You mentioned a plan?"

"Yeah. You and I declared the Moonrise Inn neutral ground, remember?"

Ana wrinkled her forehead. "Yes."

"It's perfect neutral ground for Lacey and Jake's conversation. Her hotel room? No. His? No way. Any restaurant, coffee shop, park, public place in Seasalter is full of memories for both of them, good or bad. This whole place is their home turf—except for *this* inn. It just opened this weekend. Neither of them has been here."

"And it's peaceful," Ana said. "The first moment I walked in here, I exhaled for the first time in like a month."

"Exactly," Roman confirmed. "But there could be guests in the common area, or Lacey and Jake might not feel like it's private enough. So I propose we have them meet to talk in my room."

"Not mine?"

"Let's look at both," Roman said, leading her up the porch stairs and into the inn. "See which is better for a tension-filled meeting."

"Mine's pretty nice."

"Mine, too."

Ana unlocked her door—and hesitated.

"I can just look from the door," Roman said. "I don't have to come in."

"N-no. It's fine. You can't see it all from the doorway."

She opened the door, and he followed her inside, taking in the tall open windows and the unzipped bags on top of a chest at the foot of the bed. The bed—was not something to stare at. He turned away from it. "You have a whole other *room*?"

"It's the Stardust Suite," she said. "Emphasis on *suite*."

He went into the adjoining room and theatrically collapsed on the sofa, flicking on the remote.

"Don't be shy," Ana said. "Make yourself at home."

"I don't think this will work for Lacey and Jake," he said. "Mine's just a room, not a suite. They've had enough space between them since everything happened. Probably best if they have to physically face one another to talk, and don't have the escape of a second room."

"You're probably right. But let me see your room anyhow. If only so I can rub my scent all over it the way you're doing here."

"When I go to the channel guide," Roman said, adjusting a pillow under his head and clicking through screens, "HGTV is highlighted. Was that you? Were you watching HGTV, or was that the guest before you?"

"We're the first guests in this inn's history," Ana said. "And what's wrong with HGTV?"

"Nothing at all," he said. "I love it. Never thought I'd get a kick out of watching people put in new insulation or sand their living room floors, but now that I'm in real estate, I admit I'm kind of fascinated. But why would you watch it?"

"It's—" Ana searched for the most accurate adjective. "Satisfying. I like watching houses get put into order. Fixed. Because it shows me …" She trailed off, staring out the window.

Roman flicked off the TV and sat up. "What?" he asked after a moment.

"That it's possible to clean up a big mess," she said. "That order can be found in chaos if the right people attack it the right way. I … I like watching it happen."

Not for the first time since meeting the adult Ana yesterday, Roman considered that Ana was quietly struggling with something difficult, something dark. He was being truthful when he told her yesterday that working in a convenience store was nothing to be ashamed of, but there was no avoiding the fact that anyone who had known her as a brilliant, driven teenager would have suspected—expected—that she'd be making seven figures and be famous by now. It wouldn't matter what she was doing for work if she were happy, but she didn't seem to be.

And if he allowed whatever was happening between them to grow larger, he would one day make her even unhappier.

He flicked off the TV and stood. "Okay, let's go to my room."

As Ana locked the door behind them, they both waved to Selene, who was dusting the sitting room while listening to headphones. Roman wondered if Ana was uncomfortable being seen leaving her room together, or going into his room together, or both, but her face gave nothing away.

He opened the door to the Sea of Tranquility and rushed in before her to gather his strewn-about clothes from yesterday. The last thing he wanted was for fellow HGTV fan Ana to discover that he wasn't a very organized traveler. But Selene had folded everything neatly and stacked it on the dresser, inadvertently making him look like a neat freak.

Unlike Ana, he just had one room, and the bed took up about half of it. The walls were painted a soothing sky blue, and the wall opposite the king bed was covered with a large framed star chart, with constellations and coordinates shining in white on a midnight background. The floor was a gleaming hardwood with a braided deep-purple throw rug, and his bedding was the same regal purple. The TV in here was in a large entertainment unit in the corner. He turned on the central air as Ana studied the stars in the poster. Then he darted into the bathroom to line up his toiletries in size order, in the event she decided to go in there. He didn't think she'd judge him, but if she preferred order to chaos, if it soothed her soul, he wanted to give it to her.

"I think you're right," Ana said, her gaze still in space. "This room is a better idea." She turned and evaluated her surroundings. "There's a nice armchair and the bed, so they both have somewhere comfortable to sit without having to be right next to each other. The bathroom is good enough if one of them needs a minute to walk away and gather their thoughts. But this room encourages physical proximity, and you were right—they've had none of that since yesterday. Maybe even the day before, if they followed the protocol of the groom not seeing the bride before she walks down the aisle."

Roman went to sit on the bed, but hesitated and sat in the velvety black chair instead. "I'll let Selene know we're going to have a couple of guests for a while, then we can give them my room, and I'll tell Jake to call me when they're done talking. Hopefully, they leave together with all their problems solved."

"And if not," Ana said, "we tried."

"Right."

"Where will you go? While the peace summit is happening."

"I'll hang out in the sitting room. But I think you should hang out with me. Just in case of—something."

"Of course. I'm not leaving you to deal with this alone." She raised her brows. "I guess we'll have to confess to them that we're both staying at the inn."

"I'm sure they won't even ask," Roman said. "They'll be so stressed out over seeing one another that none of that will compute."

"You're probably right. Let's plan for tomorrow night at ... seven? After dinner?"

"Good idea. If Jake goes into a serious situation like this while hungry, I can't be responsible for his actions. Or words. Or both."

"I don't want to be hungry either, especially if they take a couple of hours and we don't want to leave them here alone."

"Find out if Lacey's game," Roman said, "and if she is, we'll text them both the time and place."

"They'll know we coordinated this together."

"Well, they asked for our help, so it shouldn't surprise them."

"Yeah, but ..." Ana said, and Roman waited until she finished, "I kind of liked that this was our place."

Roman felt warm under his shirt. "When they make up and clear out, it will be again."

She nodded and whipped out her phone, leaning against the wall. He did the same and went to the bathroom to give her privacy to call Lacey. After about three minutes, she yelled, "We're on!"

Roman emerged from the bathroom. "Let's text tomorrow at seven, Moonrise Inn."

They both squinted at their phones, typing furiously. They both hit send, looked at one another for about ten seconds, then their phones beeped nearly simultaneously. "Confirmed." Ana held up the screen.

"Same. Maybe this time tomorrow, we'll be packing to leave instead of staying the week."

His words were optimistic, but his enthusiasm didn't match. She just nodded.

Peace talks scheduled, they lapsed into silence again.

Silence that screamed loudly, *we kissed we kissed we kissed.*

"I'm ..."

She could go anywhere with this. *I'm sorry about the kiss,* or *I'm not sorry about the kiss,* or *I'm wondering how you feel about the kiss,* or *I'm freaking out about the kiss.*

Whatever she was about to say, he would have no good answer. For his best answer had to be, *it won't happen again,* and he didn't trust himself to either say that or follow through on it.

"I'm ... tired," she finally said. "Thank you for inviting me to your family dinner. Theresa and Tony are ... they're the kind of family I'm not used to, and I wish I were because they're so kind and funny. You're close. I'm envious but also grateful you asked me to join."

"Of course. Any time, and I mean that. Now that they've met you, they're going to ask every week for the next ten years if you're coming back, and now you're going to have to sometimes, if only to let me off the hook."

Ana laughed, and her smile had him almost leaping from his chair to swoop her off her feet and lay her in the bed and—

"I will," Ana said. "It has nothing to do with you, though, and everything to do with her ravioli."

"I warned you."

"You did, and no warning could have prepared me for the mouth goodness."

She turned a little pink, no doubt realizing what she said—that there was other mouth goodness that happened this evening.

Roman became aware that he was hyper-aware of each breath she took, each blink of her eyes, each twitch of a finger. Then he became aware that though he couldn't kiss her again, if she made the first move again, he didn't have the strength he'd need to back away.

"Um," Ana said, searching his face, then quickly looking away. "Long day," she said. "Tea shop standoff, your mom's, the Monster Smash—"

"The what?"

She waved away the question. "Never mind. I'm ready for bed. Sleep," she clarified. "I'm ready for sleep."

"So am I," Roman lied.

"Tomorrow is Labor Day," she said in that nonchalant way someone says something unnecessary when they don't want the conversation to end.

Roman didn't want it to end either. But what were they doing now? Friendship? It was a fast and fun friendship, but he'd assumed the kiss had derailed it. Ana's continued conversation gave him hope. He wanted Ana in his life, and if friendship was all he could give her, he'd give her the best friendship she'd ever had.

"The first thing you said to me was that people should get to spend a holiday from work relaxing the way they want to," Roman said.

"I did say that, but it was a more meaningful sentiment when I had an actual job," Ana said. "Now that I'm unemployed, it's just a day and not a holiday."

Roman scoffed. "You'll get another job as soon as you get back to New York. The pressing question is, how do you want to spend your holiday here in Seasalter?"

Ana cocked her head and twisted her mouth, thinking.

"The sky's the limit," Roman added.

"Nice cliché. But it's woefully inaccurate. My wallet's the limit."

"Fair enough. But plenty of fun can be had. When you're a little kid, you have no money but lots of fun. What does kid Ana want to do tomorrow?"

"There's a small gym on Broad Street," Ana said. "And I noticed they're open tomorrow morning. I want to take a class. But … I want to go alone to that. Working out is something I … prefer to do by myself."

"Totally understood."

"Then I want to go to the bookstore. They're usually open on Monday holidays for all the tourists. I can probably afford one book. Supporting local business and all."

"Good plan."

"You can come if you want."

"I do want."

"Then I want to find some barbecue for lunch."

Roman nodded. "We can do that."

"And I want to go to the beach. After lunch, when all the out-of-towners start hitting the road so it will be quieter than the morning."

"You read my mind."

"And maybe some games while we're waiting for Lacey and Jake to hash out their stuff in your room. I don't like how we left checkers last night."

"You won twice in a row."

She waved it off. "I prefer a hat trick of three in a row. And you?" she asked. "What do you want to do tomorrow?"

"Did you even leave me eight minutes in the schedule?"

"You asked me what I—"

"I'm just kidding."

"We'll fit it in, whatever it is."

"I want to be with you," he said simply.

She paused, seemingly taken aback at his honesty. Then she said, "I'm not going to kiss you again."

His heart dropped to his sneakers, even though he couldn't kiss her again, and her decisiveness was making it easy for him. He swallowed hard. "Good to know," he heard himself say, "so that I won't hesitate to order double onions on whatever I get for barbecue lunch."

She scrunched her nose. "Double onions? I'll still be *next* to you all day. Have a little mercy on my nasal passages, will ya?"

"You can take it."

"Just because I *can* take it, doesn't mean I *want* to take it."

They both chuckled. Then Ana closed her eyes, took a deep breath, and slowly opened them. "Yeah. I'm tired."

"Me too. I'll see you in the morning after your class. I'm going to have a lazy, slow, carb-heavy breakfast. To be honest, even if you asked me to go to the gym with you, I'd probably skip it. My days of getting up early to pump iron—or really, pumping iron at any hour of the day—are behind me." He patted his belly. "As I'm sure you can tell."

"Don't make me convince you how hot you are, Montgomery. You know you are."

"I know I *was*—"

"What are you saying? That you're a little softer now that you're not seventeen and playing baseball every day?" Ana said. "Maybe so. Big deal. We're not kids anymore. You're an adult, and hotter now. Way hotter. I couldn't be bothered with you in high school."

Roman fought the urge to laugh. She didn't need to tell him that; he'd spent every day dreaming she'd bother with him.

"Now, though ..." she said.

"Now?"

"Now I'm spending Labor Day with you."

"You wouldn't spend it with me if I weren't hot?"

"Nope." Her eyes sparkled. "Sorry. I'm just too shallow to be seen with an average man."

He pretended to look shocked. "I am *not* a piece of meat."

She shook her head. "Good night, Roman."

"Good night."

Neither of them moved.

"Oh," Ana said finally said. "I'm in your room. I suppose I should leave."

"Unless you want to sleep here."

Ana cleared her throat. "I couldn't displace you."

"No, you couldn't. This bed is awesome. I'll throw a pillow on the floor for you and try not to step on you when I get up to pee."

"Fine. I'm going to try to get you to talk in your sleep. Tell me all your secrets."

"That's the line," he said. "Get out."

Ana laughed and pushed herself off the wall. "You're funny. Anyone ever tell you that?"

"Did you not get a yearbook? I was Class Clown."

"I'd assumed that was probably more for your propensity for making fart noises with your armpit than for clever comebacks."

"It was," he admitted. He put a hand under his arm and stood from his chair. "Listen."

"No." She walked to the door.

He walked closer to her. "Wait! I'm really good at it!" He lifted his elbow.

"No!" she shrieked, giggling. She threw open the door and ran out. "Niiiight!"

"Night," he said softly, watching the door swing slowly shut.

He didn't move for what felt like a half hour, but was probably only three minutes or so. Waiting to see if she'd return for some reason. She wasn't tired after all, or she decided a board game was a good idea, or she wanted to—

No. Because even if she did want to, and he certainly did want to, he couldn't, and they couldn't, and that was that.

He thought a cold shower would be beneficial for the way he felt now, so he went into the bathroom, stripped down, and stepped into the spray. Nice pressure. But when he turned the knob away from the red and into the blue, he said out loud, "Nope." He loved hot, hot showers, so instead, he turned it way into the red and he closed his eyes, surrendering. He tried to erase the pictures seared into his brain: Ana's face, Ana's body, Ana's smile, Ana's lips. He tried to dissolve the sensations of her mouth, her tongue, her skin, her fingers.

Roman tried. He did. But he gave up, leaned against the tile, and stroked himself. He imagined sliding her shorts down her perfect legs, pushing into her willing wetness, grabbing her hair on both sides of her face and sucking on her neck as her mouth fell open in wordless ecstasy and he poured all his liquid heat into her.

He gasped as he released into his hand, then relaxed under the water, letting the heat cleanse his soul.

He toweled off and slid naked into bed, turning on the TV but muting the sound, squinting as he listened. Then he immediately felt like a creep. His bed was on the opposite wall as hers, and her TV room was on the other side of her room. Unless a large piece of furniture fell over in her room, he wouldn't hear anything.

After flicking through about fifty-eight channels, he landed on HGTV, but even the elaborate kitchen redesign didn't hold his attention. Ana could be watching it now, too, and if she were, he hoped it soothed whatever hurt her heart.

Roman turned the TV off and rolled over, looking out the window, realizing that after ten years, he was once again falling asleep wondering what Juliana Capuano was doing: listening to music, looking at stars, writing in a journal.

But now there was one possibility that didn't exist then.

Maybe she was wondering about him too.

CHAPTER 10

On Labor Day, Selene pushed the broom vigorously through the common rooms on the first floor, as well as the hall-way. She'd nervously made waffles for the guests this morning, but they came out nearly perfect. Only one of them burned a bit, and one guest, catching an acrid whiff from the kitchen, asked her if he could have it. Apparently, he liked waffles "well done." So even that worked out well. She'd cleaned the kitchen and run the dishwasher when breakfast hours were done, and now she had a ton of cleaning to catch up on after about half her guests had checked out. She'd had to stay on top of it every day, which was even more challenging than she'd worried it would be.

She sat on the sofa to rest a moment, leaning back and closing her eyes.

The rest of her guests would check out at lunchtime, and only Ana and Roman would remain. She smirked a little, thinking of the way the two of them danced around one anoth-er's space and watched each other when they thought the other wasn't looking.

They'd figure it out. Maybe this week.

Roman had eaten breakfast alone again today, telling Selene that Ana had gone to work out. Selene already knew, though, because Ana had stopped in the kitchen very early for coffee, and Selene had talked her into taking a fresh croissant with her.

Selene opened her eyes and almost squealed in surprise to find Owen at the door, about to walk in. "You."

"I deserve that less than hospitable greeting," Owen said, coming in but lingering in the doorframe. "But I brought you a peace offering."

She got up and crossed the room to him, and he handed her a small plant. The leaves were thick and juicy, and the flowers were a lush tropical pink. Selene admired it, turning it one way, then the other.

"Normally, I don't give plants as gifts," Owen said. "I feel like when I gift a plant, I'm saying, 'Here's a responsibility for you.' I'm not great at caring for plants myself. But your garden is pretty, and you have some potted plants in here that look like they're thriving, so I took a chance you might like another. And I did ask at the garden center for a plant that was easy to take care of, just in case, and they suggested this. It's a—"

"Christmas cactus," Selene finished for him. "Yes, these are easy to care for, and they can live for years and really grow in size. Thank you. This is very sweet of you." She glanced at him and allowed him a smile. "Come in."

"Thanks."

The room felt different with him in it. It was as if the space molded around him. He wasn't a stranger like the guests who had come to stay. The house welcomed him in a different, more familiar way.

Selene was sure that Dan also would have.

"Did you need—" she began at the same time he said, "I was hoping—"

"For what?" she asked.

"I was hoping maybe I could have a little tour? I'd like to see what you've done, what everything looks like now."

"Of course." She set the broom in the corner. "It will have to be brief, though, because I have a Snow White amount of housework to do."

"Understood."

"And I can't let you into any of the guest rooms. Many are still occupied, and the others need cleaning. But if you come back during the week—"

"They might be full then too."

"Only two are, after today," she said, trying not to let her concern filter through. Her next booking was two weekends away. She had savings, and she was aware it took a while to get a new business off the ground, but none of that logic had been able to ease her mind.

She hadn't been sleeping well.

She looked at Owen, who was watching her as if he could read her mind.

"Lead the way," he finally said.

Selene walked him around the inn, showing him the new wallpaper and bump-out window in the dining area, the updated kitchen appliances, the fresh blue carpet runner on the stairs between the first and second floors. It was stranger to show Owen around than to show guests around. Guests were seeing it for the first time, and they were impressed with the love in the details, and the amenities, and the proximity to the ocean. But showing this man his childhood home with its changes and "improvements" seemed wrong, in a way.

Owen didn't give any indication of disappointment or melancholy. He nodded and even smiled a few times and asked a few questions. She brought him to the second floor, though there was not much else to see except the hallway. She didn't want to show him her own living area, and he didn't ask.

Owen pointed to the smallest room at the far end.

"That was my room," he said. "When I was a little kid. When I was high school age and my brothers and sister began to leave home, I moved to the third floor, but this room was my real childhood space."

His face was suddenly younger, softer. Vulnerable.

"Do you want to go in?" Selene asked.

He hesitated. "No. Not today."

"Then that completes your tour of the Moonrise Inn. I live on the third floor."

He followed her down the stairs. "Nice name, Moonrise."

"Yes," she said, remembering something Dan had told her. "You know how the moon sometimes seems to rise during daylight?"

"I do."

"It's because the moon revolves around the sun, and sometimes it's in the right position for the light from the sun to reflect back, and it looks like the moon is glowing during the day."

"I appreciate the explanation," he said, "though I knew about the phenomenon already."

"I'm sorry, I didn't mean to womansplain the moon to you."

He laughed. "It's okay. You'll probably have plenty of guests who ask you moon questions."

They arrived at the first floor, and Selene checked the time on her phone. "You're welcome to stay and relax," she said, "and there's tea and coffee for the guests in the nook in the dining area that you can consider yourself always welcome to. But I need to keep working, if you don't mind. I need to finish sweeping and dusting before I go into two rooms and make the requested change of sheets and towels."

"I don't mind, and thanks for the coffee and tea offer, but there's something I want to talk to you about. I can talk while you clean, or I can dust if you want."

Selene tried not to narrow her eyes in suspicion. She should have known there was some kind of ulterior motive to this unannounced visit. "No, I'm not going to put you to work today, but yes, go ahead and talk."

She picked up her broom and continued to sweep, collecting all the debris into a little pile near the entrance to the dining area.

"I was thinking," Owen said.

"That's a bad habit."

Owen paused and she said, "Sorry. Just a thing I say."

"It's okay. What I was thinking was, you have this business to run, and you just opened, and you don't have experience, and you admitted you're over your head."

She stopped sweeping and pointed a finger at him. "If you're here to make me another offer on the house, you can forget it—"

He held up a hand. "I'm not going to offer again. Not like that, anyway. Let me finish."

She rolled her eyes and went back to sweeping, perhaps a little more aggressively.

"You could very well make this place a success," Owen said. "It certainly is beautiful, and I assume you're a gracious and generous hostess. It's a prime location in a gorgeous little town, and I'm sure everyone who stays here will enjoy it."

Selene set the broom in a corner and fetched the dustpan and little brush. She bent over the small pile of dust and crumbs. "But?"

"But business is unpredictable, right? No matter how clever and experienced the entrepreneur, about one in five businesses fails in the first year. Even if they had a solid business plan, and even if the market seemed perfect and all the pieces fell into place."

Selene brushed the dirt into the pan, realizing these statistics would guarantee another sleepless night ahead. "What's your point, Owen?"

"My point is, I'd like to offer you an out."

Selene straightened to standing, dustpan in hand.

"Here's my offer: If your business is not profitable after one year, I'll buy the house back from you."

Selene nodded slowly, then walked into the kitchen to toss the dirt. She grabbed the fluffy little duster from behind the door and went back into the sitting room.

She wasn't sure what to say, really.

"Think about it," Owen said. "If you're in the red after a year, you're going to be losing money. Some business owners call the unprofitable year a wash, and go another year only to find themselves deeper in debt. Then there's the sunk cost fallacy; many will stick with it because of the time and money they've already invested." He cocked his head and gave her a genuine sympathetic look. "And some have too strong a sentimental value to let go. Until it's too late."

Selene moved through the room, picking up little frames and lamps and dusting every little surface, as well as lampshades and windowsills.

But she was listening.

"I'm offering you something most businesses don't get," Owen continued. "An out. An option. If, by the end of summer next year, the Moonrise Inn is in the red, you can spare yourself more debt by selling to me. You'll recoup your losses, plus you'll be welcome to negotiate with me for more so that you come out ahead. Then you'll be free to move anywhere, do anything you want."

He softened his voice. "And you'll have given it a really good effort here. You'll know you did what you and your late husband wanted to do."

Dan. Dan wouldn't want her to go into debt, not even to keep his dream alive.

He would want her to try, and she was.

But he wouldn't want it to break her.

Would he take this deal if it was offered?

Probably not. But it wasn't being offered to him.

It was being offered to her.

"Are you looking to draw up a formal agreement?"

"No," he said. "I could try. I could make you sign something and hold you to it. But I don't want to do that. If the inn isn't profitable in a year, I want you to sell it to me because I'll be willing, and because you'll know it's the right thing."

"How do you know that in a year, you'll even be here? Maybe you'll follow your own dream of—I don't know, moving to Switzerland."

"This is my house, Selene." He swallowed. "I'm sorry, no. I shouldn't say that. It's your house. Yours and Dan's. But it was my house, and I will always be invested in what happens to it. If you close in five months and split town, I'll be here. If you are profitable for twenty-two years, then decide to move on, I'll be here. I'm not going anywhere."

Selene moved into the dining area and began dusting there, but Owen didn't follow her, seemingly giving her some time alone with her thoughts.

It was a good compromise, for her and Owen. But even considering it, she felt like she was betraying Dan.

She sat in one of the dining chairs and closed her eyes.

"This is going to work, Selene." Dan held her close to him under the blankets, his eyes an inch from hers, then touched his lips to the tip of her nose.

"I don't know," she said. "It's so much. The renovations, the website, the—"

"We can do it. And if we fail—"

"We fail spectacularly."

"I was going to say we fail together, my moon goddess."

Would he understand if she placed a safety net under the inn?

She rubbed her eyes with one hand and headed back out to the sitting room, where Owen was looking out the open window in the direction of the ocean. He couldn't see it from that window, but he gazed into endless space as if he could. As if the horizon stretched before him.

"Owen, I will take your offer into consideration."

"Thank you. That's all I can ask. I'll give you … a week?"

"Come back tomorrow," she said. "I don't need a week. If I don't know tomorrow, I won't know in a week."

"I don't want to pressure you."

"You're not. You made me an offer. I'm going to think it over and tell you tomorrow."

"Well, all right. I'll stop by."

"Okay." She nodded once, as if punctuating the end of the discussion. "I need to start on the guest rooms now."

"I'll be going, then." He moved to the door, then turned.

"Don't say 'thank you' again," Selene said. "Not yet. Tomorrow you can thank me or not thank me, depending on what I've decided."

"All right." He tipped an imaginary hat and left.

Selene stood for a moment, her thoughts tumbling around like pillowcases in a dryer.

Then she continued dusting down the hallway. When she was done, one of her guests approached her to check out, and she spent some time checking everyone out except for Ana and Roman.

Then she went into each vacated room and replaced sheets and towels, made the beds, vacuumed, and freshened and replenished the bathrooms.

CHAPTER 11

Although Ana had had to borrow clothes from Theresa for the week ahead, she had brought a pair of nylon workout shorts, a sports bra, sneakers, and a T-shirt from home. When she'd packed on Friday, she couldn't have anticipated the specific kind of stress this weekend would yield, but she'd assumed the wedding and being home in Seasalter and seeing everyone for the first time in years would provoke anxiety of some sort, and on her therapist's recommendation, she had checked online for a nearby fitness studio's holiday weekend class schedule. She'd thrown her gear in her large duffel bag.

It was unusual for her to attend a live class rather than just doing her own programs at home, but she was hitting a lot of firsts lately. Might as well.

She could say one thing about working out: She might be broke and generally unsuccessful in life, but whenever she looked down at herself in her underwear, she was gratified at her own results.

Not that anyone but her would see her in her underwear.

A shiver went through Ana as she remembered that … kiss.

She'd tossed and turned all night in sweat-covered sheets. She'd even gotten up and closed the window, opting to turn on the air conditioner, even though she hated AC. She needed some relief from the images and sensations and Roman. He was one room away from her, and in one hazy, sleepy moment, she had even entertained the idea that her arousal would carry to his room somehow, a pheromone that would have him pounding her door down.

Ana picked up her pace now, on her way to Blue Ocean Fitness Club. The coffee Selene had given her sloshed around in her stomach. Not a good idea before a workout, and ordinarily she would have saved her caffeine fix for her cooldown after class, but she was weak and sleep-deprived. She had to perk up somehow before jumping around in a room with a bunch of other fitness enthusiasts.

When she arrived with only about ten minutes to spare, women were crowding the lobby, chattering as if something was wrong, furrowing their brows.

"What's going on?" Ana asked a woman in her early sixties.

"The teacher isn't here," the woman said, shaking her head. "She's always here about thirty minutes early. Can't be traffic. People are off today."

Ana politely wound her way to the desk. "I thought there was an 8 a.m.," she said to the frazzled receptionist.

"There is," the brunette said. "Or, there's supposed to be. But Cassie hasn't arrived yet."

"Is it possible she didn't realize class happening today because it's Labor Day?"

"Yes," she said slowly. "It's … very possible. We emailed all the teachers last week to confirm morning classes are still on today, but if she didn't see it, she might not be coming."

It was a testament to Seasalter's residents and visitors that no one was particularly angry, but there were about twenty women here and most of them were unhappy and disappointed. They all waited, though, in the event that Cassie overslept and came running in.

"I was really looking forward to this," one student said. "With all the beer and hot dogs I plan to put away in about eight hours, this was supposed to balance it out."

"I don't think that's how it works," her friend said, laughing.

"Let me rationalize my own way, please."

Another woman circled the perimeter of the room, glancing at her watch, clearly trying to get steps in now that her class was likely not happening.

Ana checked her watch: seven fifty-three. She squeezed next to a woman about her age who was sitting in the cushioned window seat and frowning.

Ana gave a polite half-smile, and the woman returned it. Her eyes were red, though, as if she'd just paused a crying spell.

"Are you okay?" Ana asked.

The woman nodded, then wiped her eye with the flat of one palm. "Yeah, sorry. It's so stupid. Things happen, right? But my boyfriend broke up with me this week and I ... I haven't left my apartment in a few days and ... I really kind of needed this today. I forced myself to get dressed and walk out the door. And now there's no class. I'm not very lucky these days," she said with a sad shrug.

Ana patted her arm, and her own eyes welled up. She knew. She knew what it was like to not want to get up, to watch a mess pile up around you, to be unable to move to do even the most basic thing for yourself. Working out got her out of those phases, which were fewer and farther between once she'd started creating programs for herself.

The woman swiped at her eyes again, and Ana's own throat closed the way it so often did, her possible words choked off by a lump of futility. If Roman weren't here in Seasalter, it would be.

Then she remembered that when she'd informed Roman last night that she wouldn't be kissing him again, he hadn't missed a beat.

Ana went to the reception desk. She heard the brunette finishing up a voicemail to a local teacher, pleading with her to please come and cover if she was available. "No one's around," the brunette muttered to no one when she hung up. "It's a holiday."

"Hey." Ana forced the next words out of her throat. They scratched her mouth uncomfortably. "I can cover. I can teach."

"What?" the brunette asked. "Who are you? Are you serious?"

"I have a fitness program I created," Ana said. "It's kind of a High Intensity Interval Training slash cardio slash stretch class. It's fun. I have a playlist. I can fill an hour."

"Do you have any teaching experience?"

"I took an online fitness training course," Ana said, naming the company she was certified with and politely sidestepping the actual question. She got certified in fitness instruction a year ago so she could keep creating classes for herself with authority, but she never really taught anyone other than herself.

She glanced at the sad girl in the window. Ana could do it for her. Ana could push herself through discomfort for one hour to keep that girl from going back home and going to bed and staying there for more days on end.

"If you're serious," the brunette said, "I'm taking you up on this. What's your name?"

"Ana Capuano."

"Okay, Ana. Go down the hall and into Room 2, and I'll hold them off for ten minutes so you can set up." She scribbled on a little piece of paper and handed it to her. "Here's the Wi-Fi password so you can connect to the speakers."

Ana walked down the hallway in a stupid daze.

Was she insane?

No. No, she wasn't.

She stepped up for Lacey this weekend after years of zero communication. She could step up for a girl who needed a fitness class to pull her out of sadness. Ana was a loser in every other way, but she *could* do this thing for someone and be valuable, meaningful, impactful, for one hour out of her life.

Ten minutes was not enough time to panic or freak out, so Ana pushed it aside. She could have a delayed reaction later. She now had a job to do.

She slipped into Room 2. It was a big room, but Ana told her nervousness that it would look smaller when people were here. The wood laminate floors were spotless, and she pulled a mat off the wall. She chose three sets of dumbbells, different weights, and put everything at the front of the room.

On her phone, she found her little file of programs and their corresponding playlists, because keeping the beat to the music was part of the fun. She selected a program, one she'd created recently so it was mostly fresh in her mind. She connected to the speaker and put on a motivating song that the students could walk in to.

From the window on the door, Ana could see the first students walking toward her room.

How could she do this? Talk everyone through this?

The anxiety crept in around the edges of her mind, and her vision.

She shook her head. No.

No time to regret this. No time to panic. As the door opened, she smiled widely.

"Good morning!" she said to each student. "I'm Ana. Grab a mat and two or three sets of weights—make sure one set is heavy enough to feel like a challenge for you. Good morning! I'm Ana! I love your top! Good morning! Spread out, plenty of room. We'll get started shortly. Good morning! Oh, you're welcome. No, there's no canceling class for a holiday. A holiday is the perfect day to feel great, right?"

The sad girl from the window still seemed sad, and moved a little slowly, but she was moving. "Thanks," she said quietly to Ana, who squeezed her arm.

"My friends," Ana called to the room. "Ready to sweat?"

"Yes!" they called back happily.

For the first time in years, Ana was *on*.

★ ★ ★

"Oh, my word," one woman said, "I feel like I'm going to collapse into a puddle of perspiration. Happy perspiration."

Ana laughed as an hour later, nineteen tired students sprayed down their equipment and stored it on the wall units.

"Don't you feel good?" her friend asked. "I do. I feel … invigorated."

"I feel strong. Like I could pick up my car and throw it across the street," a third woman said.

"Don't do that," Ana said. "I don't want to be responsible for the damage."

The three women laughed. "Ana, was it?" the first woman asked. "Why do you look familiar?"

"I grew up here. Juliana Capuano."

"Oh!" the woman said. "Your father is Angelo Capuano, the cardiologist?"

"The retired cardiologist, yes."

"He was my husband's doctor. He's the best."

"That's what they all say." Ana couldn't be annoyed at the reminder. It was the truth. He *was* the best.

"Never mind that," her friend said. "Talent obviously runs in her family. When's your next class, Ana?"

"I don't have a next class," Ana said. "I'm just the substitute teacher."

A woman wearing a matching sports bra and shorts swirling with neon colors said, "If we have anything to say about it, you'll be teaching here permanently. No disrespect to the other teachers here, but that was the best workout I've had in … forever. I'm not kidding. I went from working so hard I wanted to be put out of my misery to relaxed and gooey, and it went back and forth, and so perfectly."

"I feel electric," another student said. "Like, humming all over."

"Is this some sort of workout style I never heard of?" the neon woman asked.

"I … it's my creation," Ana said.

"We need more. What's it called?"

"Yes, what's it called? Hopefully you named it after yourself."

"Y-yes." Ana's mind worked harder to come up with an answer than it had since her first-year law school exams. "I did. Ana … Ana—tomically Fit—er, Fun. Ana-tomically Fun."

"Aren't you clever?" one woman asked. "I love it."

So did Ana, surprisingly enough.

"I'm calling the owner tomorrow," the neon woman said. "I need Ana-tomically Fun on the permanent class schedule. At least twice a week, but three is better."

"I don't—" Ana started to say she didn't live in Seasalter, didn't even live in Rhode Island, but the woman grinned and was out the door.

"Woo!" another student said. "That was *so* Ana-tomically Fun! Bye, Ana!"

"Bye, Ana! Thank you so much!"

"Happy Labor Day, Ana!"

When the last student left with a wave and a smile, Ana collapsed to the laminate floor, lay on her back, and closed her eyes.

Exhilarating.

Workouts always filled her with energy. But to teach her techniques, to walk around the class as they put their bodies through the movements, to offer encouragement and praise and assistance—she had no idea how this would light her up from the inside.

She grabbed her phone off the mat next to her, extended her arms to hold it over her face, and texted Roman.

I'll be back at the inn in about twenty minutes

He answered almost immediately—almost as if he'd been waiting for her. *Good. Let's attack this holiday.*

Also, she texted, *I have a feeling that tonight's meeting is going to go really well*

You do, huh? Why's that?

I just think so. Things are on the upswing

I like this confidence, Ana Banana ☺

Seriously, don't call me that

Make me not call you that

She put her phone on her stomach and stretched.

It was unusual to feel this … yes, confident.

It was unusual to have someone to text about that confidence.

It was … unexpected that that person was Roman Montgomery. She could have texted Lacey about it, or Sarai, or Kate. She did have her friends back, but it was Roman she wanted to share with first.

She took a deep breath.

What had that student said about Ana? *Talent obviously runs in her family.*

In her memory, Ana saw her mother's disapproving frown, her father's disappointed eyes, her law professors' concerned eyebrows, her ex-Conveenience Store boss's dismissive scoffs, and laughed. She laughed and laughed.

There was no talent here. This wasn't anything that any person couldn't do. This wasn't special. Just a fluke good performance under pressure.

Her laughs died down, and she stared at the drop ceiling as the final song on her playlist faded to silence.

It was fun, though.

Ana-tomically Fun.

She laughed again.

★ ★ ★

She texted Roman that she was headed to the bookstore, and he said he'd meet her there. She paused outside the door, her hand hovering over the handle. This bookstore had been here since she was old enough to read—which was a couple of years earlier than most children learned how to read. She'd bought a lot of books here and spent hours and hours studying at a table in the tiny café in back, knocking back cup after cup of hot chocolate or, later, coffee, which the sweet owner, Meg, put on a tab that Ana's parents had there.

That tab was long gone, and probably so was Meg—in Ana's senior year, she remembered Meg sharing her plans to retire to Virginia in the next year or two. The mood of the shop was different also; instead of a cozy-mystery-with-tea décor, the windows now were bright with colorful posters and stuffed animals, and the beachy women's fiction novels were joined by young-adult fantasy stories and children's adventure stories and candy-hued romance novels.

Too bad Ana couldn't afford so much as a comic book today.

Her phone buzzed in her pocket. She slid it out and glanced at the screen.

"Lacey."

"Hi."

Ana waited a moment but her friend didn't elaborate. "Are you okay?" she finally asked.

"Yes. No. I don't know. I'm sorry. I was hoping to give you a break today, so you could at least have a few hours of holiday."

"I'm in Seasalter for you," Ana reminded her. "You're my priority. Tell me what you need."

"I'm—scared about tonight. Seeing Jake."

The new bookstore owner had put out two benches in front of the store, under a striped awning. The paint on the bench was perfect, so much so that Ana smoothed a hand over it to make sure it wasn't wet. Then she sat in the shade of the candy-cane-striped overhang.

"Maybe you should call Kate," Ana said. "I'm not very good at this. Feelings, and expressing feelings, and ... having feelings."

"I almost called her. I could have called Sarai, but ... Ana, you're the one who helped me on Saturday. You told the guests. You arranged this meeting. You're ... my person right now. Is that okay?"

Something warm blossomed in Ana's chest where her heart used to be, as if it were growing back. "Of course it's okay." She watched tourists walk happily along Broad Street. "I'm no expert on anything anymore, but Jake is on board with talking to you tonight, and I think you can assume that means he's ready to listen to you."

"Do you think so?"

"Yes, and I think that you need to not only be ready to say what you need to say, but you need to be ready to listen."

"I am."

"Are you sure? What if it's something you don't want to hear?"

"Why? Do you know something? Do you—"

"No, I don't know anything at all," Ana said honestly. Roman hadn't betrayed his friend, and neither had Ana. "But whatever he's thinking, it was enough for him to want to call off the wedding also. You need to be prepared for whatever it is."

Lacey was quiet for a while. "Do you think it's figure-outable? In the end?"

"Do you love him?"

"Yes."

"Do you want to be with him?"

"That's not the same thing."

"That's right. That's why I asked."

"I'm not sure it's possible."

"Forget possible. Do you want to?"

Lacey said nothing for a while again. Then, finally, "I don't know."

"That's not a bad answer," Ana assured her. "It's an honest place to be, and that's where you can learn what you need to know."

"He's so angry."

"So are you."

"Yeah, I am. I wish—I wish I knew how to do this, Ana. I don't know how to hold up my end of a marriage."

"Don't you think it's probably similar to holding up your end of a relationship?"

"Sort of," Lacey said. "Not completely."

"I think you need to tell Jake this. Tell him how you feel. See what he says."

A shadow passed over the sun, and Ana looked up to find Roman. She pointed at the phone and mouthed, "Lacey." He nodded, pointed at the bookstore, and went in.

"I wish I had all the right things to say to you," Ana said. "But you're articulate and honest, and I think once you start opening up to him tonight, you'll be able to say what you need to say. I really do."

"I've missed you so much, Ana."

"Me too." Ana's eyes welled up, but she sniffled the tears back. "And no matter what happens, you've got me."

"And you're pretty wise about relationships."

Ana rolled her eyes, not at Lacey, but herself. Who did Ana date the last few years? That was a big, fat no one.

"Seriously. Don't disappear again. I need you in my life. I couldn't stand losing you again too, not after all this."

The bookstore door opened quickly, bell clinging, and Roman popped out, holding up a copy of *Frog and Toad Are Friends*. "I *love* this book," he dramatically mouthed with a hand on his heart, and as Ana grinned, he popped back in and the door shut behind him.

Then Ana's grin disappeared. "Stop talking like that," she said to Lacey. "I won't ever leave you. Trust me."

"I do."

★ ★ ★

Roman and Ana left the bookstore, Ana shaking her head.

"I can't believe you bought me this book when I wasn't paying attention," she said, waving the bag holding the new thriller novel.

"Why not?" Roman asked. "It's just a book. I didn't buy you a Rolex."

"Just a book, he says flippantly. Like a book isn't the greatest gift in the world."

"I saw you looking at that book like it interested you. You need something to read on the beach later while I bumble through a sudoku."

"It's a hardcover."

"Yup. I'm a big spender."

"I'm going to get sand in it."

"I hope so," Roman said. "Then it won't just be a book. It will be a souvenir of the holiday wedding weekend that went completely sideways. Every time you pull that book off the shelf, it will sprinkle this memory all over you."

Ana felt the same warmth in her chest she'd felt earlier talking to Lacey. It was like having been trapped in an ice sculpture for so long, and suddenly this weekend was blowtorching her to liquid.

"Everything okay with Lacey?" Roman asked. "She doesn't want to cancel tonight, does she?"

"No, no. She's nervous, that's all."

As Ana said it, she realized she herself was also nervous, scanning the streets for any sign of her friends, fearful they'd see her consorting with an enemy.

"Are you okay?"

"Yeah, sorry." Ana forced her shoulders to relax. "I can't help being on high alert. If any of our friends see us—"

"If they do, we can just act cordial and say we ran into each other while out walking," Roman said reasonably. "And Seasalter is small, but it's not that small. You said Sarai and Kate are staying in the same hotel as Lacey, and that's nowhere near downtown. Mark's with his family today at home, and Pete said he had to work a holiday shift at the pharmacy this afternoon. I doubt any of them will be around."

"Okay." Ana's nerves were only slightly reassured.

"I found barbecue on Surf Road," Roman said. "But I propose we take it to go. I want to get on that beach."

"Good idea. I love eating on the beach. It's extra salt."

"Exactly. I had a feeling I wouldn't need to convince you. We have a lot in common."

"Can we walk up the beach and set up not so close to downtown? Sitting on the beach together would be harder to explain if—"

"Of course. We'll keep a low profile. How was your workout this morning?"

"You won't believe it. Speaking of everything this weekend going sideways." She filled him in on her morning, from offering to sub to teaching the class to all the effusive praise from the students afterward.

He stopped in his tracks, took her arm, and gently guided her closer to the consignment shop, so pedestrians could pass them. "You just taught a room full of people off the top of your head?"

"Someone had to do it."

"No," Roman said. "No one *had* to do it. They could have just canceled. But ... you did it. Do you teach fitness classes in New York?"

Ana scoffed and waved her hand. "Please. No."

"Why are you just blowing it off?"

"Why are you not?"

"Because you are amazing. You are Wonder Woman. You've always been."

"No." The word came out more forcefully than she'd expected it to. "I used to be. I'm not anymore. I'm nothing."

"Ana, you can't—"

"We've hung around together for a couple of days," she interrupted. "And it's been fun. But don't talk about me like you *know* me. You don't. You don't *know* that Wonder Woman was hospitalized for losing it in law school. You don't *know* that she gave up superheroing because she couldn't cut it. You don't *know* she quit everything."

She stopped, breathing hard. "Well," she said slowly, "now you do know."

"Ana—"

She held up her hand. "I'm fine today. I'm fine a lot of the time, as long as I don't do anything too stressful or take too much on or … care about anything too much."

"Is that why you—"

Her hand was still held up, so she quickly waved it to stop him again. "No. You promised me a fun day."

"I did." Roman paused a moment before he said, "Let's get on with it."

★ ★ ★

Gazing at the ocean was peaceful and lovely, but that wasn't the reason Ana resolutely kept her eyes on the horizon where the blue of the sky met the blue of the ocean.

It was so she didn't have to train her optical attention on shirtless, swim-trunked Roman.

His shoulders and arms were spattered with freckles, and his chest had just the right amount of dark hair. He reclined on the blanket beside her, propped up on one elbow, one leg extended, one leg bent, and his quadriceps were so tight, she was tempted to try to bounce a quarter off one of them. If she had a quarter to her name, she might have.

She self-consciously glanced down at her own modest navy tank one-piece. She attempted to draw in her abs a bit, but it was impossible with the barbeque sandwich taking up an inordinate amount of internal space.

She stared at the horizon, unblinking, until her vision blurred, and she turned to look at Roman again. He lifted his chin to the sun and closed his eyes, and his enviably long lashes fanned along the thin skin. The sea breeze ruffled his hair. Ana allowed her gaze to stray slowly, very slowly, down his chest, down his stomach, below his waistband—

"So—" Roman said, suddenly opening his eyes and turning his head toward her.

"I wasn't looking," Ana said quickly.

"Looking at what?"

She scanned the beach quickly. "I wasn't looking at that guy in the red Speedo."

"I should hope not. He's about eighty-five." He lowered his sunglasses and peered over the top. "Wow. If you were looking at him, I don't blame you."

Ana pulled her own sunglasses down and squinted. "He *is* hot, isn't he?"

"Smoking. If I somehow look like that at eighty-five, you'd better make me wear a red Speedo. I'll have earned it."

"You say that like I'll be there."

Roman shrugged one shoulder, one corner of his lips curling up. One corner of the lips she'd kissed curling up.

Her heart thumped in her ears, so she turned her head and stared at the ocean again. Seasalter Beach was certainly holiday busy, but yesterday, it was probably crazy with tourists who had an entire day of leisure. Today, many of them were already on their way back home to go back to work tomorrow.

Work. Ana scowled as she thought about not going in to Conveenience tonight as originally planned, but her face relaxed as she thought about all the happy women at Blue Ocean Fitness Club. Women *she'd* made happy, even if just for an hour.

"I can't wait for tonight," Roman said, and when she looked at him again, he was scratching in a puzzle book with a pencil.

"Lacey and Jake, you mean?" She twisted her mouth. "You're not worried?"

"They obviously want to talk to each other. This was a good idea."

"Says you, because it was your idea."

He frowned for a second, half concentrating on the puzzle. "You don't think so?"

"I'm not predicting anything," Ana said. "I'm taking the wait-and-see approach."

"Boring. I'm taking the winning approach."

"You think they'll get back together?"

"What I think is that they'll have a conversation they should have had a long time ago, and they'll understand each other better. I don't know if getting back together can be the outcome, but finding some peace is a reasonable expectation."

"Huh."

"Huh what?"

"Huh, I agree."

He nodded, flipped his pencil, and erased something, brushing the eraser dust in her direction.

"What are you *doing*?" she asked. "You can't just *erase* answers in a sudoku. If you are erasing, it usually means your mistake goes further back than that one number."

"I agree, smarty-suit. I've only filled in two numbers so far, so I erased them both."

"Good," Ana said, mollified. "Smarty-suit?"

"You're not wearing pants."

She nodded, but her cheeks heated up. Obviously she wasn't wearing pants on the beach, but hearing his voice state that fact was a bit disconcerting.

"Remember what Jake blurted out in Jasmine Pink's?" Ana asked. "That he doesn't think he's enough for Lacey?"

"I remember."

"Don't you think that's a legitimate concern?"

"I've given this a lot of thought, and I've come to the conclusion that it's a misguided concern," Roman said. "That's his self-assessment, not necessarily what Lacey thinks. It's a him problem, not a them problem."

"But if he's saying it this early in the relationship, don't you think it's likely to become a them problem?"

Roman slid the pencil behind his ear and dropped his spiral-bound puzzle book onto the blanket between them. Ana tried hard not to look at the perspiration along his hairline, and tried even harder not to imagine licking it. She rubbed her face. Must be the heat. Of the *sun*. Not him.

"It's not real," Roman said. "He's a smart, capable, funny, and caring man."

"I'm not saying he's not. But maybe he has other shortcomings that he can see better than you can. Or Lacey can. And maybe he's simply trying to stop a big problem before it starts."

"Do you really believe that? I don't."

A tear leaked out of the corner of her eye. Though it was from the bright sun and not despair, she hoped Roman didn't see it.

"Lacey, though," Roman continued. "If what she said in the tea place is true, that she doesn't know how to hold her up half of a marriage, that's a bigger concern."

"No, it's not. I've been thinking about this, and I've decided it's crap. How would she know she can't be a wife if she hasn't even tried yet? You never know what you're going to be good at if you don't try. She must have been good at being a girlfriend if she got as far as a wedding gown."

"Marriage is different. Marriage is forever."

"Marriage is a piece of paper." When Roman raised his eyebrows, she said, "I'm sorry, but it is. An important piece of paper, but a piece of paper that is placed in a drawer somewhere, then they're just two people again who might fumble and fight a bit, but that's normal."

"And if they fumble and fight a lot?"

"Then they do. But writing off marriage without even making an effort?"

"It would save them a lot of heartache."

"It would also deprive them of greatness." She shook her head. "Do you really believe not trying is the way to go? Did you step into the on-deck circle every time with a certainty you'd strike out? Or did you step into it with the hopefulness that you'd hit a homer?"

Roman cleared his throat and gazed out to sea. Without taking his eyes off the waves, he quietly said after a moment, "You know what an on-deck circle is?"

She kicked sand onto the corner of his blanket. "Of course I do. Just because I didn't like baseball boys in high school doesn't mean I don't like baseball."

She picked up his puzzle book and reached over to slide the pencil out from behind his ear, but before she could take her arm back, he took sudden but gentle hold of her wrist.

Still, he kept his eyes on the surf. But he rubbed the delicate skin on the inside of her wrist with his thumb once, twice.

"It's a risk," he said.

"Wh-what is?"

"Trying to work it out."

She blinked and he turned his head, catching her eyes with his. Neither of them moved a muscle, until he finally said, "Lacey and Jake."

He released her wrist and she dropped her hand, still holding the pencil between two fingers. Her skin tingled where he'd touched her.

"Want to do the puzzle together?" he asked. "It's in the 'difficult' section. I'm more of a medium-skill sudoku-er. But maybe … I can figure it out with you."

CHAPTER 12

Even after a shower and dinner, Roman continued to luxuri-ate in that day-at-the-beach sun fatigue. He and Ana had sat on the beach, talking and doing puzzles and napping. Well—he was pretty sure she had succumbed to slumber for a few min-utes. He was too acutely aware of her to fall unconscious beside her. At one point, as she prepared to flip to her stomach, he nearly offered to put sunscreen on her back, but she reached into her tote and slid on a cotton shirt before flopping facedown.

She'd said she wouldn't kiss him again.

He respected her wishes. Long term, they were also his wishes. Maybe not wishes—requirements.

He liked being Ana's friend.

But it was not easy to remind himself he couldn't be more.

He sat on the blue sofa in the Moonrise Inn's sitting room. They'd picked up light salads for dinner after the beach and ate them on lounge chairs in Selene's rock garden, sunflowers sway-ing over their shoulders. Then they'd parted ways to freshen up and wait for Jake and Lacey.

Selene breezed into the room from the back hallway. "Hey, Roman! How's your day?"

"Great. Hey, is it all right if Ana and I have a couple of friends over for a while?"

"Of course," Selene said. "You don't have to ask."

"I'm just making sure, because the situation is a little unusual."

"How so?"

"It's the bride and groom."

"From the wedding that wasn't?" She raised her brows. "Have they gotten back together already?"

"No, but they want to talk, and I thought this is a good place for that. New for both of them. And really peaceful."

"As long as it stays that way," Selene said, and frowned. "Do I need to worry about breakables?"

"No, no," Roman assured her. "They are having problems but they're both civilized, reasonable adults."

"I heard a little differently when I saw Delilah today at Jasmine Pink's."

"They were angry," Roman admitted. "But they weren't violent."

"I'll allow it. But I'm counting on you to keep them quiet and contained. All the guests except you and Ana have checked out, but that doesn't mean I want to hear yelling."

"Yes, ma'am. I'll take full responsibility."

"Why you? Was this meeting your idea?"

Roman nodded.

Selene opened her mouth like she was going to say something, then closed it.

"I didn't have to convince them," Roman insisted. "Both of them were mooning around last night missing each other." He glanced at the moon-decorated light switch cover. "No pun intended. They wanted to talk. They just needed a little encouragement."

"Mm."

"Ana and I aren't going to mediate or anything. We're just going to leave them alone in my room so they can chat."

"'Ana and I,' is it?" Selene sat on the coffee table across from him, perching on the edge.

"Wait, is it 'Ana and me'? No, 'Ana and I' was correct, right?"

"It's not the grammar that interests me," Selene said, "though yours was correct. It's the easy association. Sounds like you two are getting—close."

Roman shifted. "It's complicated."

"It always is."

"I don't know what I'm doing."

"No one does."

"No," Roman said, frustrated. "I *really* don't know."

"Well, then, you learn by trying."

"Ana said the same thing today."

"Sounds like she wants you to try, then."

"We were talking about Ana and Jake."

She cocked her head. "Were you?"

Roman paused. "Are you some kind of psychologist?"

"No." Selene half smiled. "I was an advice columnist."

"Ah. A know-it-all."

He was horrified at himself as soon as the insulting words left his mouth, but Selene laughed genuinely, even doubling over and holding her stomach. "Yes, I knew it all. Until," she said, her laughter quieting, "I didn't." She sighed. "Here's what I've found. Life is like a … classroom. It offers you countless opportunities, lessons, to learn what you don't know."

Roman knit his brows together. "You're saying I need to show up for my lesson?"

"You said it, not me. I'm not an advice-giver anymore."

She slapped her thighs and stood, and as she did, Ana's door opened. Ana stepped out, barefoot and damp-haired, wearing yellow cotton shorts and a red T-shirt depicting the famous red powdered-drink pitcher crashing through a brick wall.

"Hi, Ana!" Selene said. "I hear your friends are coming by."

"We'll keep things under control," Ana promised quickly.

"Roman already reassured me. I trust you. Good luck."

"Thanks," they both said, and she went out the front door.

"I really like her," Roman said. "She's the cool mom we wish we all had."

"What are you talking about? Your mom is incredibly cool. This is her shirt. My mom is the uncool one."

"Why's that?"

"She's … she's a very high achiever."

"That's uncool? That sounds like a girl we all knew."

"Shut up. That girl … is gone."

"I don't believe that for a second."

"What's that supposed to—"

The door swung slowly open, and Jake walked in. "Hey." He shoved both hands in the pockets of his khakis. His blue button-down shirt was neatly pressed. It was a step up from Jake's summer casual, and Roman was gratified to see that his friend had made an effort that Lacey would be sure to notice.

"Hey, buddy." Roman went over and hugged his friend, and they exchanged a few back pats before they stepped away. "You remember Ana."

Jake narrowed his eyes at Ana, and something rose in Roman's chest—an instinct to defend her. He clenched a fist, but Ana just smiled benignly at Jake. "Hi, Jake. You look good."

Clearly considering her an enemy, he didn't answer her. But after a moment, he gave a curt nod of acknowledgment.

"Nice place," Jake said, glancing around. "Smells amazing. Like cookies and incense and stars." Then he blinked, as if surprised by his own eloquence.

"You're not wrong," Roman said, just as the screen door opened again.

Lacey walked in, the hem of her pink flowered sundress swishing around her ankles. Her hair hung in loose blown-out waves around her head and shoulders, and pile of thin gold bangle bracelets tinkled on her arm. Roman could easily see how Jake would have been captivated by her. She was the walking manifestation of the art and glamour of Broadway.

"H-hi." Her timid voice contrasted with her confident presence. She didn't look directly at Jake—or at Roman, for that matter—but instead engulfed Ana in a hug. When they separated, all four stood in the thick, awkward air, shuffling their feet.

This was Roman's idea, so he needed to take the reins and encourage this reluctant horse forward. He cleared his throat. "My room is just down this hallway. Make yourselves comfortable and talk as long as you want, okay?"

"We're in no rush," Ana added.

"That's right," Roman said. "Jake, text me when you leave so I can go to sleep, but in the meantime, I'll keep myself occupied. And I won't go far."

Jake and Lacey both nodded, still not looking at each other.

"Follow me." Roman started toward the hallway. He glanced over his shoulder. Jake waved Lacey through first, and after one last blink at Ana, she followed Roman, Jake trailing a few paces behind.

Roman unlocked the door, pocketed the key, and showed them inside. They walked around the room; again, not looking at each other.

"This inn is lovely," Lacey said. "Even just the little edges on the curtains. Every little detail shows … love."

Her last word was small but loaded, and Jake finally did meet her eyes. Lacey bit her bottom lip as she gazed up at him through her eyelashes.

"I'll leave you to it," Roman said, and escaped, shutting the door quietly behind him.

Ana hadn't moved from her spot in the sitting room. "Are they … good?" she asked in a quiet voice that wouldn't carry to his room.

He matched her low volume. "I think so. Should we play some board games?"

"Sure, but I don't think we should hang out in here. If one of them opens the door, they will see us only a few feet away and think we're eavesdropping. They'll also know we're … together, getting along. I don't want Lacey to think even for a second that I'm consorting with the enemy."

"Are you saying you don't want to wait together?"

"No," Ana said slowly. "I want to but I don't want to upset my friend. I've been a crappy enough friend in the past."

"Does she know you're also staying here?"

"I'm not sure she ever asked. I told Sarai, but I don't know if she remembers or told Lacey."

"Let's just grab some games and go in your room, then," Roman said. "If … if you don't mind me inviting myself."

"No. We were planning on hanging out anyway, right? Doesn't matter where."

"When Jake texts me, I'll confirm they're gone before I leave your room so no one gets the wrong idea."

She raised a brow, and Roman instantly knew she was thinking what he was thinking. That this wasn't one hundred percent about Jake or Lacey seeing them together.

It was about being together in one bedroom.

And though nothing should happen, or could happen, it gratified him that at least she was thinking about it. If he were the only one thinking it, he'd feel like a fool.

"I could also just leave," Roman said. "It's a nice night. I could sit on the boardwalk with some podcasts and wait."

"No, it's fine. Grab some games and come to my room. I'll get some cookies from the kitchen."

Roman grabbed five games—ones they'd played the other night and a few they hadn't—and headed through her open door, closing it behind him. Then he went into the sitting room off the bedroom and plopped on the sofa. She sat on the opposite end and pulled her knees into her chest, her bare toes curling under.

"I feel good about this," Roman said. "I think they're going to work some things out."

"Not everything."

"No, not everything, but … you should have seen them in there. The space between them was crackly with chemistry. They're crazy about each other."

"And you know what that looks like?"

Roman paused. "I do," he said softly.

They stared at one another. Roman had to mindfully restrain every biological urge in every one of his body parts, but it wasn't easy. He worried she'd see him gritting his teeth in frustration and get scared. Or, worse, turned on. Because if she turned on, there was no way he could turn off.

The sound of the front screen door opening and closing startled them both. Ana frowned and checked the time on her phone. "That was not even ten minutes."

They heard the door open and close again, then a third time about two minutes later. Roman watched his phone. "No text." He twisted his mouth. "There are no other guests tonight."

"It could just be Selene coming and going. Taking care of things. Or maybe she has friends visiting. She does live here, after all."

"True."

"How about I beat you at checkers while we wait for Jake to text?"

"You sound pretty confident."

★ ★ ★

They played four board games, numerous card games, and watched a few shows on HGTV. They laughed at everything—the terrible dice rolls, their new legendary checkers rivalry, the televised closet-organization crises.

Five hours later, they weren't sitting on the sofa so much as sprawling on it, staring at the ceiling.

"I can't believe I'm so tired," Roman said. "I'm twenty-eight. Isn't this the prime of my life? Should I even be thinking that midnight is late?"

Ana muted the TV with the remote, the picture still flickering in the dark room. "I haven't gone out past nine o'clock in years. And I do feel better about that if you're as socially pathetic as I am."

Roman checked his texts and shook his head wearily.

"Do you think," Ana asked, "that maybe things with Jake and Lacey might be going a little ... too well?"

"How do you mean?"

"I mean ... maybe they are solving their problems in a less verbal way?" She lifted her head and raised both eyebrows.

Roman's head fell to the side and he slapped his palms over his face. "Ugh, no. In my room? In my *bed*?"

Ana giggled. "You're so scandalized."

"I'll have to ask Selene to bleach every sheet and towel."

Ana giggled more. "It's good, though. Right? For them to rekindle, to reconnect."

"Rekindling and reconnecting in my *bed*, though?"

Ana sighed. "Do you want to knock? It wouldn't be unreasonable."

Roman thought a moment. "No. You're right. What if they are rekindling and—I don't want to interrupt that. They've been through enough. Plus, I did tell them to take as long as they need. Maybe they … need until morning?"

They stared at one another.

"You can stay here," Ana said quickly.

"Oh … no, I—"

"I doubt Selene would love it if she came down here in the morning and saw you sleeping on the sofa in the main sitting room. And you don't have any other option."

"I could go over to Mom's."

"You'll only end up on the sofa there too, right? Because of the renovations? And I'm sure she has work in the morning. No need to wake her."

"You sound like your mind is made up."

She snorted. "There's nothing in this for me. Except being a nice person."

"It is very big of you, considering I came out on top in checkers tonight."

"Shut up." She got up and crossed through her bedroom on her way to the bathroom.

The room seemed to collapse a bit at the loss of her presence.

Could he stay here overnight? Ana was taking the mature point of view, but every cell in Roman's body hummed with knowing he'd fall asleep near her, wake up near her …

She returned and as she lingered in the doorway, he said, "If you can spare a pillow, you won't even know I'm here."

She paused, then said something very quietly.

Roman stood and walked slowly over to her. "What?" he asked, almost as quietly.

"I said, yes, I will."

They stood face to face, and his gaze grazed her chin, her cheeks, her lashes, her lips.

Her lips.

"Come to bed," she said.

He began to laugh, to tease her about that coming out the wrong way, but she shook her head once. "I know how it sounds," she said, "and I mean it exactly how it sounds. Come to bed."

"I—" Roman swallowed hard. "I've always been a lot cooler than this when a woman was interested in me. But ... that woman has never been you."

Ana's smile was quick but crooked.

"Are you sure?" he asked.

"No. I haven't been sure of anything for years. I've been lonely and directionless and sad. But this weekend, I came back to Seasalter, and suddenly I reconciled with my friends by telling them the truth, I taught a workout class that a bunch of people loved, and I was bold enough to walk up to the most popular boy in school and start talking to him—and he made me laugh, really laugh. When it comes to achievements, I'm on the kind of roll I haven't been on since college. Might as well keep it going. As long as it's ... something you might be interested in. As long as I'm someone you're interested in."

"Do you sincerely think that you're not?"

"No, I think I am. I wouldn't put myself out there so bluntly if I didn't think the odds you're into me are pretty damn good."

"I am, Ana. I ... God, I *so* am. I want all of this. Of course I do."

Was he protecting her heart, or his? Or both?

Maybe someone had to.

"Think about it for five more seconds," he said. "Then, only if you're sure, kiss me. If you do, I warn you, I will kiss you ba—"

His word was cut off forever when her lips crashed onto his.

Roman wrapped his arms around Ana, and he backed up, still kissing her, until the backs of his knees touched the sofa. He pulled her into his lap, leaning forward so she could wrap her legs around his waist.

This was *Ana*.

And it was smooth, natural, right.

They kissed for minutes, hours, or somewhere in between. The frames of her glasses pressed into the thin skin around his eyes. Her breasts pressed against his chest as they kissed like teenagers—desperate, frantic—grabbing and clutching at each other as if each were afraid the other would come to their senses.

Roman tore his lips from hers, inhaling raggedly.

"Roman," she gasped as he ran his tongue in a hot trail down her neck.

"Say my name again," he said, because though he'd heard his name in her voice before, it had never sounded like that.

"Roman," she breathed again, and he had her T-shirt off and on the floor in one swoop. He unhooked her bra with one hand, and Ana dragged it away from her body, tossing it in the direction of her discarded shirt. He bent to take one nipple into his mouth, rolling it around, and she tightened her arms around him, pressing her pelvis into his—hard.

He groaned and, spurred on by the sound, she ground into him.

"Ana," he said around her nipple before letting it go with a wet pop and moving to the other one. She clutched at the hem of his shirt and he leaned back from her so she could pull it over his head before kissing him again.

He stood from the sofa, supporting her ass with his hands, and carried her to the bed in the adjoining room, not taking his mouth from hers until she unwrapped her legs from his waist, crawled onto the bed, and pulled him on with her. She unbuttoned his shorts and pushed a hand down the front, sliding down his skin to grasp his length.

He moaned, lifting his chin to stare at the ceiling while she worked him with her palm. The shorts limited her range of motion, but the feeling of her hand stuffed into his shorts, moving her fingers just enough, had him biting his lip hard.

When he couldn't take any more, he pushed his shorts down to his knees, freeing his erection. The tip was wet, and he coated two fingers with it and rubbed the tips of his fingers across her bottom lip. Her tongue darted out and slowly, deliberately, licked the moisture he left there. Then he pushed the fingers into her mouth, and she sucked them in greedily, her eyes locking with his through her glasses.

He almost told her this was a dream; this was *his* dream. He almost said it—but he didn't want to say anything, afraid it would break the spell they were both under.

She unzipped her shorts and took her hands away, lifting her hips so he could drag them down her long, soft legs. He tossed them aside and grabbed her ass again, holding her hips aloft while he kissed up the inside of her left thigh. She bucked as his lips came close to the edge of her panties, and he hovered over her skin there, breathing hot onto her damp skin.

He heard her breath catch, and neither of them moved a muscle until he moved away and began to kiss up her other thigh, again nearly touching the edge of her panties but not quite—just hovering close and breathing hot.

The tart smell of her wetness filled his nostrils, and he clenched his buttocks with the need to plunge into her. But he didn't. Not yet.

She struggled to push her little opening up to his mouth, but he held fast to her hips, not letting her.

Then, without warning, he dove his tongue under the silky cotton covering her.

She cried out a profanity that sounded to him like the most beautiful song. He lapped at her, tasting her so-long-forbidden juice. He pulled the material roughly aside so he could get more of it.

She threw her head side to side, making little sounds of agonized pleasure.

He parted her folds with his hands, found her little bud, and drew it between his lips, sucking it, rolling it. She pounded a heel on the bed behind him once, twice. He felt her stomach quivering, her legs shaking.

He sucked harder as he slid a finger inside her, pumping it in and out, loving the little slurpy sound of it. Her body shook harder.

His mouth and chin were soaked with her. He moaned into her, and again, and again.

Ana's body went stiff and tight, then she roared, her voice hoarse.

He kept licking as the spasms pressed against his tongue, and when they slowed, he pulled away. He crawled up her body, and she kissed him, heedless of the remnants of her desire on his face and mouth. Then she pressed her lips into his ear and whispered that she was on the pill. He whispered back that he was clean, and she nodded.

He used one foot to push his shorts off his feet and put one hand on each of her shoulders, bracing himself over her. She reached down between them and clasped his erection in her hand, working him up and down.

"S—" he said, then didn't. He didn't want to tell her to stop for fear she'd think he wanted to stop everything, when he only wanted her to stop moving her hand because he didn't want to come yet.

Instead, he reached down and took her wrist. He brought her hand up to his mouth, kissed her palm, then pressed her hand into the bed as he drove into her in one movement.

They both opened their mouths in silent shouts and stared at each other with wide eyes. She moved first, setting the pace with her hips, and he followed.

He didn't know which one of them sped up, but only after a few thrusts, they were frantically slamming into one another. He bent down and took her mouth in a hot kiss before he dragged his mouth away.

"I'm—" he said, before he felt himself burst into her. He saw stars for a moment and when his vision cleared, he caught her staring at his face with something that looked like a cross between surprise and amazement.

He withdrew from her carefully and collapsed beside her.

They lay there quietly as the yellow streetlight bathed them. Ana closed her eyes, and Roman watched her face relax, muscle by muscle.

Finally, he stood very slowly, unwilling to disturb her, and walked into the sitting room. He packed the games properly in their boxes and stacked them on the coffee table. He picked up their clothes in both rooms and folded them, placing them in his-and-hers piles on the chest at the foot of the bed.

Ana liked tidiness and order, and he wanted her to wake up feeling wonderful and carefree.

As wonderful and carefree as he felt now.

Finished straightening up, he turned the TV and lights out in the sitting room, then came into the bedroom. Ana had fallen asleep on top of the bedspread, so he folded her side of the bedspread up to cover her. Then he slid into the bed beside her and folded his side up over them, so they were wrapped like a burrito.

He'd take her for a burrito again tomorrow. The joy on her face in eating a big burrito was close to the joy on her face just a few moments ago. Close, but not quite exactly the same.

Putting his hands on each side of her head, near her ears, he gently and slowly slid her glasses off, folded the arms, and stretched to put them on the nightstand on her side of the bed.

She needed sleep, and he didn't want to wake her by hugging her, so he simply lay beside her, smiling up at the ceiling until he fell asleep beside the girl he'd dreamed about for many, many nights.

CHAPTER 13

"Luna," Selene said into the phone. "I don't care if you think I'm nagging you. I'm saying you could call me once in a while."

"I'm fine, Mom," Luna huffed. "*God*. What could possibly happen to me?"

Everyone thought that, didn't they? That nothing could happen. "For your information," Selene said, "I'm not worried about you at all. I just want to know that the education I'm paying for is still happening, that you haven't jumped into a rock band's bus and ditched school to be a roadie."

"Like I'd do that."

"I don't know what you'd do," Selene said. "That's as likely as anything else."

Selene wasn't sure why she was playing into a nineteen-year-old's petulance, answering surliness with sarcasm. But Luna didn't exactly inspire warm and fuzzies from her these days.

She reached out and untied a curtain sash, retying it prettily. "The inn was full this weekend," she said.

"I didn't *ask*."

"I know you didn't."

"I don't want to talk about the inn."

"Clearly. You didn't want to help before you left, you don't want to talk about it—"

"Mom!" Luna yelled. Selene grimaced and added an inch of space between her ear and the phone. "This was *Dad's* dream. I was the one who helped him the most."

"I know that, Luna," Selene said with a patience she didn't have. Her daughter was still grieving, but Selene wasn't going to pretend she understood why Luna didn't feel the same way she did about the Moonrise Inn.

"It wasn't *your* dream," Luna said. "You didn't even want it."

Selene's heart caved in. Then she stood up straight. "Listen to me, Luna," she said evenly. "I'm your mother, and you will not take that tone with me. You have no right."

"*You* have no right to be *running* Dad's *inn*."

"Because it was Dad's dream," Selene repeated. "Well, you know what? Your father was *my* dream."

She hung up, her hand shaking more than her voice had.

Her chin fell to her chest in regret and resignation. She shouldn't have said that, no matter how much Luna pushed, no matter how much she hurt her.

She swallowed against the sob that threatened to choke her and began to count to ten as slowly as she could. At eight, she heard the screen door open gently, but she made herself finish all the way to ten.

When she lifted her head and turned around, Owen was standing there. His hair was windblown. He wore a green T-shirt and jeans that weren't fashionably torn but were honestly worn at the knees and ankles. He carried a toolbox, and even though he was casually dressed, it wasn't so casual that he looked like a fix-it man.

"I didn't mean to startle you," he said.

Selene realized her hand was on her chest as if she had been startled, but it was possible she had placed it there when she'd said what she had to say to Luna. She couldn't remember. She put her hand in her front pocket, feeling the heat of her own skin through the thin cotton pocket of her denim shorts.

Selene cleared her throat. "You didn't startle me. I hope you didn't have to hear my phone call."

"I heard a few sentences," Owen admitted. "So I backed down the stairs, but when I didn't hear your voice again for a few minutes, I assumed you were done."

"Note to self," Selene said. "Do not make personal phone calls in the common area of an inn I'm trying to make inviting and pleasant."

"I'm sorry. If you want to—"

"No. I don't want to speak to my teenage daughter again right now."

His mouth curved up in a half smile. "Probably a good idea. You won't get anywhere."

"Do you have kids?"

"I have two sons, twenty-seven and twenty-five."

"Do they drive you nuts? Or are you the nice parent, and your wife is the parole officer?"

Owen rolled his eyes. "I was always the parole officer. My ex-wife was Santa Claus, the Easter Bunny, and the Tooth Fairy all mashed up into one benevolent being."

"Ah."

"They're adults now, though. If just barely. Don't get me wrong, I liked being a father when they were kids, but I'm so happy now to go for days at a time not talking to them, being able to trust they can put their pants on right side out and pay their rent and make friends I don't need to meet."

"That means you raised them right," Selene said. "You don't have to be as involved in minutiae anymore."

"Your daughter—"

"Luna."

"Luna. I'm sure losing her father still hurts."

"Of course it does," Selene said. "But I'd hoped—" She stopped herself from saying, *I'd hoped we could get through this together. I'd hoped we could at least be closer. I'd hoped she wouldn't blame me every day for carrying on the best I can.*

Because this man didn't know her. He didn't need to hear all that. "Anyway, here you are," she said.

"You said to come back today."

"I did," she confirmed. "I don't know if I'll be able to talk for long. I only have two guests this morning, and they haven't been out for breakfast yet, so if they emerge from their rooms, I'll need to attend to them."

"That's all right." He shifted his weight from one foot to the other. "I shouldn't have come so early. I can't help feeling like I'm pressuring you. You really should take a few days to think about my offer—"

"The answer is yes," Selene interrupted.

"Yes?"

"Yes, in one year, if the inn is losing money, I will sit down with you to discuss a sale."

Owen hesitated, maybe waiting to see if Selene would add conditions or caveats, but when she didn't, he put his hand on his heart. "Thank you. I mean it."

"Thank you as well. Hopefully, it won't come to that," she added and realized she meant it. She didn't want to have to be in a position to unload the inn. She wanted to make Dan's inn a success. He'd believed in her.

Of course, he hadn't foreseen her having to go it alone.

Owen and Selene nodded at one another, since there was nothing else to say. But he didn't make a move to leave.

"On your way to work?" she asked, to break the silence that was, at least for her, too long and awkward. She nodded at the toolbox.

"Oh, no, I don't need tools for work. I'm an accountant. I work from home, though. So my schedule is a little more flexible. I just have a chore to do."

"I see."

"If you don't mind, then, I'll get started."

"What—" Selene started, and Owen headed out the screen door. He crouched on the porch near the stairs. He put his hand on the second stair from the top and pushed it with his palm a few times. Then he opened the toolbox and started rummaging.

Selene stepped outside. "What are you doing?"

"I noticed both times I was here this weekend that this plank is a little loose. I'm going to fix it."

He opened a little drawer and sifted through a little pile with his finger. He drew out a nail, examined it, then palmed it and went searching for another.

"You're going to fix the step?"

He didn't look up. "Yes, of course."

Of course? "Um. Why?"

He did lift his head then, and his green gaze bored two holes through her eyeballs. "Because it's loose. It could pop up more and hurt someone."

"I ... I didn't even notice it."

"I wasn't suggesting you were negligent. It's not obvious. Yet. I just—"

"Know this house," she finished for him.

"Yes, I do." He closed the little drawer in the toolbox and pulled out a hammer.

"But why are you helping me?"

He moved from a crouch to his hands and knees. "I didn't mean to assume you're not handy with tools. I apologize because that's not very enlightened of me. Are you handy with tools?"

"As it happens," Selene said, "I'm not."

"Okay, then."

"But why would you help me after we made the kind of deal we made?"

He positioned the nail and held it steady, then hammered it in. Then he pushed his hand on the step again, testing. "I don't understand your question."

"We agreed I'd sell you the house if the business fails." Selene blew a strand of hair off her forehead. "So why would you help me by fixing a step? Why not just walk away and watch the inn fail? Watch me fail?"

He sat up. The sun hit his face and he squinted, then shielded his eyes with one hand. "That wouldn't be right," he said simply. Then he hammered another nail.

He didn't offer anything more, and Selene didn't press. She just watched as he moved down the steps, examining each one. Then he stood.

"I can take a lap around the exterior. See if there's anything else."

"I—"

"The place looks great overall. The contractors did a great job. But it was neglected for about a year after that, right?"

Eighteen months, to be exact. Eighteen months that she lay in the bed she'd shared with Dan, day and night, refusing to roll over to his side because it was still his side.

"I'll make sure nothing small is out of place," Owen continued.

"I—I need to finish up some laundry."

"No problem. I won't take up any more of your time today. I'll just check things out and go."

He hopped back up the stairs with the vigor of a man thirty years younger. He picked up his toolbox, gave her a little half wave, half salute, and headed down the steps and around the left of the house.

Selene stared at a sunflower for a long moment before going back into the inn.

★ ★ ★

Awareness crept into the edges of Ana's mind, but she kept her eyes closed as she floated out from the dream state. Opening her myopic eyes each morning offered a fuzzier experience than the actual waking did, so unless her alarm blared her eyes open, she lingered in the darkness behind her lids until she was fully alert.

She searched her memory for where she was: the Moonrise Inn.

In the Stardust Suite of the Moonrise Inn.

In her bed in the Stardust Suite of the Moon—

Her eyes did pop open then. In her bed with Roman Montgomery?

She registered her nakedness under the wrap of the comforter on top of the bed. She must have fallen asleep right after they—

Oh, God, after we—

Despite the warm, humid air breezing through the tall window, her whole body flushed with heat.

She turned her head slowly, slowly, centimeter by centimeter.

Roman was a back sleeper, like her. His arm was thrown over his face, his eyes buried in the crook of his elbow. His other hand was holding the edge of the comforter that he'd wrapped over himself. His naked self.

Ana was torn between watching him sleep—like a bit of a creeper—and closing her eyes again to replay the night before, starting with the moment she kissed him and ending with …

Her body flushed again, remembering.

As she lay there, other details came back to her, including Lacey and Jake. When did they finally leave Roman's room? Did they leave Roman's room? If they hadn't, they'd all need to see to it that Selene got paid for the extra guests.

Moving like a sloth so as not to jostle Roman awake, Ana pushed up on one elbow and rolled to the edge of the bed. She folded her side of the blanket over Roman—though covering him up should be illegal—and stood.

She instinctively crossed one arm over her breasts and scanned her blurry surroundings for her glasses. She found them on the night table beside the bed, and slid them on, walking on exaggerated tiptoe into the adjoining sitting room. She never slept naked; she was never naked except for the shower and between clothing changes, and it was just weird to have everything hanging out.

She rustled through the bag Theresa had given her and threw on a long nightshirt. The game boxes were stacked neatly on top of the coffee table, with their cell phones side by side on top. She smiled briefly, grateful that Roman had thought to straighten up after she fell asleep. She wasn't good at sitting amid chaos. She settled on the sofa and checked her texts.

Nothing from Lacey. Hopefully Jake had texted Roman, but she didn't want to look at his phone. She did have a few new texts. The first few were from an unfamiliar number.

Hi Ana. This is Sydney, the owner of Blue Ocean Fitness. Any chance you could sub again today at 11am? I know it's last minute but an instructor called out sick, and my clients have been calling me and texting me for twenty-four hours straight about how much they love Ana-tomically Fun. Let me know if you can make it. When you get here, I can pay you for yesterday and today, and we can talk about putting Ana-tomically Fun on the permanent schedule if you're game.

Ana realized that at some point in the middle of reading Sydney's texts, she'd started smiling, and the smile remained after she texted, *Yes, I'll be there at 10:15.*

She looked at her other texts.

Sarai: Morning, Superfriends! Sorry for the early text, but now that all the holiday tourists are gone, I think a group breakfast is in order

Kate: Agreed. Lacey, you were lying low yesterday. Everything okay, sweetie?

Lacey hadn't responded yet. Ana didn't know if the others were aware of Lacey's meeting with Jake, so she'd let Lacey tell them later.

Ana: Morning, all. Can we meet later in the day? I'm teaching a class at Blue Ocean Fitness at 11. Long story

Kate: You're teaching a fitness class?

Sarai: I second that shock. Is this the first horseman of the apocalypse?

Kate: You hated gym

Ana: May I remind you, I got all As, including gym

Sarai: Your As were for effort, not for any kind of actual skill. You couldn't dribble, swing at, or kick a ball to save your life

Ana: What can I say? This is a new me

She got a little thrill, seeing those words come from her.

Kate: Sure is. And you know what? I love it

Sarai: Me too

They agreed to meet at the Seasalter Shopping Pavilion at one o'clock, and Ana added a heart emoji.

Had she ever sent a heart emoji to anyone in her life? Never. She added one more for good measure. Then she dropped the phone in her lap and let her head fall back to rest on the top of the sofa.

Was this what normal felt like?

Anticipating going to work?

Devoting herself to a group of friends?

Having a love life?

Wait—love life? Er, sex life.

Either way, it was new.

It was all new. Wanting things. Doing things. *Caring* about things.

Friday seemed so long ago. Just one long weekend, and she was suddenly waking up, excited about her day and its possibilities.

She heard shuffling in the bedroom, and she lifted her head in time to see Roman step into the doorway and lean against the frame, the comforter wrapped around him and pooling at his bare feet.

"Nice toga, Roman," she said, and giggled. "Did you hear what I said? Toga? Roman?"

"I heard you," he said with a grin. "What a nerd."

"Guilty."

"Are you okay?"

"Why do you ask?"

"You're in here early."

"I wanted to check my phone to see if Lacey gave me a hint of what went on last night, but no news."

"I'll check too," he said, but remained where he was, his gaze lingering on her face. "Ana, last night—"

"Last night was every superlative in the dictionary," she said. "The best of everything."

He walked over to her and knelt at her feet as she leaned over, putting her elbows on her knees.

He took her face in his hands. "I want to be the one to kiss you first this time."

"I want that too."

He kissed her, his fingers splayed on each side of her head. She peeked her eyes open, but his were closed, his lashes brushing the lenses of her glasses. His lips were soft, and when he ran his tongue over her bottom lip, her breath caught. They parted slowly, and he rested his forehead on hers, bringing his hands to her shoulders.

"Everything feels different today," Ana said. "I've been struggling for a long time. I probably still will. But I'm happier, and less lonely, and less resistant to … everything."

"Good, because this world is full of everything, and Ana Capuano deserves it all."

They stayed like that for a few more moments, then he sat back on his heels and reached for his phone. He clicked it on, and frowned at the screen. "Nothing," he reported.

"Nothing? At all?"

"He must have forgotten to text me when he left." Roman winced. "But that's not like him. If there's one thing about Jake, it's that you can always count on him to execute a game plan."

"Let's check your room. But then I have to plan a class and go teach an eleven o'clock at Blue Ocean Fitness."

"Hey, what? That's awesome."

"Agreed. Yesterday I had to teach off the cuff, so having an hour or so to plan today means I can do an even better class."

"I thought you said everyone loved class. How much better can you make it?"

"Everything can be improved upon," Ana said.

Roman smiled.

"Get dressed." Ana pulled back, patting his upper arms.

Roman's smile faded. "That's literally the opposite of what I'd hoped you'd say."

"We have to check your room," Ana reminded him.

Roman grabbed the pile of his clothes he'd worn yesterday and stood, letting the bedspread drop to the floor. "Oh, how clumsy of me." He bent over, giving her a full view of his ass.

She wolf whistled. He stood, holding a corner of the bedspread, turned and winked at her, and sashayed out the door into the bedroom, wiggling his stupidly tight and perfect butt.

After a few minutes, they were both dressed and left the Stardust Suite.

"Hi, Ana!" Selene said, turning from where she'd been dusting an end table, then said a soft, "Oh!" as Roman emerged from the room behind her. Ana's face got very hot.

Selene recovered quickly and gracefully. "Breakfast?"

"Yes," Ana said. "We'll be there in a moment."

Selene nodded with a smile and disappeared into the kitchen.

"Oh, God," Ana muttered as she followed Roman to his room.

"She owns an inn. I'm sure she's seen it all."

"This is her very first weekend in business," Ana pointed out.

"Then I'm sure she *will* see it all. Starting with us."

He went to unlock the door but Ana stopped him with a hand on his wrist. "Knock first," she whispered.

"Good idea," he whispered back, and knocked twice, then twice more. When he got no response, he opened the door.

His room was vacant, the bed perfectly made. He went to the bed and lifted the quilt off the pillow. "The shirt and boxers I sleep in are on the pillow where I put them," he reported. "So I don't think this bed was used and made back up."

"They left without telling you?"

He shrugged. "I guess."

"That's probably a good sign. Maybe they worked it out and left together, and were so happy, they forgot to call you."

"Do you think so?"

"I do," Ana said firmly.

"That means I helped them."

"Yeah."

A huge grin broke out on his face. He picked Ana up and spun her around. "I helped them! I was right!"

Ana laughed, wrapping her arms around his neck. "Yes," she confirmed. "You're a good friend."

He kissed her neck as he lowered her to the floor and let his lips linger on her skin as she shivered. "Maybe I know something about this, after all," he said softly.

Before she could ask what he meant, he stepped away from her. "You need breakfast," he said, and flinched.

"What's wrong?"

"Nothing." He flinched again.

"Are you in pain?"

"No. Yes," he admitted. "Between my ... vigor last night and my spin just now, I aggravated my back." He waved away her concern. "It's an old injury that acts up. I'll go to the urgent care clinic while you're at class."

"Take your time. I told the girls I'd go shopping with them. Hopefully Lacey will give me all the romantic details of her reconciliation."

"Okay. I'll check in on Jake and the guys. And after, maybe we can—" He leered at her theatrically.

"Ice your back?"

"Yeah, probably," he said.

"Sounds amazing."

"You're amazing, Ana."

She cocked her head. "Say that again."

"You're amazing, Ana."

Fireworks exploded in her heart, pink and yellow and purple and green. Her blood crackled, igniting every cell of her body and sharpening her eyes, her ears, her tongue.

But instead of jumping up and down and squealing, she reined it in like an adult. She smiled and nodded in satisfaction, then dropped all pretense and skipped out to the dining room, motioning for Roman to follow.

For the first time in years, she *felt* amazing.

CHAPTER 14

An urgent care waiting room wasn't a place where most people sat in a state of giddiness, joy, and anticipation of greatness. As a former athlete, Roman had had his share of broken bones and sprains and physical therapy sessions, and those doctor's visits were less than fun. Even now, his back twinged painfully when he rotated his torso this way or that.

But despite the inconvenience of pain, Roman was sitting on a cloud of fluffy sugar.

Ana.

He hadn't told her flat out that last night wasn't a one-off for him, that he wanted it to be the first of countless, but she seemed to know, and she seemed to agree. She seemed to want the same.

He'd gotten it … right. Somehow.

And when his best friend and his brother needed help in their relationships, Roman had come through for them, counseling both successfully. Maybe it was possible that he did have an instinct for romance, that he was fully capable of holding up his end of a relationship and of being a worthy and caring partner. Maybe his father's shortcomings weren't hereditary, his lessons not transferable. Maybe Roman only had to continue to try. What had Ana said on the beach yesterday? A homer wasn't a sure thing, but it would never happen if he didn't swing.

He closed his eyes, hearing all his inner voices in his brain—the voices that usually criticized him or warned him—swelling for once into a confident chorus: *Roman, Roman, Roman …*

"Roman Montgomery?"

His eyes popped open, and he stood a little too quickly, wincing in pain. "That's me."

"Come this way," the nurse said.

After his vitals were taken, he waited about five minutes in the exam room before the doctor knocked quietly.

"Hi there. I'm Dr. Angelo Capuano."

Roman blinked.

"You're here for a back injury?" the doctor continued, consulting a printout in his hand.

"Um. Are you—are you related to Juliana Capuano?"

The doctor looked up from his pages and studied Roman, searching for a hint of recognition. "Yes," he said after a moment. "Juliana is my daughter."

Angelo Capuano had neatly trimmed salt-and-pepper hair and dark-framed glasses that had slid down a bit on the bridge of his long nose. The hand gripping his pen sported a thick gold wedding band. He had laugh lines around his eyes and a deep furrow between his brows that no doubt his studious, skeptical daughter would one day inherit, along with her intellect and weak eyesight.

Roman realized the doctor was waiting for him to explain. "I know Ana from high school. We graduated in the same class."

"Ana," Dr. Capuano repeated, then smiled, but it was without mirth. "I keep forgetting that she decided a few years ago to go by Ana."

A few years ago wasn't exactly a recent change, so Roman wondered why it was still something Ana's father forgot.

"I haven't spoken to her in a while," Dr. Capuano said, as if reading Roman's mind. "But not for lack of trying." He went back to reading the notes. "I see here you have an old back injury that you've irritated?"

Roman squelched the embarrassment and the irony that he was sitting with the father of the woman who'd unwittingly helped Roman "irritate" his back.

Roman succumbed to questions and the physical exam, which included Dr. Capuano manipulating him gently into some uncomfortable movement. "I can live with some pain," Roman said, "but in my experience it gets worse before it gets better, and since I'm only in town a few days, I'd like to do what I can to minimize it."

"I'll prescribe a steroid for seven days. Should help for the short term, but when you get home, follow up with your doctor."

"I will, thanks."

The doctor sat on a little stool with wheels and began typing on the computer.

"I ran into Ana at the wedding on Saturday," Roman said.

Dr. Capuano swiveled around in his chair and leveled his gaze at Roman. "What wedding?"

"Lacey and Jake. Ana's friend and my friend from Seasalter High."

"That must have been nice."

"No. It was kind of a disaster." He realized as he said it that if Ana hadn't told her father about the wedding, they probably hadn't talked at all since she came to town.

But she also hadn't blinked when Roman said he was coming to the clinic. "Do you not usually work here?" he asked.

"I'm retired from my own cardiology practice," Dr. Capuano said, "but I fill in here occasionally when needed. I like to work. It's a short drive for me, so it's easy."

"Ah."

"Is Jul—Ana still in town?"

Roman opened his mouth, then closed it. Ana's father clearly still lived in Seasalter, but Ana was staying at the Moonrise Inn. There had to be a reason he didn't know she was here.

"I only ask," Dr. Capuano added, "because her mother and I have a gift for her, and we've been trying to call and arrange a visit, but ... well, you know how kids are."

Roman didn't, and he wasn't sure why the doctor would think he did, but he nodded anyway.

"If you see her, would you ask her to come home? Or call? Her mother misses her. I ... do too."

Roman didn't consider himself a particularly adept student of human nature, but his instincts had been pretty reliable the last few days, and what he saw in Ana's father's eyes was not malice or meanness. Only hurt and sadness.

And Ana had told him that this morning she felt happier, less lonely, and less resistant to everything.

Roman was only beginning to wade into the waters of being in a relationship, but part of a relationship meant making a woman happy, right? Helping her resolve issues? Encouraging her to embrace all life had for her? Her parents missed her. They had a present for her.

The printer spit out a few sheets of paper.

"You can fill this over at Seaside Pharmacy on Evanston Street," Dr. Capuano said. "If things suddenly take a turn for the worse, head over to the ER, and we can do an MRI."

"I will, doctor." Roman's mind was racing.

"Are you—are you visiting your family while you're home?"

"I did," Roman said, and if he weren't paying attention, he'd have missed the cloud that quickly passed over the dark eyes that were as cartoonishly large behind his lenses as Ana's were.

Roman gingerly slid off the exam table, put his T-shirt back on, and shook the doctor's hand. It was firm and warm.

"Do you have any questions for me before you go?" Dr. Capuano asked.

"As a matter of fact, I do. Do you and your wife have dinner plans tonight?"

* * *

Ana was sweating by the time she reached the Seasalter Shopping Pavilion. It was about a mile-and-a-half walk from the Moonrise Inn, where Ana had gone to change clothes after class. She could have driven to the shopping center—the streets were far less clogged with the holiday weekend vacationers gone—but Ana had told herself a walk was healthier. It was, but it was nearly ninety-two degrees, so it was also hotter.

She crossed the park and saw Kate and Sarai waiting for her on a bench near the large flower arch that heralded the entrance to the open-air pavilion. The carousel sat quietly beyond them, in the center of the circle of shops, the painted horses apparently taking a well-deserved break after running for three days straight.

"Hey!" Sarai called.

"Sorry I'm late," Ana said.

Sarai glanced at her phone. "You're not late. We're just early. I haven't gone shopping in a while, and I haven't gone shopping *here* in forever."

All three of them studied the stores. "Is it my imagination or are like half these stores not what they used to be?" Kate asked.

"Malls evolve," Ana said. "Like people."

Kate narrowed her eyes at Ana. "That's oddly wistful."

"I didn't mean it wistfully. I meant it pragmatically."

"That's more like it," Kate said. They stood, and the three of them walked under the arch of jewel-toned flowers. In a few weeks, this arch would change over to fall leaves and pumpkins, then twinkle lights and pinecones for the holidays, then flowers in spring pastels. Summer was Ana's favorite season, though, and how could it not be, growing up at the seashore?

"As a matter of fact," Sarai said, "I'm willing to bet that the last time I was at this mall was with you two, shopping for college dorm accessories. Lacey was here too."

Ana hadn't checked her texts. "Anyone hear from Lacey?"

"She's lying low today," Kate said. "I called her. She seemed extra down today but didn't elaborate. Her mother and sister are taking her out to lunch somewhere. Hopefully, they'll be nice to her. She said she might call us to meet for drinks after dinner."

"That sounds good," Ana said. "Did she—is she okay?"

"Other than having to spend the day with her family, she seemed the same. Which, of course, isn't that great at the moment. Why?" Sarai turned her head to study Ana. "Is something up?"

It seemed as if they didn't know Lacey and Jake had met the night before to talk, and if Lacey didn't tell them yet, Ana didn't want to be the one to spill it. "I'm just worried about her, is all."

"She did stay underground all day yesterday," Kate said, "which is a little worrying, considering that we are still in Seasalter for her, but she said she just needed to think for a while alone. We never know how we're going to feel in a situation like this, until it happens to us."

"I know how I'd feel," Sarai countered. "Pissed and homicidal."

"We saw her angry at the smash room," Ana said. "But Kate's right. She's probably buried under a barrage of mixed emotions."

"Can we talk about you for a minute?" Sarai asked Ana, then drifted over to a shop window and tapped the glass. "Ooh, cute shoes." She opened the door and they followed her in. She asked the clerk for the shoes in a size eight, and sat on a cushioned seat with Kate and Ana on either side of her.

"Are you about to ask Ana about this fitness teaching thing?" Kate said. "Because I'm looking for details too."

"Speak," Sarai commanded Ana, who laughed and explained her fitness journey over the last few years, creating a program, and unexpectedly stepping up to teach it yesterday, and coming up with a name on the fly.

"So after my class today," Ana said, "Sydney, the owner, offered me a job. A … a real job."

She realized as she said it that she'd wanted to tell Roman first, but she didn't have any time to consider what that meant before Sarai and Kate both looked at her with startled and thrilled open-mouthed expressions.

"As an instructor?" Sarai asked.

"Part time, teaching a few classes a week, and full time at the front desk because the current receptionist is going back to college in a week."

The clerk brought Sarai her shoes, and Kate asked for the same ones in a size six. Sarai gave her a look. "What?" Kate asked. "They're cute, and we don't even live near each other. No one will notice." Sarai nodded, appeased. Then Kate asked Ana, "How do you feel about teaching, Ana?"

Ana didn't bother to hold back the smile that crept across her face. "I feel … I feel good about it." Then she shrugged. "But I don't live here."

"Move here," Sarai said, and Kate nodded.

"What, just like that?"

"Just like what?" Kate asked. "You said yourself that you've been moping around for years, not wanting to do anything or care about anything. This would hardly be an impulse move. It's a long time coming."

"Go to the real estate office on Broad," Sarai said. "They've always listed apartments."

"Ha!" Kate said. "You'll be closer to me! I'm in Boston, only an hour away. Thanks," she said to the clerk who brought her a box.

"Roman's in Boston too," Ana said, before realizing that should have been inner dialogue. She resisted the urge to slap her own forehead.

"Roman Montgomery?" Kate asked. "Interesting. You know that how?"

"Oh, I was talking to him before the wedding was called off," Ana said, trying to infuse a careless breeziness into her tone that ended up sounding a lot more like a careful defensiveness.

"Don't let Lacey know you were getting chummy with Roman," Sarai said. "He's the enemy."

"We're not chummy. And 'enemy' is kind of a ... strong word."

"Canceling a wedding is a strong gesture," Sarai said.

"She canceled it too," Ana pointed out.

"Stop with the logic," Kate said. "At least, don't let Lacey hear it. Let her hate who she needs to hate right now."

Ana's heart twisted a bit as she considered the real possibility of Lacey hating her too.

"Anyway, Roman Schmoman," Kate said. "Who cares about him? Do you want the job?"

Today's Ana-tomically Fun class was even smoother and better than yesterday's, and Ana thought about how she was good at this, and she thought about how much fun she gave her students, and she thought about how teaching a few times a week would keep her smiling in anticipation on the days she didn't teach.

And she also thought about Roman, and how he lived four hours away from Staten Island but only about an hour from Seasalter, and how if they were starting something ...

"Yes," Ana said firmly. "I want the job."

"Yay!" Kate cheered. "You'll be a New Englander again, like me. We can get together every weekend if we want."

"Dammit," Sarai said. "I'm on Long Island and Lacey's in Manhattan. You're closer to us where you are now, Ana. We could have hung out all the time."

"Tough luck," Kate said. "She got a job offer here. I'll have custody of Ana."

"Fine," Sarai stood and walked around in the pink suede ankle boots. "We can meet in Seasalter every couple of months for a girls' weekend. Are these the cutest shoes or are these the cutest shoes?"

"They're cute on you, but they're *super* cute on me." Kate stood also. "Move." She gently shoved Sarai away from the mirror on the floor. Sarai pretended to be affronted. "Oh, yeah, these are perfect. Don't wear them when we meet in Seasalter next. People will think you're copying me."

"You copied me!" Sarai said. "I saw them first!"

Kate snickered, and Sarai rolled her eyes, grinning.

"You get them too, Ana," Sarai said. "Might as well look like the Three Pink-Booted Musketeers."

"No way. This week is costing me tons, and now I have to scratch up money for first, last, and security."

"So, you're doing it?" Sarai asked excitedly.

"Yeah," Ana said. "I think I'm doing it."

"How long will it take for you to round up the money?" Kate asked.

"Well, I got fired from my job when I told them I was staying in Seasalter, so I need to find something new in New York and save up. A few months, at least. I might have to turn down the reception job since I can't move right away, but I can still teach there and find another job nearby."

"Nope," Sarai said, glancing at Kate.

"What do you mean, nope?" Ana asked.

"I mean, nope, you can't wait that long, Blue Ocean Fitness and their students can't wait that long, and we can't wait that long," Sarai said. "I'll float you a loan, so you can find a place to live right away. Tell Sydney you're aiming for the twenty-first of the month."

"I'll split it," Kate said. "She'll probably need a moving truck, too."

"What?" Ana asked as they sat down and put their own shoes back on. "You can't—you can't do that."

"Why not?" Kate asked. "At the risk of sounding far richer than I actually am, it's just money."

"Money is for investing," Sarai added, placing the cover on the shoebox and holding it in her lap. "And what better investment than in Ana Capuano?"

"I'm … I'm not a sure thing," Ana said.

"No good investment ever is," Sarai said. "But I have insider information that this stock is about to go way up. It's worth the risk."

"Also," Kate said, brushing her black hair out of her eyes and standing with her shoebox, "I think we can all agree that my social media game is on point, and we're going to break the internet with Ana-tomically Fun. I'll help you. Look at you, you hot little thing with your adorable glasses and your stupidly perfect body. People will want everything you're selling, and they'll be breaking down the Blue Ocean Fitness doors to take your classes in person. Not least of all, me. Sydney will have more business than she knows what to do with, and you'll have all kinds of side moneymaking opportunities."

"I don't know what to say." Tears sprang to Ana's eyes. "Except that I don't want to let you down again. I couldn't stand to let you down again."

And she couldn't stand to let herself down again.

"You didn't let us down, Ana," Kate said. "You had a mental health crisis."

"And if it happens again," Sarai said, "you don't have to be alone. Because you told us, and we'll all be there for you. Just like you're here for Lacey, and like you'll be here for me and Kate whenever our lives fall apart."

"I love you guys," Ana said. "I never stopped. You know that, right?"

"Yeah, we do," Sarai said. "And we never stopped either."

"Hey, not to ruin a tender moment, but do you think that frozen yogurt place in the mall is still open?" Kate asked. "I'm in the mood for some gummy bears."

"That's right!" Ana said. "You used to fill the cup like one-quarter yogurt, three-quarters gummy bears."

"Yogurt is merely the gummy-bear delivery system," Kate said. "No one actually *likes* frozen yogurt."

"I do," Sarai protested.

"No way," Kate said. "It's the toppings that everyone likes."

They walked up to the counter with their boxes, playfully bickering, and Ana's phone buzzed in her pocket.

Roman: I hope you're having a fun day. Dinner tonight at Muscatel's?

Ana: Muscatel's? Did you suddenly turn into a retiree overnight? Are we going for the four thirty early-bird special? My parents used to take me there at least once a month. That place hasn't changed in decades. Unless … it has?

The three little dots appeared as Roman composed his text.

Roman: It probably hasn't. But the spaghetti with clam sauce is a solid choice. With garlic bread

Ana: I'll bite, but only if you're paying

Roman: I am. Four thirty?

Ana: ???

Roman: I'm just kidding. Six?

Ana: Six at Moonrise or six at Muscatel's?

Roman: Which do you prefer?

Ana: Six at Muscatel's gives me a chance to make a sexy entrance at the restaurant

Roman: Your wish is my command. I'll try not to worry you'll meet a hotter guy on the four-block walk and leave town with him

Ana: What if he promises me dinner somewhere other than Muscatel's?

The three dots appeared again for a few minutes, and Ana wondered if her teasing was too harsh. She didn't dislike the restaurant; it was just a little stodgy and old school, with no windows and 1970s wallpaper. But if he liked the restaurant, and he was paying—

Roman: I think you'll be surprised tonight, is all I'm saying

Ana: I'm just teasing anyway. Okay, I'll see you there. I'll wear my nicest clothes, though you'll likely have seen them on your mom

Roman: File that under things I never thought I'd hear a girl say to me

*Ana: *smiley face*

"Who are you texting with a moony look on your face?" Sarai asked.

Moony. Ana grinned and pocketed her phone. "No one's moony."

"Now I need clothes to match these shoes," Kate said. "Onward, ladies."

Ana walked along, a woman breezily giggling with friends, a woman with plans to move, accept a job, and meet a man— her boyfriend?—for dinner.

What a difference a day made.

CHAPTER 15

Roman folded and unfolded his napkin over and over, placing it in his lap, then on the table, then in his lap again. It was ten minutes to six, and he didn't know if Ana would be early or late. It was something he would eventually learn about her, if she would let him. He wanted to learn everything about her.

If he'd had to guess, though, he'd peg her for someone who arrived early. So he'd arrived extra early to spare her any time waiting alone. A woman like her should never be kept waiting. Well, no woman should, but particularly not her.

The waiter refilled Roman's water glass for the third time, and Roman glanced around the room at the tables covered with wine-colored tablecloths. It was definitely an older demographic; he was the youngest here by about forty years. Even Ana's parents would be youngsters here. The restaurant was about three-quarters full, with diners arriving steadily. They'd be full in thirty minutes. Every few minutes, a customer came in and instead of going to the hostess stand, went to the pickup counter for a takeout bag.

Muscatel's might not have been hip or cool, but it was a long tradition in Seasalter that had yet to show signs of slowing.

Ana swept in and spotted him right away, giving a little wave and a smile. She wound around tables, the long black skirt swishing around her ankles and flashing a bit of calf through a summery side slit. She wore a dusty-pink lace tank top that showed off the beach color on her shoulders and collarbone.

He stood as she approached the table. "Hi!" she said.

"I like my mom's outfit." He gave her a soft, lingering kiss on the lips. She tasted like vanilla lip balm.

"I like it too. I was surprised to find it. I think she threw it in when I wasn't looking. She probably expected you to take me to a nice dinner."

The waiter came over. "Can I start you off with drinks?"

"Water's fine for me, while I look at the menu," Ana said, and Roman nodded in agreement. "Oh," she added, "there's only two of us tonight, so you can clear the other two place settings."

"No," Roman cut in. When the waiter gave him a questioning look, he added, "We are expecting two more."

"What?" Ana asked. "Is that the surprise?"

Roman shrugged and picked up his menu.

She reached over and slapped it back down on the table.

"Your manners," Roman said, trying not to smile, "are nonexistent."

"Is that the surprise?" She gasped. "Is it Lacey and Jake?"

Roman's phone buzzed in his pocket.

"It is, isn't it?" Ana pressed. "I haven't heard from Lacey today. She was waiting until dinner to tell me the details of last night, I guess."

Roman's phone buzzed again, and he didn't want to be rude to Ana in public, but it would be an effective way to fend off her questions until the real surprise showed up. He held up a finger. "I have to check this." He slid his phone out of his pocket.

"Oh, you do not. But it's fine. I guessed the surprise anyway." She flopped back in her chair, but leaned forward immediately when the waiter brought a bread basket. "Ooh. I forgot how good the bread is here."

Roman glanced down at the phone in his hand.

Tony: Hey, just so you know

Tony: Phoebe is pissed beyond belief at me. She talked to Meredith, and they got in a fight, and now she's blaming me for everything. Probably won't ever talk to me again. And now Meredith has sent me a barrage of evil texts reminding me of what a loser I always was

Tony: Don't know why I asked you for advice. You're as useless as I am with relationships

Roman's brow furrowed. Oh, no. It must have backfired. His mind raced to find an answer, an alternative, a plan B, when he realized he also had a voicemail. It must have come in when he was at the doctor's office, and he didn't see it.

Jake.

Roman held the phone to his ear to listen to the recording. "Roman, yeah, thanks for last night. It was an absolute disaster. We didn't last ten minutes in the room together before we both stormed out."

Roman remembered the doors of the inn opening and closing right after they'd left Lacey and Jake, but he and Ana had assumed that it wasn't Lacey or Jake.

"I didn't think things could get bleaker than they were on my wedding day," Jake continued in the voicemail. "So, yeah, thanks for a big, fat nothing." A loud click ended the message.

"Roman," Ana said. "You look like someone just sucker punched you in the face."

Roman shook his head mutely, then started typing, *I'm sorry, buddy. I was only trying to help*

Jake's response came quickly, and with a number of typos that suggested furious finger tapping.

This was NOT a good idea. Thanks a lot. I don't know why I let you talk me into this. It's not like you have a serious girlfriend. Have you had any serious girlfriends as an adult? What do you know

Roman slid the phone back into his pocket. Nothing.

That was what he knew. Nothing.

Behind Ana's shoulder, the door opened, and Dr. Capuano walked in, followed by a very pretty woman with Ana's light-brown hair.

"Oh, no," he muttered, because he had just made two big mistakes that affected two people he cared about, and it was suddenly very clear to him that his third and biggest mistake was about to explode in his face.

Ana's brows drew together as she continued to watch his face, oblivious to her parents approaching behind her. "Roman, you're worrying me. What is going on?"

"Juliana!"

Ana didn't turn at the sound of her name. She just went very, very still. Something passed over her eyes, then something else, and neither was good. Her lips parted, and she said without turning around, "Mom?"

Roman quickly stood.

Angelo and his wife circled around the table, and Ana swallowed hard as her mother kissed the top of her head and her father, on her other side, rubbed her arm affectionately.

"Nice to see you again, Roman," Angelo said, reaching out to shake his hand.

"Again?" Ana repeated weakly.

"I—your dad was my doctor today," Roman said. "When I went in for my back."

"I've been filling in at urgent care occasionally," Angelo explained to Ana. "Roman, this is my wife, Gabriella."

"Nice to meet you," Ana's mother said. The resemblance between mother and daughter was striking, from the sassy chin tilt to the sprinkling of freckles over their noses and cheeks. However, Gabriella's smile was warm, and Ana's was nonexistent.

Ana finally cleared her throat. "I was going to call you ..." she started, then faltered.

Gabriella cleared her throat as well, when it was apparent Ana wasn't going to offer an excuse. "Well, it worked out," she said with a forced cheerfulness.

"I'll come by after dinner. We're meeting friends."

Roman, his heart pounding, shook his head almost imperceptibly.

"We're not meeting friends?" Ana asked.

"Your mother and I are your double dates tonight," Angelo said gently. "It appears Roman decided to surprise you."

Big mistake number three. Roman looked at Ana and winced to acknowledge that he was aware of his faux pas, but Ana's return look flattened his heart into the carpet. Hurt. Confusion. Betrayal.

Then she pressed her lips together, stood, and came around to his side of the table so her parents could sit beside each other. Roman pulled out her chair, and she nodded regally before sitting.

He wanted to touch her for reassurance, but he was almost afraid to, so he just patted the back of her chair like an idiot before sitting.

The waiter took their drink orders, and they didn't say anything more to one another before the drinks arrived. Angelo and Gabriella had ordered martinis, but Ana had ordered a soda, so Roman followed her lead. He felt goofy sipping from a bendy straw in front of her sophisticated parents.

When Ana's mother placed her menu down, Roman asked, "Are you a doctor as well, Mrs. Capuano?"

"No." She waved the question away, as if the idea of being a doctor was as frivolous an idea as being a supermodel. "I'm a professor at Rhode Island College. Physics."

She was happy to discuss this semester—the course load and the students—so Roman's awkward questions and her confident answers at least broke the icy silence until the waiter took their dinner orders.

"Ana," Gabriella said, "how are you?"

"Fine." Ana twisted her fork and refused to make eye contact with anything other than the empty plate in front of her.

"Despite what you may think," Angelo said slowly, "we do want to know what you're doing."

"I was working at a convenience store." Ana finally looked up and leveled her gaze at both of them. "But I got fired."

Her parents glanced at each other.

"Yup," Ana said. "I couldn't even do that right."

"Well, that's not—" Roman started, and he felt Ana turn her head to glare at him. But even with the red-button warning, he forged ahead. "That's not exactly what happened. She got fired because she decided to stay and support Lacey, whose wedding was called off. But she's been teaching fitness classes that people really love."

"I taught two classes," Ana muttered.

"What kind of fitness classes?" Angelo asked.

Though Roman didn't detect any disdain in Ana's father's voice—only curiosity—Ana scowled as if insulted he would ask.

"It's a program she created herself," Roman said. "Ana-tomical, um ... what is it, again?"

A few uncomfortable moments passed before Ana said, "Ana-tomically Fun."

"Ana-tomically Fun!" Gabriella laughed with what seemed to be genuine delight. "I love it!"

Ana looked at her mother as if she were six and her mother was trying hard to explain that Santa Claus really did exist when Ana had known for a year that he didn't.

"Tell us about it," Angelo said.

"About—about what?" Ana said.

"About Ana-tomically Fun. What are the core principles? What's a class like? What's the goal?"

It seemed a strange way to bond with a daughter, but Ana sat up a little straighter, lured in by the prospect of intellectually explaining her class. "Well," she started slowly, "I wanted to incorporate the concept of proprioceptive neuromuscular facilitation ..."

Roman had been an athlete much of his life, but he was too far in over his head in the discussion that followed to do anything more than nod. Angelo asked Ana about the scientific studies she'd used, and about the way different muscle groups were worked. Gabriella asked her about her teaching methodologies, and if she'd considered creating a textbook, or a teacher certification program.

Roman should have known—and he supposed he had known—that Ana wasn't merely leading a class through jumping jacks, that her program was the result of deep research and experimentation. But he was still impressed. And secretly relieved. Because whatever not-good stuff that caused Ana's initial reaction at seeing them seemed to be dissipating, and that meant maybe he hadn't been completely in the wrong with this surprise.

Until dessert.

"Ana," Angelo said after the waiter presented him and Roman with tiramisu, Ana with a slice of lemon meringue pie, and Gabriella with a cup of herbal tea, "I'm so happy we got this opportunity to spend time with you. And your mother and

I have something for you, something that you seem ready for now."

Ana narrowed her eyes.

Angelo looked at his wife.

"We'd like to give you money to finish law school." Gabriella leaned forward and looking intently at her daughter. "And it turns out one of the men in my department at RIC is married to a dean at Columbia Law. She's reviewed your transcript and she has said that despite the … issues that kept you from finishing for a few years, she can back you up and recommend what you need to graduate. It's only about three and a half semesters."

Roman turned his head to find Ana with her mouth hanging open, shifting her gaze between her mother and her father.

No one said anything for a long minute.

Until Ana swung her legs sideways in her seat so she was facing Roman. "You know." Her remarkably calm voice did nothing to assuage Roman's trepidation. "When they first walked in, and I realized you'd orchestrated this surprise, I thought, well, he didn't know better. It was a misguided attempt to manufacture an opportunity for me to see my parents because he thinks I'm lonely or sad."

"You said you were, in those exact words," Roman started, then stopped when her nostrils flared.

"But," she said, "it's becoming clear that this was not a ruse to bring a family together, but to talk me into going back to school. To make an actual something of myself, instead of what I am now."

"No," Roman said quickly. "I mean, yes, your father said they had a gift for you, but I didn't know until now that it was—"

Ana held up her hand. "Save it. I'm not good enough for any of you the way I am. I get it. Don't make it worse by trying to explain."

Quicksand, according to many classic cartoons, was a real threat. Once stuck, it would hold you fast and slowly suck you down, and there was no way out. When one became an adult, one learned that quicksand wasn't a legitimate everyday threat, yet Roman's feet were sucked in now, and flailing only drew him in deeper. Helpless, he grabbed her hand with both of his, trying to make his true intentions shine through his eyes.

"Ana," he said.

Something in her face softened the tiniest bit, and he wondered if she'd believe whatever he thought to say next.

But something caught her attention, and Ana turned her head, looking beyond her parents to the takeout counter. Roman followed her gaze.

There, with one hand clutching a stapled brown-paper bag, was Lacey.

Lacey, wide-eyed and open-mouthed, staring at Ana, Roman, and Ana's parents. At Ana's hand engulfed in Roman's two hands on the table.

Ana yanked her hand back and stood so abruptly that her chair fell over.

"No," she said, shaking her head. "No. None of this."

She grabbed her purse and rushed toward the front door.

"Ana," Gabriella said, half confused and half admonishing.

"Ana," Roman said, but she was already almost to the door.

"Ana!" Lacey called.

"I'm sorry," Ana said over her shoulder to Lacey as she ran out the door.

Lacey stood frozen for another few moments, staring at the door. Finally, without one more brief glance at their table, she slowly walked out, the door slamming behind her.

"I don't understand," Angelo said. "Wasn't that Ana's friend from school?"

"Yes," Gabriella murmured. "I don't know what's going on." Then both of them turned back to the table.

An uncomfortable silence fell over the trio.

"I don't want to overstep," Roman eventually said. "But I've already got one foot in this mess. I might as well go all the way. You said that Ana sounds healthy, and ready to work now. And maybe she is ready ... to move forward, not back. Maybe law school isn't what she wants anymore, if it ever was. Maybe Ana-tomically Fun is what she wants now, and that's what she's ready for."

"I think her class sounds wonderful," Gabriella said. "And useful and different and interesting. But it's not a career."

"With all due respect," Roman said, "Ana gets to decide that."

"Ana decided as a child that she wanted to be more than most people," Angelo said. "We're not forcing her to be a different person. That's who she is."

"That's who she was," Roman said, "and it was too much for her."

"She told you?" Gabriella asked.

"Very little. But enough for me to understand that she needs to find a different way for herself. And she found"—*me*—"this."

"We want her to be happy," Gabriella said. "That doesn't mean being a professor or a doctor or a lawyer. But for Ana, it would mean challenging her mind. That's always when she was happiest."

"She is challenging her mind with Ana-tomically Fun," Roman said. "You heard her talk about it. But maybe happiness for her also means ... protecting her mind. Staying calm and in control."

"Is Ana—" Gabriella stopped and swallowed before continuing. "Is she healthy, Roman?"

"I don't know her medical details," Roman said, "and if I did, it wouldn't be my place to tell you, but I can assure you that she's vigilant, and taking proactive care not to be in an unhealthy place again."

He stood. "I'll take care of the bill. I'm sorry that this went awry. It wasn't my intent."

"No," Angelo said. "You didn't know the situation, and I could tell you didn't, yet I allowed you to set this up, so I'm sorry we put you in the middle of it."

Gabriella nodded.

"And I'll take care of the bill," Angelo said. "You go take care of Ana. Please tell her we love her, and we were only trying to help."

Roman nodded and left the restaurant.

He wanted to tell Jake how he'd messed up with Tony. He wanted to tell Tony how he'd ruined everything with Ana. He wanted to tell Ana how he'd make a big mistake with Jake. But after a lifetime of avoiding any situation in which he might break a heart, he'd broken three in one week.

For an athlete who used to love setting personal records, outdoing himself proved to be a miserable experience.

CHAPTER 16

The full moon hung low in the sky, its orange glow threatening autumn's imminent approach, cold and ice on its heels.

But the air was still thick with summer humidity, like sticky cotton candy, lifting and frizzing Ana's hair as she stomped out the front door of the Moonrise Inn and marched in the direction of the beach.

After her nervous breakdown had sent her to the hospital, she'd stopped caring. She'd stopped dreaming. About school. About friends. About relationships. About everything. She'd hidden in her small bedroom in her Staten Island apartment, only emerging to go to a simple job she didn't have to think about when she went back home again.

Was it a happy life? No.

Was it a safe life? Yes.

She slammed her feet down on the boardwalk steps, risking shin splints in her pissed-off state.

One weekend was all it had taken to tear down the carefully crafted walls around herself. One weekend of allowing herself to revive her friendships, to try teaching her class, to plop her heart right in the path of destruction.

She stalked to the railing and stared out at the water.

Why? Why had she done all this?

She slammed her hands on the metal and screamed to the ocean, "Roman!"

"Yes?"

She whirled, and he was there.

"You," she said, advancing with a pointed finger. To his credit, he didn't back away. "You did this."

She interpreted his stony-eyed silence as it still being her turn to speak. "Everything was under control. I was handling everything, for years. Then suddenly, I'm talking to you at a wedding, and four days later everything has gone up in flames again."

"Are you kidding me?" Roman burst out, and the sudden volume made Ana wince. "*You* talked to *me*, Ana. If you hadn't, I would have just stood there and stared at you the way I did in high school, never saying a word. But you talked to me. You started this."

Ana took such a sharp breath, she coughed.

"And you're right," Roman continued. "This is all my fault. In four days, I've ruined my brother's chance at a new relationship, I've ruined Jake's chance at reconciliation with the woman he loves—because it turns out they were at the inn only ten minutes before they both stormed out—and it's pretty clear you and I are not going to ride off into the sunset together. My dad was the only role model I had, and thanks to that, I'm never going to be able to be a boyfriend or a husband without hurting someone, and oh, look! It took less than a week for me to prove myself correct. I hurt *you*."

"Yes. You did."

"But at least I'm owning my responsibility here. You can't even be bothered to do that."

"What?" Ana said. "How dare you say that to me?"

"How dare I not, when it's staring me right in the face? You were 'handling everything'? Everything was 'under control'?"

"Don't use air quotes with me!"

"You pushed everyone and everything away. You think *that's* an effective way to live your life?"

"Yes!" Ana yelled. "I do! I was doing fine!"

"Oh, pardon me. So you were deliriously happy, with no friends and a job you hated and estrangement from your parents? You were living in Smurfy My Little Pony candy perfection? Give me a break, Ana."

Tears blurred Ana's vision but she refused to swipe them away, instead letting them roll freely down her cheeks. "This *is* your fault, because *you* made me *care*!" she screamed, then looked away when a curious biker glanced at them as he sped past. "You made me care," she said, more quietly. "Don't you get it? Isolation, loneliness, apathy ... none of that hurts *nearly* as much as caring does."

After a few quiet moments, Roman said, "You don't want to end up in the hospital again."

"It's not that. I have a therapist. I've learned coping strategies. I take medication. I don't think that would happen again, and even if it did, that wouldn't be the worst part." She shook her head and turned around, gripping the railing. The full moon reflected on the water, rippling on the blackness.

Roman stepped up beside her and followed her gaze to the water. "What would be the worst part?"

"Putting myself in a position to fail. Again. I don't want to fail."

"Yeah," Roman said. "I don't want to fail either."

A few silent moments ticked by.

"For what it's worth," Roman said, "I was wrong to surprise you when I didn't understand the rift between you and your parents. I should have asked you. And I swear I didn't know your parents were going to offer you money to go back to school. I was as surprised—and disappointed—as you were."

"I don't want it."

"I told them that when you left. Though at the risk of saying something you're not willing to hear, I don't really believe that they were trying to pressure you to be like them. I think they just want you to be happy and healthy, and they thought law school was still a path to that."

"It's not."

"You're allowed to make that call for yourself. Just like you're allowed to make the call that a relationship with me isn't a path to that either."

"It isn't that. It's that you deserve better than me," she said. "I'd drag you down with my lack of ambition."

"That's funny," Roman said, "because I'm of the firm belief that you deserve better than me. I'd break your heart with my lack of competence."

"We should never have done this anyway. We should have stayed loyal to our friends. Now Lacey probably hates me after I'd somehow managed to win her friendship back. You and I should have stayed in our social lanes. Like we did in high school."

"Maybe," Roman said. "But you made me feel like I knew what I was doing. I should have remembered I don't."

"Well, you made me feel good enough, and I should have remembered I'm not."

Roman raked a hand through his hair. "I want to kiss you," he said. "I want to kiss you now and insist that you absolutely are. And I want you to kiss me back and insist I'm not a bumbling idiot."

Ana's heart thudded. It would be so easy to kiss him now, to go back to the inn together, to the same bed. It would be so easy to let the warm, cozy fantasy overtake the reality. But reality would win eventually. It always did.

"It's too much," Ana said. "Lacey and Jake realized it's too much. As hard as it was for them, they acknowledged it and broke up, like responsible adults. We need to take a cue from them, and realize that it's too much for us too, before we invest as much as they did."

But even as she said it, Ana knew the investment was just as deep. It had only been a few days, and only one magical night, but her heart was gone. Roman could try to give it back to her, but it would follow him to Boston, never to be seen by her again.

"Yeah," Roman finally said with a small, sad shake of his head. "You're right. This … this isn't going to work. I don't bring enough to the table."

"Neither do I."

Ana's phone rang in her skirt pocket, the ringtone and the buzz against her thigh startling her. She ignored it and turned to Roman. The wind off the water whipped her hair across her eyeglasses and her mouth, but before she could brush it away, Roman's hand was there, tucking the strands behind her ear.

When the phone stopped ringing, Ana said, "I'm sorry I blamed you. You're not my problem."

"You're not mine. And I'm sorry too."

Ana's pocket rang and buzzed again. And again. And again.

"Who's blowing up your phone?"

"I … I don't know." Ana fished the phone out of her pocket.

"It's Lacey," Ana said, swallowing back a lump of fear that she was about to be yelled at.

Roman nodded at her to take it.

Ana willed her voice to not shake. "Hello?"

"Ana!" Lacey shouted into the night air, and laughed. Ana realized she'd accidentally answered with speakerphone, but before she could fix it, Lacey went on. "Ana, we're eloping!"

Ana blinked. "What the f—" she murmured. She looked up and saw Roman's eyes were wide.

"Wh-what—?" Ana tried.

"Jake and I are about to board a plane to Vegas to get married, then we're going on our honeymoon a few days late."

"Hi, Ana!" Jake called.

"We've been *so* stupid!" Lacey giggled. "We *love* each other. We want to be together. We're going to work on our issues, but we can do that married, right? Love is what's important."

"Um, right—"

"When I saw you at Muscatel's, I was on my way to bring dinner to Jake so we could talk, but I did not expect to see you. Why did you run away? What is going *on* with you and Roman Montgomery? Why was he holding your hand in front of your parents?"

"Wait, what? Roman was holding her hand?" Ana heard Jake ask.

"He totally was. Ana, you need to tell me everything when I get back. I have to call Sarai and Kate before we board. I love you, Ana. So much."

"I love you too," Ana said, and she was sure Lacey didn't even notice the bewilderment before quickly disconnecting.

Roman slid his own phone out of his pocket and scrolled through what looked like many texts.

"Looks like Jake's not mad at me anymore," Roman said.

"And I guess Lacey wasn't mad at me at all. Just surprised."

She walked to a nearby bench and sat, suddenly too weary to hold herself upright. After a moment, Roman sat next to her.

"Now what?" he asked.

"What do you mean? Now nothing. We can go home tomorrow."

Her heart stung at her own words.

"You said we need to take a cue from Jake and Lacey," Roman said. "They acknowledged that this wasn't working and they broke up. But now they've decided to try, despite their fears. They're willing to let love lead the way."

"Well, they've been together a while. They're *in* love. That's an advantage."

"So am I."

Ana sprang off the bench and glared down at him. "*What* did you just say to me?"

"I said, I'm in love with you, Ana. I'd be willing to try, to work on our issues, but be together while we do it."

He stared into her eyes with a half-shocked, half-confident expression. "I love you," he repeated.

She could say it back.

She could say it back, because it was true.

I love you, Roman.

I can't believe it, but I love you, Roman.

I love you.

"I don't care," she said. "And you're right. You don't know the first thing about relationships."

She crossed the boardwalk, hopped down the stairs, and walked quickly back toward the inn. She didn't shed any more tears, but her glasses fogged, shrouding her view.

CHAPTER 17

The Moonrise Inn was quiet that night, with its only two guests avoiding each other in adjoining rooms as the mini decorative full moons all over the house continued to smile.

Roman was almost certain he'd hear Ana dragging her suitcase across the gravel driveway and squealing her wheels in a rush to check out the next morning. He did hear her door open and close, and the front door open and close, but when he emerged later, her car was still parked outside. She might have gone to Blue Ocean Fitness, or anywhere, really.

There was no logical reason for Roman to not go back to Boston today. But leaving Seasalter meant leaving Ana, and he just wasn't ready for it yet, so he decided to wait one more day.

He went to the bookstore, he got a burrito, he walked along the boardwalk. He let the fresh memories surround him. The pain in his back had subsided, but a new ache in his chest moved in time with the crashing waves of the Atlantic. He logged miles on his fitness watch, walking and walking and thinking and shaking his head.

In the afternoon, Roman pushed open the door to Jasmine Pink's Tea Shoppe. It was as quiet as he'd have expected on a weekday afternoon, with only a back corner table occupied. When he saw who was at sitting the table, he pivoted to leave, but not quickly enough.

"Roman," his mother said. "Get back here."

He turned very slowly and smiled amicably. "Ladies," he said to his mother, Selene, and Delilah. "I'll let you get to your tea."

Delilah stood, walked over to him, and squinted up into his face. "Lemon rosemary." She went behind the counter.

"I didn't know you were all friends," Roman said, trying to push the attention off him.

"I've known Delilah for ages, and Delilah's known Selene, and Selene and I met a half hour ago, though I can tell already we're going to be good friends." Ma rubbed Selene's shoulder. "She owns the inn you're staying at."

"Yes, we've met."

"Now, what's wrong with you?" Ma asked Roman. Then, to Selene, "What's wrong with him?"

"I can't say for sure," Selene said.

"Ana and I broke up." What was the point in holding back? If three women over fifty were determined to find out what was wrong with you, you'd break sooner or later. No use fighting it.

"What did I tell you?" Delilah said. "Lemon rosemary."

"Oh," his mother said. "I'm so sorry."

"I'm so surprised," Selene said. "Speaking as someone who's been watching the Fourth of July sparks fly between you two the last few days."

"What happened?" Ma asked.

"A lot happened," he said. "But mainly, I screwed up. Just like I knew I would."

No one answered him right away. "What do you mean, like you knew you would?" Ma asked.

"I set up a surprise meeting with her parents because she hasn't seen them in a while. As it turned out, I shouldn't have done that."

"No," Selene agreed. "Probably not, if you want her to be able to trust you."

"But why did you assume you'd make a mistake?" Ma prompted again.

"I don't know anything about how to be any kind of partner," he said. "How would I? Dad—" He cut himself off. He couldn't hurt his mother, not on top of everyone else, but she widened her eyes.

"Dad what?" she asked.

He shook his head.

"What were you going to say?" she insisted. "It's okay."

"Dad left you and broke your heart, and clearly he didn't model relationship behavior for Tony and me."

"Is that why you haven't ever had a serious girlfriend? Because you think you can't?" Ma asked.

Roman blinked. "Can't. And shouldn't."

"Oh, honey," Ma said. "You are not your father in any way. He's lazy and disrespectful and dishonest. You didn't inherit any of *that* from him. You're the opposite in every way. What could possibly make you think you'd treat a woman the way he treated me?"

"I ... I saw how much he hurt you."

"Yes, he did."

"I don't want to chance hurting someone else that way."

"What way?"

"In a ... catastrophic way. You never got over it."

"Didn't I?"

"What?"

She shook her head. "You're my child, so you only see me as your mother, not as a fellow adult. I've been dating the last few years. And the man I'm dating now ... we've been together a few months. I was thinking of introducing him to you and Tony."

"But ..." Roman's head was spinning. "Dad's stuff is still in your room."

"Yeah." She looked embarrassed. "It's been years, so at this point, it's kind of superstitious. I keep his things there to remind me to stay vigilant and to honor my intuition when I see red flags." She smiled. "But I *was* thinking recently that it's time to take all that down. I really like this guy. He plays the saxophone."

"Ooh," Selene said. "A musician."

"That's why we haven't seen you around as often," Delilah said, setting the lemon rosemary tea on the table and pulling a chair over for Roman.

"Yeah, I've been ... busy," Ma said, and the other two women smiled encouragingly.

"Well," Roman said. "I did screw up with Ana, though."

"That doesn't mean you're not meant to be in a relationship," Selene said. "It just means you're clueless. Like all men."

Delilah and Ma laughed.

"Men who want to make a woman happy often go through trial and a lot of error," Selene said. "It's normal."

"Also." Ma hit his arm with a napkin. "I'm rather insulted you presume to take after your father's gutless ways, instead of taking after me. After all, I did a bang-up job raising you for years without him. And unless you've really got everyone who knows you fooled, you're a kind, caring, giving man."

Roman hung his head. "I can't trust that."

"Can you at least trust that the mistakes you make are well intentioned?" Selene asked. "And that any woman who gets close to you will see that? If you're so concerned about hurting someone, doesn't that mean you're someone who doesn't want to, someone who will do his best not to?"

"Yes," Roman said slowly.

"I'm willing to bet," Delilah said, setting a cup of steaming, fragrant tea in front of Roman, "that your mother doesn't even regret marrying your father."

"No, I don't," Ma said quickly. "He gave me my sons, the joys of my life." She took Roman's hand and held it tightly. "Do you see? Yes, there's risk and there are mistakes and there's loss—sometimes terrible loss—but there are good things, miraculous things, that make your efforts worth it. And the good things can't happen if you close yourself off."

Selene and Delilah nodded.

"You've convinced me," Roman said. "But Tony is angry at me for giving him lousy love advice. And Ana—I don't know."

"Speaking as someone who used to give advice for a living," Selene said, "I happen to know that most people who ask for advice already know what they're going to do, no matter what you say. You don't have as much influence, or as much blame, as you think."

"And Tony loves you," Ma said. "Don't worry about him. I'll talk to him. He'll get over it. As for Ana—did you apologize?"

"Yes."

"Good," Delilah said. "Now, drink your medicine."

Roman lifted the cup and inhaled the delicious citrusy scent.

★ ★ ★

Ana walked into the inn around seven o'clock, and found Selene on the blue sofa in the front room, reading a paperback thriller.

"I read that one," Ana said. "It was pretty good. I didn't see the twist coming, and I usually do ..." She faltered, realizing what she'd said.

Selene dropped the book on her stomach, facedown. "Come sit."

Ana perched on the other end of the sofa, but it was easy to relax around Selene for some reason, and after a moment, she kicked off her sneakers and curled her feet under her, cross-legged. She picked up a deep purple velvet throw pillow and hugged it to her chest. Dusk was darkening the room bit by bit, but they didn't need lights yet.

"What did you do today?" Selene asked.

"I went to the beach with Sarai and Kate. We went about a mile up the beach, though, in case … I didn't want to run into anyone."

"By anyone, do you mean Roman?"

Ana nodded. "Is—is he here?"

"I saw him at the tea shop this afternoon. He mentioned he was going to dinner and a movie with his friends tonight. I think he'll be out at least two or three more hours."

Ana nodded, sighing. She wasn't sure if the sigh was relief or disappointment. Probably more disappointment than relief, and she was disappointed in herself to realize it.

"Do you want to talk about it?"

Ana shook her head, but even as she did it, her mouth opened and everything came spilling out. Law school, the hospital, her parents' disappointment in her. The wedding, getting to know Roman, rekindling her friendships with the girls, the tension between Lacey's and Jake's friends, going to Roman's mother's and kissing him, Blue Ocean Fitness and the job offer, spending the night with Roman—though she omitted the details—his spectacular blunder with her parents, her parents' offer, Jake and Lacey's elopement, and the last angry then sad conversation she'd had with Roman.

"Was it a breakup?" Ana asked. "I don't think so. We weren't officially a couple. Yet."

Finally she stopped, and she could sense the sweet warmth of the room absorbing her pain and confusion.

"So I'm going home tomorrow," Ana said.

"Just like that?"

"Well, it's not 'just like that.' I was supposed to leave Sunday. I've been here four more days than I'd planned. It's time to go back to New York, to what I was doing before."

They sat in silence for a few moments. The wind blew suddenly through the window, snuffing out a little candle on the bookcase beside Selene. She stood, lifted the candle, moved it across the room, and relit it. Then she took a crocheted blanket off an armchair and carried it to Ana. Ana spread it around her, tucking the edges under her legs, as Selene took her seat again.

"Did you know that every monthly full moon has a name?" Selene pointed out the window. "My husband told me all the names, and I remembered them all. September is the harvest moon."

"Probably the only one I've actually heard of."

"The message of the harvest moon is, well, harvesting," Selene said. "Reaping all that you've sown."

"I haven't sown anything in a long time. I've got nothing to reap."

"Really? Because it seems to me that this week alone, you reaped three new old friendships and a brand-new job that you sound like you really enjoy."

Ana didn't say anything.

"Seems a shame to throw away those opportunities you created just because things with Roman aren't working."

Ana knit her brows together.

"And maybe it's not even that things with him aren't working," Selene added. "Maybe what you've sown there isn't quite ready to harvest yet. It needs a little more time to grow. You need a little more time to grow."

Ana's eyes filled with tears, and she blinked them away.

"When you've closed yourself away for so long, coming back to life is so challenging and frightening," Selene said. "Trust me,

I know. I shut myself away for many months to grieve, and suddenly I had to open an inn."

"I'm sorry. I can't imagine."

"I'm doing it, though. It's hard. But every day, I find a tiny bit more peace. You can do it too. I can see how smart and strong and good you are."

The tears finally fell then. "Why can't I see it?"

"Can't you?" Selene asked gently, handing her a tissue from the box on the coffee table. "I'm willing to bet in the last few days, you've caught glimmers of it in moments, here and there."

She was right; Ana had seen it when she taught class, walking around the fitness room confidently, and when her students praised her after class. She had seen it when Lacey asked her for help before the wedding. She had seen it every time Roman looked at her, smiled at her. Kissed her.

"Move forward," Selene said. "And soon you'll recognize yourself again. When you've become reacquainted with Ana Capuano and all she has to offer, you might even find yourself ready to become acquainted with love."

Ana leaned forward and hugged Selene, sniffling into her blond hair. "Thank you."

"It's been a joy having you here. And I'd invite you to come again, but if you're moving here, we can see each other as neighbors instead."

Ana stood and folded the blanket neatly. "I'm going to pack."

"Okay, hon."

"Is it okay if I use your washer and dryer to clean the clothes I borrowed from Roman's mother?"

"Of course. Down in the basement. Detergent is on the shelf above the washer."

"Thanks."

Ana walked to her room. Before she opened the door, she turned and looked at Selene, whose chin was lifted toward the window, toward the moon. Her eyes were closed, and her smile was soft.

* * *

Selene walked around the sitting room, snapping on three small lamps and putting her book back on the shelf with a ribbon marking her place. She closed the window most of the way, leaving only a couple of inches. It was still too early to lock the main door.

She'd gotten a few phone calls since the weekend, people asking to book a few upcoming dates. Each call gratified her, but she needed more reservations to pay her expenses.

She thought about Roman and Ana. Sweet kids, each with a massive fear of failure. She could understand that, especially now. Maybe they could find a way to support each other, to love each other on their journeys, the way Dan would have with Selene.

She glanced up at the moon again, through the sheer curtains and the glass.

A tentative three raps came from the screen door, and she whirled.

"Owen!"

He offered a small wave. "I know it's late, but are you free at the moment?"

"Of course. Come in."

He stepped in, carrying a long thin cardboard box. A black canvas bag hung over his shoulder.

"What's all this?" Selene asked. "Did you notice something big that needs repairing?"

"Oh! No." Owen chuckled and placed the end of the box gently on the hardwood floor. "I noticed there's a nice big moon out there."

"Yes, there is."

"I thought you might want to get a closer look at it. As you know, the little brick patio out back has a great view of the sky between the tree openings. I brought a telescope."

"A ... a telescope?"

"Yes. You said your husband—"

"Dan."

"You said Dan loved the moon and the night sky. Coincidentally, I do too. I've always been a sort of amateur astronomer. I thought you might want to see some craters."

Selene didn't say anything for a moment.

"I'm ... I'm sorry." Owen's eyes shadowed over from hopeful to apologetic. "I didn't mean to hurt you. Quite the opposite."

"Dan," Selene said, and her voice broke a little on the word. She cleared her throat. "Dan did love the night sky. But not in a scientific way. He loved the myths, the legends, the beauty of the moon and stars. He didn't have a telescope."

"Well, if you're interested, I can share with you some of the things I know. I warn you, though, I'm a real geek about this stuff."

Selene slid her hands into the front pockets of her shorts. "You said you didn't want to hurt me, and you didn't. But what did you mean by you intended the opposite?"

Owen slid the bag off his shoulder and guided it to the floor by his feet. "It can be very lonely when your spouse is gone. My wife and I divorced about nine years ago, and that first year or two was very lonely for me. I imagine that Dan being gone is far more difficult for you."

He met her eyes. "I was thinking about you today, and I wondered what a friend would do for someone who was hurting, so I decided to bring you some comfort and familiarity. The moon." He held up his hands. "But again, if I made a mistake here, I apologize. I understand if you don't want to share the moon with me."

"I don't … I don't think you made a mistake." He was thinking about her today? He wondered what a friend would do? "Dan used to marvel at the fact that everyone on Earth, wherever we live, whatever our circumstances, shares the moon. If you had brought a telescope tonight and he were here, he would have been thrilled. Beyond thrilled."

Owen smiled. "Shall I set it up on the patio?"

Selene nodded. "Okay. Do you … do you want some wine?"

"That sounds nice."

Selene went into the kitchen and uncorked a bottle of white wine, pouring two glasses. She grabbed a long white cardigan off a peg on the back of the door, shrugged it on, and carried the two glasses to the red brick patio out back.

There was a small bistro table set up on the corner of the patio. She placed the glasses on the mosaic tabletop and sat in one of the chairs. The cushion was cold underneath her bottom. It was still a warm night, but the sea breeze had gotten a little stronger. The moon sparkled overhead, bathing the yard in white light. Owen had opened the tripod and angled the telescope toward the moon. He fiddled with lenses, uncapping and screwing them on and off the telescope, sometimes exchanging them with other lenses in the open bag at his feet.

She took a sip of wine and watched his hands as they worked to fine-tune the equipment. They were long-fingered and sure.

"Have you and your daughter patched things up?" Owen asked while he tinkered.

"Sort of. She called this morning to apologize, but I got the sense it was the kind of apology you make when you realize you were unreasonable and rude, and not quite the kind of apology you offer when you want to make a serious effort to repair the relationship."

"Ah."

"I appreciated it, but it also made me feel a bit worse. She hung up quickly."

He walked over to the table. "I'm sorry. For what it's worth, I think she'll come around. Emotions are still raw for both you and her."

"And she's young," Selene said. "I'm hopeful she'll want to become a part of the inn somehow. Eventually."

Owen didn't reply, giving her the room to say more if she wanted to, but she didn't.

"Anyway, I'm almost done. I want your view to be perfect so I'm just fiddling with little details." He picked up a glass. "To the Moonrise Inn."

Selene caught herself about to ask why he'd toast to the inn if the inn's failure would get him his house back, but she remembered him saying when he fixed the step that that wouldn't be fair. "Yes," she said instead. "And to the harvest moon."

They both sipped, and Owen looked at his glass with appreciation. "That's really good."

"It is, isn't it? I don't know anything about wine, but the owner of Seasalter Spirits is amazing. If I go in there and say something like, 'What's the best I can get for seventeen dollars?' he will never fail to give me something that tastes better than what I spent."

"Yeah, that's Bert. My dad was good friends with him." He went back to the telescope and fussed for about five more minutes. Then he peered through with one eye, focused, lifted his head and looked the moon directly, then bent and looked through the telescope again. He stood and gestured Selene over.

Selene put her glass on the table, buttoned her sweater, and approached.

"Look through here," Owen instructed. "Here's the focus dial in case it's blurry." He guided her hand to it with his fingers on her bare wrist.

She shivered.

Then she looked into the telescope.

And gasped. "Oh! It's … it's so clear."

"Yeah."

Selene could hear his smile, but she didn't see it because she couldn't tear her eyes away from the moon. "It's gorgeous. Tell me what I'm looking at."

He did. He told her about the seas—which weren't seas at all, but dark lava plains formed by erupted volcanoes long ago—and craters and other phenomena. He told her that the full moon was actually not the best time to observe it through the telescope because the sun was shining on the moon almost directly, but he said he added a moon filter to the telescope to reduce the glare so they could see the most.

"The best time to observe is really a few days after the first quarter moon," Owen said. "You can see all the major features of the moon then. But this inn is decorated with full moons, and it seemed the best sentimental choice to get our first look tonight."

"You're saying the view is better a few days after the first quarter?"

"Much better. I can come back then, and you can compare."

Selene straightened and met his gaze. In the dark of the evening, his eyes were nearly black, and she had to rely on her memory to fill in the green. "Come back?"

"If you want me to. I'd—I'd like to be friends with you."

A small pain stabbed her heart, and she considered it.

She was certain she'd been correct earlier. If Dan were here, Owen would be his new best friend right now, and Dan's friends were her friends.

Is this okay?

She bent and peeked at the moon close up again. *Is this okay, Endymion? To make this friend?*

The moon gazed back at her, filling her heart with peace.

She stood upright. "Yes, Owen. I'd like to be friends."

Owen grinned, and grabbed their two glasses. "Shall we toast it?"

"To new friends," Selene said, taking the offered glass and clinking it with his.

"And to the ancient moon." He sipped, his eyes sparkling over the rim of the glass.

Selene wondered if a friend should be noticing the way the shadows moved over the perfect lines of his face.

CHAPTER 18

The movie, filled with car chases and explosions and swagger, had soothed Roman's soul for about two hours, but as soon as the end credits began to roll up the black screen and Pete and Mark started to debate which expensive special effects were the most impressive, Roman was despondent again. He declined their offer to go out for drinks, and also declined to tell them about Ana when they asked what was wrong. His failure with Ana was something he needed to endure alone.

Driving home, he considered that Ma, Delilah, and Selene were all probably correct, that when it came to love, mistakes—big and small—were bound to happen. It was fair advice for his future, but when it came to the present, and to Ana, he couldn't see a way forward if she didn't.

He parked in the gravel driveway, and realized he was relieved to see Ana's car was still there. He shut off the ignition, bowed forward, and rested his forehead on the steering wheel.

Was it possible that everything had happened this week to teach him what he needed to know for the next relationship? The next woman? That Ana was his teacher, not his destiny?

He couldn't even fathom the idea of caring about another woman, touching another woman, laughing and playing board games and eating burritos with another woman.

But though he was convinced now to give his best to a relationship, mistakes or not, Ana was not on board, and he couldn't force that.

He dragged himself up the stairs to the inn. The blue sitting room was as welcoming as always, but though it was empty, he heard voices. He peered out the window to find Selene sitting at the bistro table with a man. They were drinking wine, and there was a telescope set up nearby. Roman smiled. She was an insightful and attractive woman, and by the way the man leaned forward and hung onto every word she said, it was clear he thought so too.

He glanced at Ana's Stardust Suite door but moved toward his own Sea of Tranquility door. He'd just placed his hand on the doorknob when he heard footsteps coming up from the basement, and there was Ana, pushing open the door with her shoulder and carrying a large laundry basket of folded clothes.

Roman stepped forward and took the basket from her. Their eyes caught, and hers were dark and unreadable. "Thanks," she said.

"Selene's got you working for your room now?" Roman asked.

Ana half laughed. "No. Though maybe for the sake of my credit card, I should have thought of that a few days ago. These are your mom's clothes. I was going to leave them at your door."

"Are we not on speaking terms?"

"I—" She paused. "I'll be right back."

She walked past him and into her room.

He went to the front room's blue sofa and sat, placing the basket carefully at his feet. Ana emerged from her room with the two bags his mother had given her, and sat beside him on the sofa, keeping some deliberate space between them. She began placing items into the bags. Instead of filling one bag first, she put one item in one bag, then the next item in the other, seemingly to ensure the bags were evenly distributed. The precision was oddly fascinating.

"Listen," she said, keeping her eyes on her work. "What I said to you on the beach was out of line. I shouldn't have said you don't know the first thing about relationships. And even if you don't, it's a skill you can improve. I said it because …"

She unfolded a T-shirt, shook it out, and folded it more precisely. "I said it because you said that you—you know."

I said I love you.

"And it was a shock," Ana continued, "and my emotions were already at a boiling point."

"I understand." He watched her every move, despite her refusal to look at him. "No apology needed."

"There certainly is an apology needed. Do you accept it?"

"Yes," he said quickly. "I do accept it."

Her shoulders slumped a little in apparent relief.

"I do intend to improve my skill in relationships," Roman said. "For what it's worth."

"That's good."

"Though it will be a more challenging task if I'm not in one."

Ana hesitated, holding a skirt in her lap for a moment, then placed it on the top of the bag. "Yes, it will be. But I'm sure that won't last long."

Roman wanted to ask her if she was going to work toward improvements too, if she was going to work on relearning how valuable she was, how beautiful and special and complete. But he couldn't think of a way to word it without sounding bitter at his own loss.

She nudged both full bags on the floor toward Roman. "Please thank Theresa for me."

"I will."

She finally looked up then, and they studied each other's expressions. "I don't want to say, 'it's not you, it's me.' Though it is. And I don't want to make you think I haven't been happy these last few days, because I have. I want to say something meaningful and poignant, but I've got nothing."

How about that you'll give us a chance? That you might love me too, a little bit?

But she seemed to be done speaking.

"How about a few games of checkers?" Roman finally asked. "That way, only one of us will go home truly defeated."

Ana pressed her lips together but couldn't quite suppress a smile. "You are quite the glutton for punishment. Okay."

He brought the bags of clothes to his room as she carried the laundry basket downstairs, then they set up the board.

Selene and her friend laughed outside as Roman pondered his first move.

"Roman."

He looked up. Ana's eyes were shining—with tears, or with moonlight, or both.

"I think what I'm trying to say is ... goodbye."

Roman's heart deflated into a flat, sad heap. "Goodbye, Ana."

He directed his gaze back to the board, and pushed one black piece forward with his index finger.

★ ★ ★

In the morning, Roman stepped out of his room before seven.

Sunlight streamed through the sheer white curtains, illuminating the spot where he and Ana had played four games and decided to leave the count at two-two and retire to their rooms. Dishes and glasses gently clinked in the kitchen as Selene prepared breakfast. An incense stick burned in the corner, filling his nostrils with sweet, light spice. The front door was open, allowing a full view of the garden.

Beyond that, the parking lot hosted one fewer car.

CHAPTER 19

Two weeks later

"I'm not going to lie," Roman said. "I'm equal parts intrigued and terrified by this conference call."

He sat on his living room sofa, which he'd cleared of stray pillows, remotes, and a worn T-shirt, all so Sarai, Lacey, and Kate would not see the detritus via video. Kate had emailed him this morning and requested his presence at a "meeting" with her and her friends this evening.

"Why?" Sarai peered into the camera, and Roman thought she was trying to get a closer look at him, but when she smoothed her hand over her hair, he realized she was using the camera as a mirror. "Have you done something that would anger us?"

"No, but I've also done nothing I would expect you to even know about. We're not … friends. Right?"

"As you know, we have mutual acquaintances." Kate's words were oddly reminiscent of a mafia boss. Roman winced.

"It's come to our attention that you are in love with our friend." Sarai's eyes, whether she was looking at him directly or not, were like two hazel lasers.

"How did you know—"

"You told Jake," Sarai said.

"I didn't tell him much."

"You told him enough. And he told Lacey, because she's his beloved wife and telling her information like this is part of his job as spouse now."

"That's okay. I didn't ask him specifically to keep it a secret—"

"And Lacey told us," Kate finished.

"Then we investigated you online." Sarai held up a pile of papers. "We compared notes."

"Wh-what?" Roman's mouth fell open. "There's that much about me online?"

"Luckily for you, we've come to the conclusion that you seem to be a nice guy." Kate rubbed her hands together. Roman thought it was some kind of homicidal glee, but then he realized she was applying hand cream. "You post lots of house listings for work. And a couple of pics of you and your hot brother."

"You think he's hot?"

"Never mind that. And we discovered you have a penchant for *Star Trek* spinoffs." Kate nodded.

"Don't judge me on that—"

"We sure did. But it was favorable judging," Kate informed him. "It gives you nerd cred."

Lacey, who'd been silent, finally spoke. "You and Ana aren't together."

Roman's heart plummeted to his feet. "No. I did realize I'm ready to try. But she isn't."

All three women appeared lost in thought.

"I want to tell you that things are going really well for her right now, but the details aren't ours to share," Sarai said.

"That's fair. I wouldn't ask you to."

"And we're not going to tell you how she feels about you, because that's hers to share also."

Roman's soul opened one hopeful petal. If Ana had said *anything* to them, it meant she felt *something*.

"We're calling to confirm that you'll be at the high school reunion in ten days." Lacey squinted at him. "In Seasalter."

Roman had considered it but was not ready to return to the town that he'd last experienced with Ana. He also hadn't wanted to intrude on Ana's emotional well-being if she wanted to attend. "I wasn't planning to go," he admitted.

"She said she's not either." Kate shook her head, as if disgusted. "But if you promise us you'll attend, we will get her there."

"Is she aware you're making this back-room deal on her behalf?" He sort of hoped so.

"No, and you're not going to tell her." Sarai narrowed her eye lasers, and Roman flinched.

"No, I'm not."

"We're doing this for her." Lacey pointed at the camera. "Don't screw it up."

Don't screw it up. Roman almost laughed. He could very well screw it up.

His next words were the truest he'd ever spoken. "I'll do the best I can not to."

Everyone nodded, including him.

"Thank you, everyone." Sarai clapped her hands once. "Roman, we'll see you at the reunion. Make sure you look sharp. Have a good evening." She clicked off.

Lacey smiled softly. "I believe in you, Roman. Jake does too." She clicked off as well.

He found himself alone with Kate, who laced her fingers together. "I would like to talk about this condo you listed on Beacon Street in Brookline. The third-floor brownstone."

Roman raised an interested eyebrow.

★ ★ ★

"I can't believe I'm talking to the high school's former baseball team in a conference call." Ana's voice echoed through her new Seasalter apartment. She'd just moved in this morning, and since most of her belongings were still in boxes, the unfurnished apartment's acoustics were significantly louder than they'd be after everything was put in its rightful place. She sat on a tall stool, laptop propped on her kitchen counter.

"The rest of the team is coming?" Pete's face brightened as he slid off his white pharmacist's jacket.

"No." Mark shook his head and rolled his eyes. "It's just us three. Well, us four." He bounced a cute toddler on his lap. She reached out and grabbed hold of his ear, and he chuckled.

Jake nodded and loosened his tie. Pete twisted his mouth in disappointment.

No one said anything else for a full minute.

"Guys, this is about as awkward as it was years ago when we all avoided speaking to different cliques. Can you tell me what this is about? I'm guessing, a surprise party for Lacey?"

Jake looked startled. "Oh, crap. Her birthday's in October."

Ana chuckled. "Get on it, man. And I'm happy to help you plan something."

"I will. Thanks."

"That's not the purpose of our call today. We understand you have feelings for Roman." Mark's lips twitched into a half smile.

"Oh ... you do, do you?" Ana tried to sound challenging, like when she was on the debate team, but the sudden topic blindsided her.

"You told Lacey," Jake said.

And of course Lacey told Jake, because he was her partner. Ana hadn't specifically told her not to tell anyone. She hadn't thought to, figuring the information wouldn't interest anyone else.

Apparently, she'd thought wrong.

"And so I told these men here," Jake added, "because when one of our teammates is in trouble in mud, it's our duty to also get into the trouble in the mud with him."

"That's how it works," Pete said with a fist pump.

"You all get into trouble in mud with him?" Ana squinted, thinking. "Did you just mangle the words of some motivational poster? What does that even mean?"

"Never mind that." Jake banged his fist on the table in front of him. "Roman has been in love with you all this time, and we need to do something about it."

All this time? "A few weeks?"

All three of them stared at her like she'd sprouted two additional heads.

"A few weeks?" Mark asked. "Try like eleven *years*."

"What ... what are you talking about?"

"He's been in love with Juliana Capuano since we were juniors." Jake stared at her.

Ana gripped the edge of the counter with both hands. "How do you know that?"

"How do you *not* know? All his friends knew," Mark said. "Every time you walked by, he would stop talking mid-sentence, and his face would flame up, and then when he finally talked again, he'd be stuttering. None of us said anything to him, since we figured he'd just ask you out sooner or later."

"It was obvious," Pete said. "But you were too busy being the star of everything to notice."

Ana frowned. She was always busy being the star of everything, true, but Roman—?

Mark correctly interpreted her expression as skepticism. "Hang on. I'll prove it."

He carried his daughter off camera and was gone for a few minutes, and returned carrying their yearbook instead. He flipped through it.

"What are you trying to find?" Ana was baffled. "I've seen everything in that book. I worked on the yearbook committee."

"Of course you did. Here, here it is." He opened the book wide, flipped it around, and held it up to the camera.

Ana leaned forward.

It was a picture of her, Sarai, Lacey, and Kate, huddled together on the bleachers at some school event. Their arms were around each other and they were laughing hard, their mouths open, their chins lifted. Ana was on the far left, and on the other side of her was Roman. He was sitting just enough inches away from her that it was clear he wasn't with her, but his head was turned and he was … gazing at her.

The way a high school boy gazed at a girl he found mesmerizing. He had a small smile on his face, like he wanted to be included.

She hadn't noticed him that day on the bleachers. She hadn't even noticed him in this photo, which she'd looked at dozens of times, focusing on her friends. Because she never paid attention to the popular kids and what they were doing.

Mark dropped the yearbook. "I don't know what happened between you two weeks ago, but you were his dream girl."

"I'm not a dream."

"Neither is he," Jake said. "He's a guy with plenty of faults. But they're honest faults. Small faults. He's a great guy who sees everything wonderful in you."

"Is this why you're calling? To ask me if I like your friend? That's … very high school."

"Do you?" Pete asked.

Ana sighed and closed her eyes, finding the memory picture of Roman's smile, his eyes, his laugh, his hands on her body. "Yes," she whispered, dropping her forehead into her hands and opening her eyes. "I do."

Mark grinned. "Are you going to the reunion? If you do, we'll make sure he's there too."

She straightened, and the three men watched her face with wide eyes. They were all suddenly ten years younger, waiting to see if she'd go out with their lovestruck friend.

"Yes. I'll go."

The men said goodbye and hung up.

Ana closed her laptop and sat motionless for a few minutes. Then she rolled her shoulders back and decided to unpack a box of books. Her bookcase sat in the corner of her new living room, empty, and nothing made a place more lived-in and cozy than a full bookcase.

Her book boxes were stacked beside the bookcase, and she tore the tape off the first one. She lifted a few books and placed them with care. After a few moments, she pulled out the book Roman had bought her in Seasalter.

Not wanting to think too hard about it, she went to place it in the bookcase, but it slipped out of her fingers, scattering Seasalter Beach sand all over the hardwood floor.

She knelt and ran her finger through the fine grains.

★ ★ ★

Three days later

"Why couldn't I meet you after your showing?" Tony complained as he walked with Roman down Beacon Street. "I drove all the way to Boston to have lunch with you, and you couldn't move this appointment?"

Roman peered at building numbers. "I'm sorry. This client is pressed for time, and I thought—I don't know, maybe you'd want to come."

"Is it Take Your Brother to Work Day?"

Roman grinned. "Maybe I just wanted to spend a few extra minutes with you."

Tony rolled his eyes. "Is this more of your apology campaign? I told you, forget about it. It's no big deal. Your advice was terrible, but it was ultimately my decision to take it. And it was my decision to get myself into a sticky situation in the first place."

"Yeah, but I'm still sorry." Roman walked up to the smart, well-maintained brownstone, found the front-door key on his ring, and let them in. They climbed the stairs to the third floor. "I just need to text the client—"

"Hey, Roman." Kate stood in front of the unit, wearing a cream-colored suit with a short skirt, stilt-like high heels, sparkling gold earrings, and enormous dark sunglasses.

"Hi! How did you get in?"

"The first-floor tenant was coming in. I'm persuasive." She slid her sunglasses down her nose and dipped her chin. "Well, hel*lo*," she said to Tony. She smiled with only half her mouth, like she knew a delicious secret.

Tony's jaw dropped open.

"Uh, Tony, this is Kate Yoon. Kate, this is—"

She stepped forward and slid her arm through Tony's. "Would you mind showing me around this condo?" she asked him.

Roman fumbled for the key to the condo. "You probably need me for that," he said, unlocking the door and creaking it open. The smell of fresh paint wafted out.

"It's only nine hundred square feet," Kate said, guiding Tony over the threshold. "How lost could we possibly get, right, Tony?"

Roman stood aside and waved them in.

"We'll let you know if we need you," Tony said over his shoulder, as if Roman were merely their meddlesome butler.

Roman smiled.

★ ★ ★

"Welcome to Blue Ocean Fitness!" Ana said to the next woman in line. "Ana-tomically Fun will begin in ten minutes, so please head to Room 2. Check the white board for the equipment you'll need to grab."

"Yay!" the woman said and practically skipped away.

"Hi! Welcome to Blue Ocean Fitness."

"Hi," the next girl said. "Remember me?"

Ana cocked her head and studied her. "Yes! You were in my first class." It was the girl who'd been so sad after her breakup, the one who'd dragged herself out of bed for the canceled class, and motivated Ana to offer to teach.

"I'm so glad your class is three times a week now. I'm pre-registered for every single one for the next month. Kick my butt. I'm Morgan."

Ana touched her arm. "I'm so happy to hear that. And I will." She turned her head for a second to watch Morgan head to the workout room, then turned to the next client and her mouth opened silently. "Oh," she finally managed. "Mom."

"I didn't register," Mom said. "Is there room for me?"

"Um." Ana dragged her gaze to the computer screen to check the almost-sold-out roster. "You're lucky. I had a last-minute cancellation."

"Did I hear, 'Mom'?" Sydney, the club owner and Ana's new boss, stepped up behind her. "You're absolutely welcome to always take Ana's class for free, Mrs. Capuano."

"Please call me Gabriella," her mother said, nodding at Sydney, then fixing her gaze on Ana. "And I insist on paying, because I expect it to be worth every dollar as the most well-choreographed, well-designed, well-researched class this gym offers, and I say that knowing Blue Ocean's already-stellar reputation."

She handed Ana her credit card. "Please sign me up for the monthly membership."

"Wow," Sydney said as she handed Ana's mother a tablet to sign a waiver. "That's a high bar you set."

"Ana set it herself a long time ago."

Ana paused, then smiled. "She's not wrong," she said as she entered the credit card number. "I won't disappoint you, Mom."

Her mother reached over, put a hand on the back of Ana's head, and guided her forward to get a kiss on the forehead. "You never have. Ever."

CHAPTER 20

O*ne week later*

Ana walked into Muscatel's large function room, then stopped to survey the scene. She was a full ninety minutes late, which she had no excuse for because she now lived ten minutes away on foot. But the start time for the reunion had come and gone with Ana sitting in her favorite armchair, knees against her chest, panicking.

She was going to see Roman, and she had no idea what she was going to say to him when she did. It had taken everything in her to leave him at the Moonrise Inn, and she was afraid that with one smile and one clever comment, she wouldn't be able to hold firm her resolve.

But now that she'd arrived, she was a bit calmer. The music was soft and subdued, as the guests enjoyed cocktails and little snacks. Though, the DJ in the corner and the empty dance floor suggested the party volume would eventually turn up. There was a lit stage with a microphone stand, and a sparkling banner welcomed their graduating Seasalter High class.

Suddenly Ana was surrounded. Lacey, Kate, and Sarai rushed over to her and group-hugged her.

Kate took a step back and looked Ana up and down. "You are gorgeous."

Ana smoothed her hands down the front of her sleeveless black sheath, then rubbed her own upper arms as if she were cold, though she wasn't. "Thanks."

Lacey lifted Ana's wrist and pressed a glass of prosecco into her hand. "Here. It's always good to have something to hold on to at events."

Ana took a sip and tried to peer around the room again without her friends noticing.

No such luck. "Roman is over there." Sarai gestured toward a busy table, where the baseball team and their various dates were laughing loudly, doubled over, having more fun than anyone in the room. "Oh. Well, he was. I don't see him now."

"Huh," Ana said. "This is exactly like every homecoming dance, every holiday dance, and the prom. The room is divided up into our old cliques. When do you think we'll grow out of this?"

"Who knows?" Kate chuckled. "Personally, I think a ten-year reunion is silly. The more years there are since high school, the closer you are to personal greatness and satisfaction. I should have waited for the twenty-year to show up."

Lacey shook her head, her dazzling curls cascading dramatically over her shoulders. "You're amazing now, and you'll be amazing in twenty years. And in fifty."

Kate seemed startled, as if imagining herself as a senior citizen was beyond her ability.

Ana wondered where Roman had gone. It was inevitable that he would approach her and talk to her, but she wanted to at least see him coming, prepare herself with a smile and a witty but platonic opening line.

A man approached the microphone and tapped it once, twice. "Welcome, class!" he shouted, and everyone cheered. It took Ana a second to recognize Scott, who'd been the president of their senior class. She scowled. She'd run for school president, but unfortunately a popular boy would always win over a qualified but unpopular girl. It had been just as well, since he was a mere figurehead, and she had managed to effect real school policy changes several times with eloquent speeches in front of the PTA and the school board.

She felt embarrassed to be gloating about it now, even in her head. She tried to focus on what he was saying.

"We know that our class has had its share of brilliant alumi." He gestured toward her group and the spotlight circled to her and her friends, shining a painful glare in Ana's eyes. "Right there is a meeting of the minds! Sarai the doctor, Kate the therapist, and Lacey the Broadway star."

Sarai cut Ana a glance. Kate nodded regally, and Lacey curtsied. The room applauded.

As the spotlight circled around the room to highlight a university football coach and a few others with interesting careers, Ana allowed her shoulders to relax. It was a little mortifying to be standing among her talented and successful friends, but the moment was over now, and there would be no reason for anyone to draw any attention to her.

"But let's get the woman up here who got her start as our class's Most Likely to Be a Billionaire—"

Oh, no.

"Our best and brightest, our class valedictorian—"

No. Please, no.

"Juliana Capuano!"

She turned in shock to Lacey, who bent to whisper in her ear. "Just say you're happy to see everyone and you hope they all have a great time." She gently nudged Ana toward the stage.

Ana's steps were slow. Her ears were ringing. Her vision was a tunnel to the microphone.

Scott gallantly met her at the bottom of the five steps to help her, in three-inch black heels, ascend to the stage; then he stepped to the microphone and said, "Juliana went to Yale, then to Columbia Law School. She's always represented the best of us all."

He adjusted the microphone to her height and waved her toward it.

"I didn't know I was going to have to speak," she said to Scott very quietly.

"Oh," he said. "I'm sorry. We emailed you a couple of weeks ago."

They probably had. Ana had been busy moving and fell behind on reading and answering emails. She remembered one with the subject line *Reunion*, and she'd assumed it was party details, not a missive informing her she'd be asked to speak.

She would have said no. She didn't represent the best of them all.

Ana stepped to the microphone and cleared her throat, echoing in stereo around the room.

Her former classmates watched her expectantly. She pushed her glasses higher on the bridge of her nose.

"Hi, everyone," she finally said. "Welcome to our reunion. I—"

She stopped.

At the foot of the stage was Roman. Smiling at her in the same way he'd been smiling at her in the yearbook picture. Like he wanted her to see him.

Like Juliana Capuano's attention was worth having.

She couldn't take her eyes off him now.

For so long, she'd thought she was unworthy.

But despite her reluctance to ever try again, she had it all in front of her again. Beautiful friends. A job she loved.

Roman.

She'd said yes to some of it.

Why shouldn't she say yes to all of it?

Why shouldn't she insist on her worthiness?

"Thanks for your introduction, Scott," she said, turning her head to him, then looking around the room. "But I don't have the kind of massive success story that some of you have or that you might have expected of me. I don't have the massive success I expected of myself."

She brought her eyes back to Roman. "Not yet, anyway."

She smiled. "I thought I had it all figured out in high school. I thought, work hard, earn accolades, be great. But sometimes it's not an easy, straight line. Instead, I worked hard for what I was supposed to want—too hard—and I wasn't healthy. Or happy. I pulled back for a long time, convinced that maybe if I just didn't try at all, I wouldn't fail. But I found … that didn't make me happy either."

The room was silent, listening.

"Now, though … I can see a clearer path to happy. It's not a path I expected. I didn't expect to be a fitness instructor."

"Fitness *innovator*!" Kate called.

Ana took a deep breath. "What I want to say is, if you ever catch yourself feeling unhappy, ask yourself if you're denying yourself happiness by holding on to expectations that don't fit anymore."

A few people started to clap, but Ana finished, "Then let them go. And start over with something new and different that excites you. Even if it doesn't look like what you thought it would look like. Because you *are* worthy and you deserve to be happy, no matter how you find it. Thank you."

The applause was thunderous.

Well, not really. Sarai, Lacey, and Kate jumped up and down and clapped and whistled, but the rest of the room offered polite, slightly confused applause. But it sounded loud to Ana because it had been so long since she had received any.

"Is it time to dance?" she said into the microphone. Everyone cheered, more enthusiastically. Scott nodded.

"Good," she said to the crowd. Then, still speaking into the microphone, she looked at Roman once more. "Roman

Montgomery, I waited far too long to ask you this. Will you dance with me?"

Everyone turned and stared at Roman, covering their mouths and clutching each other's arms, thrilled to witness such a public romantic display.

He nodded, exaggerating the motion so the whole crowd would see it. Everyone whooped and hollered, and the DJ launched into a slow, romantic song that was popular their senior year.

Scott escorted Ana to the edge of the stage, but Roman hopped up the steps and met Ana at the top. "I'll take it from here," he told Scott.

She took Roman's arm, warm and firm under his suit jacket, and let him lead her to the dance floor.

★ ★ ★

He put one arm around her and took her hand, and they began moving. The twinkling lights strung around the perimeter of the room reflected in Ana's glasses, but the warmth in her eyes shone through even brighter.

"I'd say you look good," Ana said, "but frankly, I'm disappointed. I was hoping you'd wear a tux again."

"I don't have the best track record with tuxedoes." Roman grinned. "I needed everything on my side tonight. Plus, the event's not black tie."

"Like Roman Montgomery couldn't get away with wearing whatever he wanted for this crowd."

"I don't have quite the star power I used to. You, though." He squeezed her hand. "Your star is brighter than ever, if that speech was any indication."

"I had no idea I was even going to be speaking. It was in an email I never read."

"I could tell." When her eyes widened, he quickly clarified, "Because I know you. No one else could tell at all. You were all poise and grace."

"Roman, I want to apologize—"

"I don't accept."

"What?" She stopped dancing and stepped back, but he held fast to her hand and her waist, and stepped forward with her. Other couples continued to join them on the dance floor, and the space around them was getting tight.

"I don't accept," he repeated. "You have nothing to apologize for. You broke up with me, which is your choice, and your choices are not something to apologize for."

"Okay, then." Her lips tightened before she went on. "I apologize for breaking up with you when I didn't want to. I didn't trust myself to bring enough to a relationship, so I ran away."

Roman nodded slowly, his heart starting to inflate with emotion.

"I was wrong." Ana's bottom lip trembled, and he let go of her hand to rub his thumb over it, soothing it. They stood still as their former classmates danced around them. "I think I have something to give. And I think I love you, Roman."

Roman's legs weakened, and he nearly melted into the floor.

Instead, he bent his head close to her ear. "I recently heard a woman give a speech in which she encouraged us not to deny ourselves happiness. I'm certain of what will make me happy. Ana Capuano, I love you too. Should we try this?"

A tear ran down her face.

"Will you be my brilliant, talented, capable-of-anything-she-wants-to-do girlfriend?"

She choked out a sound that was half laugh, half sob. "Yes."

He put his hands on her face, sliding his fingers into her hair, and kissed her. She threw her arms around him and kissed him back. Her lips were pliant and yielding, then they were harder and more insistent, then they were soft again.

The song changed to a fast-tempo hit, and everyone cheered, jumped apart, and started to whirl and sway. Roman made himself drag his lips from Ana's, then he leaned his forehead against hers.

"I heard there's an opening at the real estate agency on Broad Street," Roman said. "My mom's dating a contractor who knows people there, and they said someone is leaving."

"Huh. Interesting." Her smile was wide.

"Isn't it? I also heard you moved to town. But I do have a room at Seasalter's most magical inn tonight, in case ... you know."

"In case you need someone to ice your back tonight?"

"Yeah, that too."

"I've got your back." She giggled. "I've got your back! See what I did there?"

"You're a nerd." He smoothed his hand over her hair.

"I'm *your* nerd."

They drew apart and realized what was happening around them.

Kate, Sarai, and Lacey walked to the dance floor together, shoulder to shoulder, expressions serious. On the opposite end, Mark, Pete, and Jake stepped onto the dance floor as well, their faces just as stony.

"Oh, no," Roman said. He and Ana backed away a couple of steps.

The two sides stared each other down for a tense moment.

Then they all burst out dancing.

Ana laughed.

Kate and Sarai danced with Mark and Pete, arms waving, hair bouncing. Lacey and Jake wrapped around each other, swaying as if the song was still a slow one.

Sarai held out her hand to Ana, and Mark hugged Roman tightly with back slaps.

The blended group of friends danced together all night.

Outside, the moon was nearly full again, and it smiled down on Seasalter.

EPILOGUE

*T*he Moonrise Inn
Online Review
Rating: 5 stars
This lovely restored farmhouse is the ideal choice for your seaside getaway. We're sure that even if you just plan on a weekend trip, you'll be tempted to extend your stay!

Selene Bellamy, the owner, is a wonderful hostess. Every detail of her inn shows love and care, from the lace edging on the bath towels in the bathrooms to the moving-poetry curtains of the main room to the celestial theme in every room. Her garden is filled with happy sunflowers, and her porch has rocking chairs that will fade all your worries into obscurity after a few sways. Her breakfasts are wonderful (try the blueberry pancakes!), her board-game collection is vintage, and her wisdom is otherworldly.

Fair warning: This inn is ... well, it's magical. It's soothing and it's peaceful and it's love. Yes, we said love. We fell in love here, and we're quite sure we won't be the last guests to do so. Maybe you'll be the next?

Oh, also, there's plenty of parking, and short walks to the beach and the shops and restaurants on Broad Street.

Book your stay at the Moonrise Inn. Tell Selene that Ana and Roman sent you.

The Sunshine in a Suitcase assistant smiled at her laptop screen. "The Moonrise Inn. Sounds perfect." She pulled up the reservations page and carefully typed Mallory's name.

THE END

What happens when a sunshiny travel influencer and her man's man online counterpart find themselves at the same cozy, romantic inn at the same time? (And what about those sparks between Selene and Owen . . .?) Find out in the next book in the Moonrise Inn series, Christmas Under a Cold Moon.

photo by Mark Karlsberg/Studio Eleven

ABOUT THE AUTHOR

JENNIFER SAFREY lives in the Boston area with her novelist husband, Teddy, and their two cats, Kimura and Potus. She's a longtime freelance editor, as well as an adjunct professor at Emerson College, where she teaches a graduate course on romance novels. She grew up on Long Island. *On This Harvest Moon* is her eighth novel.

Please visit Jennifer online: www.jennifersafrey.com
FB: JenniferSafreyAuthor
IG: @JenniferSafrey_author
TT: @JenniferSafreyauthor

ACKNOWLEDGMENTS

Thank you to the entire brilliant team at Sibylline Press for not only championing the words of women over 50, but for including me in their ranks. When my own confidence is low, I know I can rely on your confidence in me and my work. I gift each of you unlimited nights at the Moonrise Inn.

Thank you to the Wolf Pack Women, my Sibyl sisters, whose endless support and encouragement can't be understated: Kate Woodworth, Pamela Reitman, Diane Schaffer, and Vicki DeArmon. If I could choose any warrior women in history to howl at the full moon with me, it would be you four. Ahhhhoooooo!

And thank you to Teddy, who for years called me Miss Lovely–but he can't any longer, because now I'm his Mrs. Lovely.

Sibylline Press is proud to publish the brilliant work of women authors over 50. We are a woman-owned publishing company and, like our authors, represent women of a certain age.

www.ingramcontent.com/pod-product-compliance
Lightning Source LLC
Chambersburg PA
CBHW032234310726
48973CB00008B/2135